HEART'S DESIRE

"WHAT happened?"

Jack squinted, blinking through watering eyes to try to see if there was any obvious damage. He couldn't see any, although the upper side of the canopy was out of view. Still, the canopy didn't seem to be deforming as he thought it would be if the lightning strike had ripped through its canvas.

"I think we just found out that we do have lightning rods!"

Carter's voice rose a notch. "Did we get hit by lightning?"

"Fix the drive!"

"I'm trying!"

Jack's numb hands were slipping on the steering column, the metal slick with ice. He spared a glance down under his feet, and then let himself slide, finding his footing on the underside of the canopy. He scrubbed snow out of his face with the back of his hand, but the icy glove wasn't much help.

Anywhere that isn't hot for our next mission, he'd said after Ne'tu. *Just send us anywhere that isn't hot.*

"I take it back!" he yelled, but the wind whipped the words away.

STARGÅTE
SG·1

HEART'S DESIRE

AMY GRISWOLD

FANDEMONIUM BOOKS

An original publication of Fandemonium Ltd, produced under license from MGM Consumer Products.

Fandemonium Books, PO Box 795A, Surbiton, Surrey KT5 8YB, United Kingdom

Visit our website: www.stargatenovels.com

STARGATE
SG·1

METRO-GOLDWYN-MAYER Presents
RICHARD DEAN ANDERSON
in
STARGATE SG-1™
MICHAEL SHANKS   AMANDA TAPPING   CHRISTOPHER JUDGE
DON S. DAVIS
Executive Producers JONATHAN GLASSNER and BRAD WRIGHT
MICHAEL GREENBURG   RICHARD DEAN ANDERSON
Developed for Television by BRAD WRIGHT & JONATHAN GLASSNER

STARGATE SG-1 is a trademark of Metro-Goldwyn-Mayer Studios Inc. © 1997-2012 MGM Television Entertainment Inc. and MGM Global Holdings Inc. All Rights Reserved.

STARGATE ATLANTIS is a trademark of Metro-Goldwyn-Mayer Studios Inc. © 2004-2012 MGM Global Holdings Inc. All Rights Reserved.

METRO-GOLDWYN-MAYER is a trademark of Metro-Goldwyn-Mayer Lion Corp. © 2012 Metro-Goldwyn-Mayer Studios Inc. All Rights Reserved.

Photography and cover art: Copyright © 2012 Metro-Goldwyn-Mayer Studios Inc. All Rights Reserved.

WWW.MGM.COM

No part of this publication may be reproduced, stored in or introduced into a retrieval system, or transmitted, in any form, or by any means (electronic, mechanical, photocopying, recording or otherwise) without the prior written consent of the publisher. Any person who does any unauthorised act in relation to this publication may be liable to criminal prosecution and civil claims for damages. If you purchase this book without a cover, you should be aware that this book is stolen property. It was reported as "unsold and destroyed" to the publisher and neither the author nor the publisher has received any payment for this "stripped book".

ISBN: 978-1-905586-58-5 Printed in the USA

CHAPTER ONE

JACK O'NEILL stepped out of the wormhole's chill and paused on the steps of the Stargate, taking a moment to take in the view.

"Whoa," Daniel said from beside him. "It's a long way down."

"We're a long way up," Jack said. He could feel his ears popping at the pressure change, even though Colorado Springs was well above sea level to start with.

The Stargate was perched on a narrow butte, a bare shelf of stone that dropped off sharply on all sides into deep ravines. Across from the island of rock, a precarious path hugged the edge of a steep mountainside, winding downward out of sight. It began in a field that might have seemed like a reasonable place to start heading down the mountainside if it hadn't been on the other side of a ten-meter ravine.

"They did say they were going to send transportation," Daniel said. "I was more thinking they meant 'because our city is a long walk from the Stargate.'"

"It looks like, from here, you'd have to fly," Sam said. "Which makes me wonder what kind of transportation they have in mind."

"I believe I have found a means of descent," Teal'c said. He pointed out what might charitably have been described as a staircase, carved out of the rock on one side of the butte. It wound around the side of the cliff toward the ravine floor somewhere below. The concept of handrails had clearly not occurred to anyone who used it.

"The idea of combining that with any kind of 'transportation' doesn't excite me," Daniel said. "I've been down into canyons on mules before, but…"

"I do not believe a pack animal would be capable of descending this staircase," Teal'c said.

Daniel frowned. "It might be, but I'm not that sure I want to descend with it." He glanced at Jack. "Or without it."

"That's what they pay us for," Jack said. Privately, though, he was sizing up the climb down and trying not to wince. He'd taken a staff blast right above the knee back on the prison planet of Ne'tu, and while Janet had cleared him for duty, he wasn't kidding himself that it was fully healed yet. If they had to climb that many steps, it was going to hurt getting down, and he didn't particularly want to think about coming back up.

The MALP was still resting near the gate, where it had been sitting when the curious locals had turned up to chat. They hadn't mentioned how much of a hike they'd had to get there. They'd seemed interested in trading, and offered to take an SG team to visit their king, who was apparently the only one around with the authority to make a deal.

Sam checked out the MALP while Daniel and Teal'c squinted down into the canyon below, looking for any signs of movement. Jack looked out across the jagged peaks, wondering where you'd put cities and farms. His eye was caught by a shadow moving oddly across the rocks, faster than the clouds, and he peered at it through his sunglasses for a moment. "Carter," he said.

"I just want to take a look at these atmospheric readings," she said. "The preliminary output from the MALP suggested some interesting weather patterns that we may want to get somebody to—"

"*Carter*," Jack said, and she finally raised her head. He jerked his head upward, and she followed his gaze.

"Oh, wow."

"I think that's our ride," Jack said.

The airship's canopy was scarlet, and banners in a dozen shades of crimson and orange fluttered from its sides and streamed from a rope trailing behind it like a long tail waving in its wake. It threaded a pass between two peaks with little room to spare, sinking lower as it approached. The gondola that hung beneath it gleamed with brass trim, although most of it looked to be made of wood, or maybe something more like bamboo.

Jack could hear the sound of the airship's propellers, now, a rumble like rising thunder. He couldn't help grinning watching its approach. He itched to get a closer look, and from Carter's expression, so did she.

From windows on the gondola's side, men were leaning out, several of them throwing hooks as they approached. The hooks caught somewhere below the edge of the butte, and the ropes attached to them drew taut, the propellers stilling. Jack backed up as far as he could out of the way, looking up as the craft slowed and rocked above them, finally stilling in the air. The ropes were being played in, now, bringing the craft down toward the surface of the butte.

Sam was frowning up at it, her hand over her eyes to shield them from the sun.

"What's the matter, Carter?" Jack asked. "You have to admit this is a lot cooler than what we were expecting."

"Definitely more interesting than mules," she agreed absently.

"And? But?"

"I don't think that ship actually ought to be able to fly."

"It looks like some kind of dirigible," Daniel said, coming to her side along with Teal'c. "Don't you think?" A man waved from one of the craft's windows, an enthusiastic smile on his face, and Jack held up a hand in return.

"It does, but the proportions are all off," Sam said. "This isn't really my field, but I'm pretty sure the canopy should a lot bigger proportionally, especially if it's a semi-rigid design, which — from here I can't tell if there's any kind of underlying framework, but if there is, it makes the whole thing even more unlikely." Jack looked at her. "It should be too heavy to fly, sir," she said. "I think."

"And yet it does fly," Jack pointed out.

"That's what's interesting," Sam said.

"See if you can get a closer look while we're in the air," Jack said. "Right now, it looks like it's show time."

The airship had settled just off the side of the butte, with a couple of its crew climbing down to lash it more tightly to whatever anchorage they'd found on the cliff side. They didn't seem much concerned for their own safety in the process, clinging to the outside of the airship as if hanging over the edge of a precipice was all part of a day's work.

"That must be fun in a high wind," Sam said.

"I would think not," Teal'c said.

Daniel smiled. "I think she means fun in the special Air Force definition of the word."

"I mean hard," Sam clarified. "There's not much wind right now, but they probably get some pretty impressive storms here."

"Greetings!" the man who had waved called down as a hatch in the side of the gondola dropped open. He scrambled down lightly, while behind him another man began unrolling what looked like foldable bamboo steps. "You are the Tau'ri?"

"That would be us," Jack said, sizing up the young man. "Colonel Jack O'Neill. This is Major Samantha Carter, Dr. Daniel Jackson, and Teal'c."

"I am pleased to make your acquaintance," the man said. "I am Tolar. In the name of the High King Anu, I am here to welcome you to Saday." He was dressed in a long wool tunic and wide wool pants, both dyed a deep red, with what looked like wool boots beneath them. The rest of the crew were similarly dressed, although most in paler undyed wool. Somewhere around here, there had to be a lot of sheep.

"Pleased to meet you," Jack said. "I take it this is the transportation you offered."

Tolar nodded. "The palace is possible to reach on foot, but

the journey is long and difficult," he said. "The low roads are far from villages and offer little shelter from the weather. We do not ask potential trading partners to make such a journey when we can transport them in comfort."

"Nice of you," Jack said. Tolar wore some kind of knife at his belt, but Jack didn't see any signs that he or any of his crew were armed with anything more serious. Hammond had assured him that these people had seemed friendly in their initial contact, and had been interested in trading for medical supplies and refined metals.

"It should be a quiet trip," Hammond had said after the briefing had broken up and the rest of the team were already on their way down to the gateroom.

"Knock on wood, sir."

"I will," Hammond said, and tapped his knuckles on his desk. "But I certainly hope this one doesn't pose much of a challenge for SG-1."

"Thank you, sir," Jack said. It had been a rough few weeks, and he couldn't honestly say that the team was at its best. They'd still been reeling from the death of Daniel's wife when they'd gotten word that Sam's father had been captured, and trying to get him back had meant going through hell, all too literally. Sokar's idea of accommodations for his prisoners had been dark, hot caverns filled with choking fumes and patrolled by guards who embraced the idea of shooting first and asking questions later.

Getting shot in the leg had taken Jack out of action for a couple of weeks, but he still thought Sam might have gotten the worst of it. Martouf had used Tok'ra technology on her to make her recall the memories of the Tok'ra symbiote she had once hosted, on the grounds that Jolinar was the only one who'd ever escaped Ne'tu. The problem was that 'recall' had apparently meant 'experience all over again,' and some of those memories were pretty nasty.

So this mission seemed right up their alley. A nice trip

to talk about trade agreements was probably just what the doctor ordered, and the presence of some interesting technology for Sam to putter around investigating was a bonus. If he could find some crumbling artifacts for Daniel to play with and thereby get him to actually take an interest in something, Jack would call this one a win.

"If you are ready?" Tolar asked, inclining his head politely toward the airship.

"All right, kids," Jack said. "All aboard."

The ride to the palace might have been impressive if you were impressed by seeing a lot of mountainsides from the air. Sam was more interested in how they were staying in the air at all, and no matter how tactfully she tried to inquire, she wasn't getting very far with her questions.

"If you would like to talk to one of the builders of ships, it is possible that could be arranged," Tolar said, sounding like he couldn't imagine why she would want to. "This is merely a small craft used to transport visitors who come through the Stargate, not worthy of your attention."

"I'm still interested," Sam said. She craned her neck, trying to see aft from the cushioned seat that she was apparently supposed to stay in. She couldn't see the propellers, but she could hear them turning, as well as the chug of what sounded like motors. The whole gondola vibrated with their force, drumming against the soles of her feet. "What kind of fuel does this ship use?"

"There is a gas which burns," Tolar said reluctantly. "It is carried in tanks which feed the fires of the engines. The process creates steam, which turns the propellers."

Sam frowned. No matter how she did the math in her head, she didn't come up with an answer that worked. "Wouldn't that kind of system be awfully heavy?"

"The gas within the canopy also creates lift," Tolar said.

"Yes, I know, but—"

"You will see on the left some of our farms," Tolar said. "It is the growing season, and you will see that our crops prosper."

Sam put on what she hoped was the kind of polite smile suitable for being shown people's farms and turned to look out the window behind her. The flatter parts of the mountainside were terraced, with rows of something green bending in the breeze and the occasional flash of what might have been irrigation ditches catching the sun. Between some of the terraces, long staircases wound their way up and down the rocky mountainside.

"Interesting," Daniel said.

"Oh, very," Jack said, politely enough, but she suspected he was being sarcastic, while Daniel actually sounded serious. Teal'c made no comment, although he nodded courteously in the general direction of the fields.

Daniel was still watching as they glided past the fields. "After they harvest the crops, I assume they have to be transported somewhere, some kind of market or storehouse, right? But with these steep hillsides, that must be very labor-intensive."

"The harvest itself takes the work of many," Tolar said. "But most crops are transported by air to the palace. The High King ensures that they are stored and distributed wisely according to the needs of the people."

"Ah," Daniel said, with just the slightest of hesitations. Jack raised his eyebrows, and Daniel glanced at him and shrugged slightly. Too soon to have much sense of what exactly that meant, Sam thought.

"Please remain in your seats," Tolar said, as if he hadn't been encouraging them to do that since they came aboard. "We must cross the Gap, and the winds will be higher."

"Cross the gap," Jack said, tilting his head to one side to make it a question.

"There," Tolar said, leaning precariously out the window to point. Ahead, one peak stood out in the sea of mountains that seemed to go on endlessly. Higher than its neighbors, its peak glistened with snow. Lower down, below the tree line, Sam could just make out buildings and walls that sprawled down the mountainside on what seemed like an endless series of terraces.

The neighboring peaks were distant enough that there was no approach except up a winding trail that disappeared far below into mist. It was certainly defensible, Sam thought, unless you had neighbors who'd also be coming by air.

As if in answer to her thought, sunlight glinted off something moving in the distance on the far side of the peak, what looked like another airship but considerably bigger. She pointed it out wordlessly to Jack, and he cleared his throat to attract Tolar's attention.

"One of yours?" he asked, pointing it out.

"Oh, yes," Tolar said. "The High King has many ships, both small ones such as this insignificant craft and greater ones used to transport goods from outlying areas. And back to them, of course."

"Of course," Jack said.

The wind did pick up in the gap between the peak and its neighbors, but Sam twisted around in her seat anyway so that she could watch their descent without having her view blocked by Teal'c's head. She could see better with her elbows braced on the bamboo sill of the open window, although the wind whipped at her hair.

"Ah, Sam…" Daniel began.

"I'm fine," she said. "I'm not going to fall out the window."

"Don't," Jack said. She chose to take that as meaning *don't fall out the window* rather than *don't look out the window*. The wind buffeted them, rocking her back and making her grab at the top of her seat for balance. The whole airship rocked and shuddered as it corrected course. It was sinking down toward what looked at first like a warehouse, and then, as the scale became clearer, a blocky, barn-like hangar that must have been at least five stories high.

She frowned again as they corrected course once more, getting the craft's nose pointed again toward the hangar. The turn felt too fast given the direction of the wind, as if the ship were more aerodynamic than it looked. On the other hand, it wasn't as if she had a lot of experience with dirigibles.

"Think we need one of these for the Air Force?" Jack asked, deadpan, as if in answer to her thought.

She smiled. "Yeah, that'd be cool."

"I hope there has not been a misunderstanding," Tolar said, his expression suddenly darkening. "We cannot possibly offer one of our ships in trade. It would be a great dishonor for the High King to reduce the size of the royal fleet."

"No, no," Daniel said, shooting the two of them a quelling look. "We're, ah — we're all set for airships, really."

"Not to worry," Jack said. "I'm sure we can make a deal for something else."

"We have many fine woolen goods to offer," Tolar said.

Sam looked at Jack, feeling a certain lack of optimism about whether this mission was going to turn out to be useful at all, but he only shrugged. "Sure. We'll take a look."

She couldn't help wondering what the colonel was thinking. He wasn't usually particularly patient with trading missions, especially ones that looked likely to end with having to find a diplomatic way of saying 'you're really nice people, but I don't think you have anything we want.' Instead, he seemed content with the way things were going. He was leaning back in his seat, his sunglasses making his expression harder to read.

Teal'c, on the other hand, did look bored, if only because his expression was the impassive one that she was learning meant that he didn't want anyone else to know what was on his mind. Probably being Apophis's First Prime had involved a lot of standing around trying not to look bored. Probably the times when he'd been fighting boredom had been better than the times when he hadn't.

For a moment she could picture it, Teal'c standing next to Apophis with that familiar impassive expression. She wasn't entirely sure if that was imagination or residual memory — would Jolinar have ever had reason to meet with Apophis? Probably not, she decided, and then realized too late that asking herself the question had been a bad idea, opening up a door she'd been trying to keep firmly shut.

She closed her eyes against the intrusive flash of memory, the smell of sulfur in Ne'tu's punishingly hot air, the screams of the other prisoners, the stone floor hard under her knees. She wasn't sure if that was Jolinar's memory or hers, and she really didn't want to know.

"Carter?" Jack asked. His tone was casual, but when she opened her eyes, he was watching her closely. Damn it.

"It's nothing," she said. "Just feeling the altitude a little, I think."

He raised his eyebrows but didn't argue with her.

"I think we're coming in for a landing," she said, pointing out the window. It was an effective distraction, since bringing the airship into the hangar involved a few minutes where it looked alarmingly like they were going to crash straight into the side of a rocky cliff. Jack looked like he was barely repressing the urge to try to backseat drive, and Teal'c didn't look much happier to be a passenger.

Instead they threaded the broad door of the hanger neatly, drifting into the enormous stone room with the noise of the propeller dying. The crew sprang into action, scrambling out and down rope ladders that hung to the floor below, where a ground crew was catching at dangling lines and clipping them quickly to huge iron mooring rings set into the stone floor.

The gondola rocked and then jerked as the ropes caught the ship, stopping the forward drift that would have eventually sent it into the far wall. It took a few minutes for the stairs to be lowered so that they could scramble down without climbing a ladder, apparently a courtesy offered to guests.

Or possibly to women, Sam couldn't help thinking; there didn't seem to be any women among the crew either on the ship or on the ground.

"All right," Jack said when they were back on the ground, spreading his hands. "Take us to your leader."

Sam gave him a look behind Tolar's back as Tolar led the way.

"I always like to say that," he said, again perfectly deadpan.

She shook her head, still not sure what had brought on this mood, but all the same she couldn't help smiling.

CHAPTER TWO

TEAL'C stayed watchful as Tolar led them through a series of twisting hallways, some built of stone blocks or bricks, others seemingly chiseled into the side of the mountain. It would be easy to lose track of the way back to the airship hangar if he let himself become distracted. O'Neill was smiling easily, leaning closer to Major Carter to make some joking remark, but Teal'c could see his sharp eyes making note of each turning as well.

Daniel Jackson was paying more attention to the figures that lined many of the walls, carved reliefs and painted images of somber great cats and broad-winged birds. He seemed entirely distracted, having to be nudged by Major Carter to make one of the turnings rather than continuing on alone down an empty corridor, but Teal'c had no doubt that he could retrace his route by recalling each piece of art or engraved inscription they had passed.

"A lot of this looks Caananite," he said, stretching up to look at the top of one weathered painting, a winged goddess whose feathers were blurred as if by the touch of many hands over the years. "The names would fit, although of course there's been considerable linguistic drift…"

"And that means?" O'Neill said, collecting him with a glance.

He began walking again, but looked at Tolar before he answered. "It's just interesting."

O'Neill rolled his eyes but did not pursue the matter, apparently accepting that whatever he had to say was best brought up when their guide was no longer present. Possibly he had formed some theory about the Goa'uld to whom this planet's inhabitants paid tribute.

According to the inhabitants to whom they had spoken, the Goa'uld came only rarely to Saday to collect divine offerings from its people. There was no sign of a permanent Jaffa presence at all, which in itself suggested the world was not promising as a trading partner. If there had been deposits of naquadah or other valuables, the Goa'uld would have occupied the world rather than apparently paying it little mind.

He suspected, though, that General Hammond had intended the mission as a chance for the team to rest. O'Neill had been wounded on Ne'tu, and although Dr. Fraiser assured him that the wound was healing well for a human, humans healed slowly enough that Teal'c was not sure how they tolerated it. Major Carter had seemed troubled ever since their return, although perhaps it was merely her worry about her father, who had remained confined to the infirmary for several days despite having his symbiote's assistance in healing.

It was harder to tell how Daniel Jackson had fared on Ne'tu. He had spoken very little of their time there, or at least he had spoken little of it to Teal'c. That might mean much or nothing. He knew from their debriefing that on Ne'tu, his friend had faced Apophis and told him of Amonet's death. It would have given Apophis pain to hear that his mate was dead, but it must also have given Daniel Jackson great pain to speak of it. His wife Sha're had died along with Amonet, struck down by Teal'c's staff blast.

He had assured Teal'c that he forgave him for killing Sha're, and that he understood that Teal'c had made the choice he had to make. Teal'c could still see it all too clearly, Amonet forcing Daniel Jackson to his knees, his body convulsing as she racked him with the ribbon device, Sha're's face twisted with Amonet's fierce smile. He had simply gazed into her eyes, ignoring his agony, searching her face for any sign that Sha're still knew him, his weapon slipping from his hand.

And Teal'c had been the one there, and he had done what he must. Daniel Jackson forgave him for it, or so he had said, his voice clear and his expression intent, urging him to believe it. It was what Sha're wanted, he had said, and Teal'c had accepted his forgiveness as balm for his own regret.

They had not spoken of anything beyond trivialities since their return from Ne'tu. That might mean much or nothing, Teal'c told himself again, and returned his thoughts firmly to the doorway in front of which they had stopped.

"Please wait in the audience chamber," Tolar said. "The minister of trade will be sent to speak with you."

"Great," O'Neill said.

They entered an airy room whose main feature was a long table that looked much like the conference tables of the Tau'ri, although it was set with low stone benches that had no arms. Along two sides of the room, wide square windows looked out across the gap that surrounded the peak, from this angle showing only the dark slopes of distant mountains against the deep blue sky, their heights glittering white.

Major Carter and Daniel Jackson pulled up benches to the table while O'Neill investigated the view out the window.

"They don't seem to believe in safety railings here," O'Neill said. "Or window screens."

"Don't fall out the window, sir," Major Carter said, with a hint of a smile.

"Thanks, Carter," O'Neill said. "I'll try not to. You'd think this place would get drafty when it rains."

"They probably have window screens, in the sense of solid screens of some kind that can be fitted into the windows," Daniel Jackson said. "Servants would do that. Everything we've seen suggests that there's a lot of manpower going into supporting this kind of lifestyle at this level of technology, even if they are using some labor-saving devices."

"We have ceremonial buildings back on Earth," Major Carter said.

"Well, yes, and how many people does it take to keep the White House looking like that? I'm just saying, carving this place out of rock has been a substantial investment of somebody's time and labor, and probably not the High King's."

O'Neill turned away from the window. "You think the Goa'uld built this place?"

"Had it built, maybe," Daniel Jackson said. "The construction techniques aren't Goa'uld, and so far we haven't seen much evidence of Goa'uld technology."

"I think there's some kind of artificial ventilation system in these tunnels," Major Carter said. "Did you hear that hum? They've got fans running somewhere. But that could fit the local level of technology. We're probably looking at steam engines running on coal gas or some other kind of mineral-based fuel."

"What was so interesting about all those paintings?" O'Neill asked.

Daniel Jackson shrugged. "The paintings themselves, not as much, but the inscriptions do suggest some connection to the Caananites on Earth. That doesn't necessarily mean anything about who rules here now, but if I had to guess, I'd say it's a pretty good bet these people were brought here by one of the Goa'uld who ruled in that region."

"Who were?" O'Neill said, sounding as though his patience with speculation that wasn't immediately useful was wearing thin. Teal'c had often observed that Daniel Jackson's definition of *interesting* did not always coincide with that used by O'Neill.

"Well, we don't really know for sure. Teal'c, do you know anything about a Goa'uld called... well, probably Ba'al, and possibly... Dagon, Anat, maybe Athtart or Asherah?"

"Ba'al was an underlord of Ra, now a system lord in his own right," Teal'c said. "I do not believe this world falls within his territory. The others I do not know."

"Some of the imagery, though, the woman standing on a lion — I think we're probably dealing with a goddess, not a god."

"Another Goa'uld queen?" O'Neill sounded less than enthusiastic. "That could be a problem."

"I hear you, believe me, but it doesn't sound like their goddess is likely to drop in. Anyway, she's probably not actually a queen in the sense that Hathor was, just a Goa'uld who prefers female hosts and playing the role of a goddess."

"There are many minor Goa'uld," Teal'c said. "I have heard nothing of this world before, but I do not believe it is within the territory of one of the System Lords."

The door to the corridor opened, revealing a plump man in a crimson wool robe. "I am Walat, minister of trade," he said. "It's an honor to meet the Tau'ri."

"We're pleased to meet you, too," O'Neill said after a moment. "You've heard of us, then?"

"Let us be frank," Walat said, settling onto a bench at the end of the table as if he spent a lot of time there. "We know that you have set yourselves in rebellion against the gods. We have heard many stories of your battles against them."

O'Neill glanced at Teal'c. "That'd be true," he said.

Walat shrugged one shoulder. "We are still interested in trading with you. After all, the Queen of Heaven is far away, is she not, and does not interest herself in the details of our business arrangements." He glanced heavenward on the words, as if repeating a truism.

"You tell us," Daniel Jackson said cautiously. "We'd be interested in trade, but not if it's going to cause problems for your people."

"Interested," O'Neill said. "But we need to find out what we both have to offer."

Walat brightened. "Let me tell you about our wool production."

He proceeded to do so at some considerable length. Teal'c suspected that even Daniel Jackson was hard-pressed to maintain an expression of courteous interest.

"That's... that's really fascinating, and I'm sure that you

have fine textiles," Daniel Jackson said, when Walat reached a pause in his description of new methods for producing dyes from coal tar. "But we produce some very similar fabrics back on Earth."

"I was actually wondering if we might learn more about your airships," Major Carter said. "I know that you're not interested in actually parting with any of the ships, but it may be that some of the technology you're using could be of use to us."

"They are very simple machines," Walat said. "I am sure nothing in their design could be of use to the Tau'ri."

"Still, if I could talk to some of the people involved in building them..."

"If you are not interested in our fabrics, perhaps our cheeses? We produce a range of aged sheep's-milk cheeses that store well for travel."

O'Neill and Daniel Jackson exchanged looks. Walat seemed to catch their expressions, because he said quickly, "You must be tired from your journey. Let us show you to a guesthouse where you can rest, and in the afternoon we can discuss the possibilities for trade between our peoples in more detail."

"Actually, we probably have to be getting back," Major Carter said. "But I'm sure we can send a team back later to talk some more."

"Oh, what's the hurry, Carter?" O'Neill said. "We'd be happy to stick around and talk this afternoon."

"I was wondering, would you mind if I took a look at some of the art we passed on the way here?" Daniel Jackson said. "The relief sculptures, and some of the inscriptions? It's really very impressive work."

"If you like," Walat said, blinking. "Really all of that is old. You should see some of our recent bronzework."

"I'm sure it is old, but it's still interesting. If you wouldn't mind..."

Walat shrugged. "I will send a servant to show you some

of the older parts of the palace," he said. "If such things interest you."

"They do."

"I don't suppose I could see someone about the airships?" Major Carter put in hopefully, but Walat was already standing to go.

"Please wait here," he said. "A servant will be sent to guide you to your quarters." He swept out, his robes brushing against the worn stone floor.

"I don't get it, sir," Major Carter said. "Do you really think there's much here for us? Leaving aside the airships, which apparently they're really determined not to let us get a close look at."

"You never know," O'Neill said. "Let's hear them out. Anyway, apparently they have interesting wall... things. Right, Daniel?"

"Right," he said, although he was also looking at O'Neill a little suspiciously.

A female servant, dressed in a simple wool robe with her hair caught up at the back of her neck, soon came to show them through more winding hallways out into a courtyard that was startlingly green after so many rooms of bare stone.

Small trees shaded a small pool of water with tiny fish flickering through it, and terraced planters were draped with vines that flowered crimson and gold. On one side of the courtyard, a low wall guarded a steep drop to the next terraced courtyard far below. Above it, the mountains filled the sky.

The guesthouse lay against the rear wall of the courtyard, with an overhanging roof that sheltered low benches. Through its arched doorways, at least two rooms were visible, their floors piled with thick woolen carpets laid one over another to form a patchwork of rusts and rich browns.

"Please rest and refresh yourselves," the woman said. "There is running water within, and I will send someone to you with tea. There is steam heat to keep the guesthouse warm in the evening, but you will not need it yet on such a fair day."

"It's nice," O'Neill said, settling onto one of the benches and resting his pack against its side. "Somebody will come fetch us when you guys are ready to negotiate some more, right?"

"Of course," the woman said.

"We'll be here," O'Neill said. Daniel Jackson was already rifling through his pack extracting a notebook. Major Carter was visibly restless, however, looking about as if in hopes that one of the airships would suddenly appear for her examination. "What, Carter, you didn't bring a book?"

"I'll think of that next time, sir," Major Carter said. "I'm going to go take a look at that steam heating system while we're just waiting around."

Teal'c settled onto a bench rather than accompanying her. He was used to 'waiting around,' and this was a more pleasant place than many to do it, but he did not think she wished to be told so.

"All we need is some fishing poles," O'Neill said, and stretched his legs out in the sun.

CHAPTER THREE

DANIEL panned his video camera across the wall, recording a lengthy inscription about the work involved in building a temple to the glory of the goddess Asherah. It would give him something to do later, working out the translation in pencil, erasing one dry word and replacing it with another more accurate one. If there had been some poetic intent behind the words, he wasn't really in the mood to try to capture it.

The servant who'd been sent to keep an eye on him was waiting patiently while he worked. He'd learned that her name was Anath, that she'd been indentured to the palace as a small child when her father had a bad year with disease taking half his sheep, and that she was far more interested in the airship docks — and, he suspected, the airship pilots — than she was in dusty inscriptions. He thought Sam might have gotten more useful information out of her.

He was starting to get a sense of personality from this set of inscriptions; the writer complained at length about delays due to weather and the quality of the stone available for building. He tried to imagine carving letters in stone, expecting them to endure for thousands of years, and being able to find nothing better to say than *we built you a temple, but it's not our fault that it isn't a better one.*

Then again, what else was there to say about most human endeavors that was honest? *We tried.* People throughout the ages had hoped that some divine being handed out high marks for effort. He suspected the Goa'uld didn't, and wondered what had happened to the unnamed architect, whether these were his last words: *it wasn't my fault, we had a lot of storms...*

He realized he'd been filming the same patch of lettering for longer than strictly necessary, and snapped the video camera off.

"Do you want to see more walls?" Anath asked, sounding as if she couldn't imagine why.

"Sure, why not," Daniel said. "As long as we're here."

They'd met with the king the night before, over a lengthy dinner in which one tiny plate had been replaced by another in seemingly endless succession. Jack had established in about ten minutes that there was nothing they needed here, and then begun transparently — at least, it was transparent to Daniel — finding reasons for them to stick around anyway.

By the end of dinner, Sam had somehow decided that it was worth collecting more data on the planet's weather, and Daniel had been promised a tour of the palace so that he could get a better look at what Jack referred to as "all that cultural stuff." The king, an elderly man with a disconcerting tendency to smile like a used car salesman, had encouraged both, apparently on the grounds that if they stayed around long enough, they'd decide they wanted to trade for something.

It wasn't likely to be sheep. Sam was starting to look annoyed whenever any kind of sheep-related product was mentioned. He wasn't sure if it was just that she was frustrated about still not having been able to get her hands on one of the airships, or that she'd finally realized that Jack was trying to give her a break after Ne'tu and was pissed off at him about it.

When they'd gotten back to the SGC after escaping from the prison planet, Janet had been busy trying to get Jack to sit still so that she could treat his leg and quizzing Martouf about the best way to treat Jacob and Selmak. It wasn't every day that she had a Tok'ra laid out in her infirmary, much less one who was sharing the body of an Air Force general. As far as Daniel knew, Sam had gotten a couple of band-aids put on and gone home without mentioning *oh, by the way, Martouf used a Tok'ra memory device to make me remember how it felt to be tortured and then forced to seduce a Goa'uld prison guard in order to survive.*

Not that Janet probably had a band-aid for that, and not that there was any point in expecting enforced rest to fix any of their problems. Still, he understood where Jack was coming from, at least to the extent of agreeing that they probably didn't need a strenuous battle against the massed forces of the Goa'uld at the moment. Jack had looked glad for a moment's rest himself the day before, leaning back on a bench in the sunlight, the brim of his hat tilted down over his eyes.

Daniel couldn't remember the last time he'd seen Jack looking relaxed. The answer might have been *before Sha're died and Jack started trying so hard to take care of everyone else,* and also possibly *never.* It was hard right now for him to remember if any of them had ever felt at ease, and if there had ever been a time since he first came back through the Stargate without Sha're that had seemed like a happy one. And if there had been, what did that say about him?

"Dr. Jackson?" Anath prompted. Daniel shook his head. There was no point in standing around asking himself questions he didn't really want to answer, and it wasn't why he'd asked for this tour.

"Right, let's move on," he said. He followed her down the length of a hallway cut deep into the stone of the mountain, with condensation collecting in patches on the wall and making the wool rugs underfoot smell musty and sour. "What are we looking at down here?" It had better be carvings, he thought; the damp would surely make short work of any attempt at painting these walls.

"Decorated stones," Anath said. "They are found from time to time when new fields are being constructed, or in high places where few people go."

"Ah," Daniel said. "Well, yes, let's look at the stones." He wished he felt more genuine enthusiasm. He should, he told himself. Every artifact was important, every fragment of pottery or shaped stone one more piece of a puzzle much bigger than himself. It was fairly indefensible to feel that he wished there were more chance of finding a *good* alien artifact here.

Anath stopped at an open doorway, pushing aside the musty hangings in the doorway for him to step through. He was expecting something utilitarian, stone tools or boundary markers no longer in use, but once she lit a lamp in the small storeroom, he could see the pair of tablets propped up on a shelf on the opposite wall. They didn't look like stone; more likely clay, by the way they were deteriorating badly at the edges.

"These used to hang in one of the audience chambers, but Walat had them taken down," Anath said. "He said they looked like something out of a temple. Not modern."

"Walat might want to keep these somewhere dryer," Daniel said as patiently as he could manage. "Or at least copy the inscriptions on them before they entirely dissolve in this damp. What do they say?" He squinted in the lamplight, and then fished a flashlight out of his pocket.

"It's not writing," Anath said, sounding amused at his foolishness. "Don't you know what writing looks like?"

So far all the inscriptions he'd found had used either a variant of the Caananite alphabet or the Goa'uld hieroglyphics. There was a great deal more of the former than the latter, which suggested the Goa'uld weren't frequent visitors. In his experience, they didn't like to be confronted with things they didn't understand.

"Well, yes, it is writing, it's a pattern of regular symbols, but it may be using an older alphabet, or an entirely different... oh, hey." He held the flashlight closer, wishing now for a lot more light. It was hard to make out where the breaks between words had been intended to go, but if the first word ended *there*...

Then the next word was an impossible string of consonants. Okay. Still, there was no mistaking the alphabet, even with some of the letters stylized a little differently than he'd seen them before, with stronger crossbars and descenders that ended in stylized points. That could have been an artifact of carving them into stone, though, without the benefit of mechanical tools. His mind was already spinning rapidly over the possibilities.

"I'd like to get some more light in here," Daniel said. "Let me... no, no, I should get some other people down here. Anath, can you show me the fastest way back outside? My radio won't work underground."

Anath gave his radio a skeptical glance but led him back through the maze of corridors to a set of steps that opened abruptly out to a small terrace, where a spindly potted tree looked like it didn't get watered as often as it would have liked.

He thumbed on his radio. "Hey, Jack?"

"Right here," Jack said. "We're being served tea. And little pastries." He sounded amused.

"That's nice," Daniel said. "I need you to bring me my pack, it's got a better light in it. And you should come see this, anyway. We're in the — where are we, Anath?"

"The gallery that runs along the outside of the Hall of the Bulls," Anath said in bemusement.

"Right, did you get that? The gallery that — do you actually have cattle here? I wouldn't think that with as little arable land —"

"Daniel," Jack said.

"Gallery outside the Hall of the Bulls," Daniel said. "I'm sure somebody can show you the way."

"Let me guess," Jack said. "You found a wall with writing on it."

"No, I found a set of clay tablets with writing on them, and I need to get pictures because they look like they're ready to fall apart. Oh, did I mention that the writing on them is in Ancient?"

"You have now," Jack said after a moment. "Okay, we'll come down."

Anath put her head to one side watching him. "You like these things?"

"Yes, they're very interesting," Daniel said, and meant it more than he had all day.

"There are more in the treasury," Anath said. "The High King collects things found in the deserted places."

"The deserted places," Daniel said. "You mean ruins? Places where people used to live?" He welcomed the itch of curiosity, intense enough to drive all other thoughts out of his head for a while. "I'd very much like to see the rest of them."

"Good," Anath said, smiling cheerfully. "Walat was sure we'd find *something* you wanted."

"So I really think their price is very reasonable," Daniel said over the video link. General Hammond privately suspected that Daniel would say so no matter what it was, given the chance to get more information about a mysterious ancient civilization, but in this case he really did think it was reasonable.

Antibiotics and information on methods of producing them were a fair exchange for the tablets, and something that they would probably been willing to provide for purely humanitarian reasons without asking for anything substantial in return. He hoped Daniel had more sense than to mention that. Besides, there was a certain inherent value to having a reputation as nice, friendly people who got along well with others.

"All right," Hammond said. "I'll get someone to work assembling those supplies."

"Yes, well, there is one slight catch," Daniel said.

Hammond resisted the urge to sigh audibly into the microphone. In their line of work, it seemed like there was always just one slight catch. "And what would that be?"

"Well, we've been negotiating with the Minister of Trade, Walat, but apparently the High King is the only one who can actually approve the trade agreement."

"That doesn't seem like a problem."

"No. The problem is that we have to have someone of equivalent rank among our people come represent us. After we've spent the last few days being really firm about the fact that we can't make any promises without checking with our superiors, we can't change our minds now and tell them that we're political leaders."

"Exactly what are you suggesting, Dr. Jackson? I can't very well get the President of the United States down here to make a deal for some clay tablets, no matter how interesting they are."

"Well, as far as I can tell no one's actually mentioned to them that we have superiors other than you. I know it's not exactly our standard operating procedure, but if you came out here yourself to sign the trade agreement, I think they'd accept you as our head of state."

"As far as that goes, there's no reason it has to be me," Hammond pointed out. "I take it you haven't provided them with names and descriptions of our political leaders."

"No," Daniel said. "And of course that's a possibility. I'm just concerned that if we deceive them and they find out about it, as unlikely as I admit that probably is…"

"That's all right," Hammond said. "I don't suppose it'll hurt me to get out of the office for a change."

It wasn't only that, although he had to admit that on a lot of days it was frustrating to sit in front of a fantastic gateway to other worlds and watch other people walk through it. There were enough situations in which they had no choice but to deceive the people they met on other worlds about who they were and what their world was really like. He didn't like the idea of lying this time just to save himself the inconvenience of taking a walk.

"Great," Daniel said. "We can go over the plans for the ceremonial signing when you get here. These things are traditionally public events here even when they're dealing with people they've traded with in the past, so given that we're more of an unknown quantity, I'm expecting this to draw quite a crowd."

Hammond frowned. "Are we sure that's entirely wise, considering that we're signing this agreement on a planet controlled by the Goa'uld?"

"Yeah, we asked them about that," Daniel said. "They said that their goddess never actually pays attention to who they trade with. Apparently she hardly ever shows up, and when she does, she usually spends the whole time visiting her temples and having everybody tell her how wonderful she is. Then they give her a bunch of tribute gifts and she leaves again. It's not a bad arrangement for them, except for the fact that the tribute is draining their economy and preventing them from having any kind of reliable agricultural surplus."

"Well, it's their funeral," Hammond said. "I just hope we don't end up causing more trouble than this stuff we're selling them is worth."

"So do I," Daniel said. He looked like he was struggling with his conscience, and also like it wasn't winning. "I really want to find out what's on those tablets, though," he said. "From the two I've been able to look at so far, I think these are copies of much older original documents or inscriptions that may have already been here long before the Goa'uld ever brought humans to this planet. I'm hoping we may find an account of how the Stargates were originally installed, or find out why the Ancients were interested in this planet to begin with, or... who knows."

"All right, you don't have to convince me," Hammond said. "I'll come out there, and we can get this trade agreement signed so you can pack up your tablets."

"Actually, I was just planning to videotape them," Daniel said. "I'm not sure how we'd move some of them if we tried; the biggest ones are huge, and half of them look like they're falling apart. They are handing over one of the oldest of the tablets in the ceremony itself, though. Apparently that one's actually engraved metal, which makes me suspect it might actually be original. I have no idea right now, because as soon as they figured out we were interested enough in this stuff that we might be willing to pay them just to see it, they wouldn't let us anywhere near it."

"Sensible people," Hammond said. "How is Major Carter's meteorological survey going?"

Daniel looked like he had no idea. "Fine, I think? She has the UAV you sent through up recording data about the prevailing winds. The locals think it's interesting. I don't think they've ever seen a heavier-than-air aircraft before."

"That's a trade for another day," Hammond said. "We should be ready to leave within the hour."

"You may want to dress up for this," Daniel said. "I think we're talking royal robes in the High King's delegation."

Hammond shook his head. "I'm a little short on those, Dr. Jackson, but we'll see what we can do."

"Are you entirely sure about this?" General Hammond said, inspecting himself in the guesthouse's mirror. Jack tried not to look visibly amused. The length of heavy wool brocade that Daniel had wrapped around Hammond's waist as a... well, as a skirt... certainly wasn't the worst thing SG-1 had worn for the sake of a mission.

"I really think it's necessary," Daniel said. "It's pretty clear to me from everything that I've seen so far that trousers are only worn here by laborers and servants, or at best by ordinary guardsmen. They're going to expect a leader to wear robes of some kind."

"I suppose I could have brought my bathrobe," Hammond said. "As opposed to putting on dress blues."

"I did say..."

"I know," Hammond said, and sighed. "All right, let's get on with the show."

"I really think you ought to have a wig as well," Daniel said. "I could see if we can arrange—"

"No, thank you," Hammond said firmly. "I'm going a long way for the sake of these tablets of yours. I think the High King can deal with the sight of my actual head."

"All right," Daniel said. "The plan is, we're part of a ritual procession through the city to an outdoor court, which is where we'll meet with the High King. I'm assuming there will be a ton of spectators, but the High King's guards are supposed to be taking care of security. Once we actually come into the High King's presence, we'll have to surrender our weapons—"

"Hello," Jack said. "That's a problem."

"There was no such requirement when we dined with the High King the other evening," Teal'c pointed out.

"Yes, but apparently it makes a difference that it's a public ceremonial occasion, and that it's taking place on sacred ground. Apparently the court is a site of the ritual worship of their goddess Asherah, and being visibly armed would be the equivalent of taking rifles into a church."

"You said visibly," Jack said.

"I don't think they're actually going to search us," Daniel said. "That would be disrespectful, and they're trying to be friendly here. I think as long as we hand over our rifles and Teal'c's staff weapon, and keep anything we don't hand over well out of sight, we'll be okay."

Teal'c frowned but didn't argue. Jack drew his pistol from its holster and tucked it under his jacket instead, his eyes on Carter and Daniel to make sure they were doing the same.

"All right," he said. "Let's go... process."

CHAPTER FOUR

WALAT came to fetch them trailing half a dozen nervous attendants, all dressed in bright skirts and robes. Jack thought he looked relieved at Hammond's altered outfit. Apparently for a while it had looked like they were really falling down in the 'impressive royalty' department.

Walat led them at a leisurely pace through a maze of gardens and corridors toward what was obviously their destination, an open courtyard that on one side ended abruptly at the edge of a cliff. The drop was a sharp one, with no protective wall or even a handrail to keep anyone from straying off the edge. Jack made a note to watch his step.

The only thing that broke the view of the mountains beyond the Gap was what looked like a tall, limbless and leafless tree with its base set into the stones of the courtyard. In front of it, a handful of people were gathered around a wooden chair and low table, one of them in scarlet robes that trailed behind him on the ground and a tall hat trimmed with gold.

"It's an Asherah," Daniel said quietly as they walked, as if that answered some question he felt Jack should be asking.

"You mean these people's 'goddess'?"

"No, actually I mean the tree," Daniel said. "Although probably 'pole' or 'pillar' would be better. It's a representation of the power of their goddess."

"Most people make statues," Jack said.

"Most people probably do, but how much wood do you see around here compared to stone? They probably figure it's more impressive. Anyway, it was traditional among the Caananites, and there are a lot of complaints in the Old Testament that some of the Israelites were—"

Jack held up a hand. "Is this relevant right now?" He'd

learned to ask that question frequently.

"No, probably not," Daniel said after a moment.

"Then it can wait until after the ceremony."

Daniel nodded, although he was getting that look on his face that suggested he felt he was being oppressed by being asked not to talk. Daniel fell back to walk beside Carter and bent his head to hers, probably telling her all about how somewhere in the Bible there was an interesting story about dead trees.

"You think that would impress a Goa'uld?" he asked Teal'c, nodding toward the courtyard and the tree.

Teal'c considered the scene. "No," he said after a moment.

"No accounting, I guess."

There was a crowd assembled around the edges of the courtyard and gathered on the terraces above and below it. Men dressed like the airship crews were keeping the crowd back from the center of the courtyard, some of them watching the terrace above with the careful eye of guards.

Walat led them down a staircase between terraces lined with spectators, some of whom threw flowers. Daniel seemed to be dodging them, but Hammond caught some with a victory-tour smile, handing a handful of brightly-colored blossoms off to Jack, who tried to catch Daniel's eye to see if he could drop them without offending anybody. Daniel was pointing out to Carter that she had flowers caught in her hair, tangled there as if she were wearing a dandelion crown.

"Here your servants must leave their weapons, Great General," Walat said in apologetic tones. "The courtyard is sacred to the goddess, and she will not permit arms to be brought into her presence."

Jack's eyes flickered to Daniel's, but he didn't seem alarmed, so Jack assumed that 'presence' here meant that the goddess was symbolically present via tree. Several guards approached, bowing deeply but keeping their eyes on the team's rifles with a caution that Jack found himself approving.

"That's all right," Hammond said. "SG-1, let the gentlemen take your weapons. As a gesture of good faith."

"Yes, sir," Jack said. He handed over his P90 to one of the guards, who took it gingerly like he wasn't used to firearms and laid it down on a wool blanket spread out on the courtyard stones. Carter and Daniel handed over theirs as well, and after a moment's hesitation Teal'c surrendered his staff weapon.

That seemed to satisfy the guards, and as they didn't ask about pistols, zats, or knives, Jack felt fine about not mentioning them either. Probably if they ended up drawing weapons in the presence of the High King, they'd be in trouble, but if it came to that it would be because things were already going badly wrong.

Walat led Hammond forward at a slow, ceremonial pace, and Jack and the rest of the team trailed him, trying to look like a kingly entourage. They stopped a respectful distance from the High King, and Walat spread his hands as if in entreaty.

"Great King, Bull of Saday, Protector of the People," Walat began, addressing the High King in resounding tones clearly intended to carry to the surrounding crowd. "You who bring forth the seed and bring forth the harvest, master of the winds and of the high places, lord of the thunder…" Jack settled into a comfortable stance and resigned himself to this being a long ceremony. Teal'c was clearly doing the same, although Daniel was listening with what looked like actual interest.

Carter was looking up instead. Jack followed her gaze to see one of the bigger airships hovering some distance above the mountainside, its crimson banners billowing like sails. Steam puffed white into the air behind it, and he could see the flash of moving brass from its propellers and gears. She was shaking her head, and he could see her itching to talk through whatever she was thinking.

He kicked the side of her foot with his instead, just hard enough to get her attention, and she lowered her gaze reluctantly and made a creditable if unconvincing attempt to look like she was paying attention. Walat had thankfully finished listing the High King's titles and was now introducing the Great General George Hammond of the United States of the Tau'ri, although he looked like he would have been happier if they'd thrown in some extra ceremonial titles. Jack made a mental note to suggest 'guardian of the orifice' for next time.

"We are honored that you have chosen to trade with us," the High King broke in finally, which Jack suspected was about a hundred words fewer than Walat would have used to say the same thing. "Please allow us to present you with this small gift as a sample of our wares." He gestured to one of the attendants standing about nearby, who unwrapped a bundle containing a couple of pieces of flat metal. They didn't look like much to Jack, but he could see Daniel practically quivering with the desire to get a better view.

"Thank you," Hammond said. "We're honored as well." He nodded to Daniel, who came forward to take the tablets as the attendant handed them over. He did so reverently, peering down at them and tilting them so that they better caught the light. They flashed in the sun, and Jack glanced away from their glare, wishing he'd made a case for sunglasses as appropriate ceremonial garb.

He heard the murmur of the crowd change, growing louder, and for a moment Jack thought it was just appreciation for the moment, a bunch of people saying *will you look at that*, until he caught the note of alarm. Teal'c looked sharply toward Jack, clearly hearing the same thing. He'd have had plenty of experience with upset crowds.

Jack glanced up at the terrace above, but couldn't see anything other than people milling around more restlessly than seemed appropriate to the occasion. Carter had her eyes determinedly forward. Teal'c was already turning to look behind them, and after a moment Jack gave up on protocol and did the same.

In multiple places, people were pushing through the crowd, knocking others stumbling out of their way. The guards were already moving to intercept them, but there weren't enough guards and they weren't heading in enough directions. At one edge of the crowd, a handful of men stepped out into the square, and Jack got a quick impression of leather coats and leather boots before his eyes fixed on the more important fact that two of them were raising zat guns and leveling them on the approaching guards.

There was the crackle of a zat'ni'ktel blast as one of them fired, and the uproar in the crowd turned immediately to screams. Hammond turned, reaching for a sidearm he wasn't wearing, and Jack went for his own pistol, hesitating with his hand on it under his jacket. If they showed they'd come to the audience heavily armed, even with the best of intentions, they'd probably screw the trade agreement.

"Pirates!" Walat shouted, apparently for the benefit of the guards, more of whom were already going down under zat fire or being backed into the crowd at knifepoint. Unbelievably, none of them seemed to have managed yet to draw weapons of their own, although several of them were throwing themselves bodily at the attackers, knocking them down and grappling for their weapons as the crowd scattered out of their way. "Protect the High King!"

"SG-1, draw your weapons," Hammond said, and Jack drew his pistol, leveling it on one of a small knot of armed men who were heading their way.

"Back off!" he called.

"No, you must not," Walat said, talking very quickly, "it is sacrilege —" He grabbed at Jack's arm, spoiling his aim, and two of the king's attendants were reaching for Carter's zat as she drew it, trying to get it out of her hands.

"God damn it, get out of the way!" Jack yelled, and never mind if that was probably sacrilege too. Teal'c fired from behind him, and one of the armed men rushing them fell, his skin crackling with zat fire. Carter was wrestling with the two attendants, clearly trying to shake them off without having to shoot one of them.

Another zat shot dropped one of the other men, that one coming from Jack's right. Daniel, he registered. Most of their attackers were armed only with knives, but one of them was raising a zat in their direction, aiming past Jack at Hammond and Daniel, or maybe at the High King, Jack didn't know and didn't much care.

He hooked his ankle under Walat's and kicked his foot out from under him, not wanting to hurt him, just to dump him on his ass to get him out of Jack's way. Pain stabbed through his knee as he remembered too late about that leg, and it made him slow to bring his pistol up, just a couple of wasted seconds as he got his feet securely under him again —

Too long, he realized as the zat blast hit him and wracked him with its crawling energy, the world going black around him.

Sam saw Jack go down, and abruptly gave up on diplomacy. "Sorry," she said, and zatted the servants who were trying to hold her back from the fight. It would probably have been a good idea to respect these people's cultural beliefs about not using weapons in a holy place, but the other guys didn't seem to have gotten the memo.

She took a step back to get clear of the fallen servants, firing as she did. Out of the corner of her eye, she could see some of the guards running toward them, presumably trying to protect the king, although how much good they could do if they weren't willing to use weapons, she didn't know. Hammond was demanding that the servants get out of their way, to little avail.

"Sir!" she called, and tossed him her pistol. He caught it with a grateful expression as one of the — okay, given their current lack of any other useful information, she was going to go with 'pirates'— closed in on him. There were too many of them, coming at them from all sides, and they were stuck in a ridiculously exposed position with no cover in sight, unless they wanted to dangle off the cliff or try to hide behind the dead tree.

Probably neither of those was an option. Teal'c was still up and firing, but when she looked for him, Daniel was down, sprawled unconscious with the tablets still clutched to his chest, with one of the pirates bending over him. She hesitated, but Jack was closer. She stepped over him to cover him, hoping he'd come around soon.

The guards were there, by then, surrounding the High King and Hammond, one of them grabbing at Hammond's pistol.

"Look here —" Hammond began angrily.

She glanced up to see one of the pirates aiming his zat at Jack, already charged to fire. There was a split second in which she maybe could have dodged or fired. In which case the blast would probably hit Jack, too soon after the first one to be anything but a killing shot.

"Damn," she said, crouching instead to shield Jack, and then saw the man crumple even as he fired, blue energy crawling around him as Teal'c shot him from somewhere behind her. The man's shot was going to go wild, Sam thought for a hopeful moment, and then felt it hit her, her chest clenching painfully at the jolt and her legs crumpling under her.

The world darkened for a moment but didn't go black. Not a direct hit, she registered, her muscles still twitching with the last painful crackling of the zat blast. She was still in the fight, if she could just make her muscles obey her. She clenched her hand, trying to hold onto her own zat, and realized she was clenching an empty fist.

Before she could make her hand move across the stone, searching for the zat, someone was hauling her up from behind and clamping something hard around her wrists behind her back. She kicked, trying to make herself as uncooperative a dead weight as possible, but she couldn't keep them from dragging her.

"Teal'c!" she yelled. She twisted as well as she could, trying to see behind her. A number of the guards were backing away toward one of the edges of the terrace, the High King protectively sheltered between them, and she thought she saw a flash of Air Force blue between them as well.

"Major Carter!" Hammond shouted. If the guards were trying to protect him by shielding him from the pirates, he wouldn't want to shoot them to get them out of his way, not with the pistol when they were only trying to help. Which made him a less likely source of rescue.

"Teal'c!"

She heard no response from Teal'c, and she couldn't see him. He was down, then, unconscious or dead. Her ankle pounded painfully on the ground as she was dragged even faster, and she managed to twist enough in the man's grasp to realize that they were headed straight for the edge of the cliff.

"You're crazy!" she yelled. "We'll both be killed!"

She kicked out with her feet, trying to tangle them around his legs, but she didn't have the coordination yet. She overbalanced and fell backwards, only the man's grip on her bound hands keeping her from going sprawling, her face turned up to the sky. The large airship was descending, she realized, too slowly to get there in time to help, but even now there was some part of her mind that said *no, it's actually moving too fast.*

The rest of her mind, more immediately practical, was screaming that they were nearly at the edge of the cliff. She could see Jack being dragged by two of the other pirates, sagging unconscious between them, but she couldn't see Teal'c or Daniel now at all. There were too many people running and shouting and getting in the way, and she couldn't tell which of them were pirates and which just frantic bystanders.

The man holding her jerked her hard toward the edge. The stone was smooth under her feet, and gave her little purchase. She dug in her heels anyway, wishing she had more time to figure out what the men wanted, and why they seemed ready to die.

She wasn't. It caught her by surprise, as it had been catching her at the worst moments since they'd returned from Ne'tu, the flash of Jolinar's memory, less images this time than raw emotion: she wasn't ready to die, not here and not like this. She'd do *anything* to survive.

"No!" Sam yelled, fighting with all her strength, trying to keep herself from going over the edge. She could still see the airship descending out of the corner of her eye. If she could just hold on until its crew reached the plateau, until Hammond broke free from his would-be rescuers, until something—

"Be still, damn you," the man growled, and toppled them both over the edge.

CHAPTER FIVE

FOR A vivid moment, all Sam was aware of was the sensation of falling as she grasped for a handhold that persisted in not being there. She forced herself to look down, wanting to see just how far they were about to fall.

She flinched, disbelieving, at the sight of a gray mass rushing up toward her far too fast — surely they couldn't be about to hit the bottom of the ravine already — and then perception caught up to reality and she realized it was the canopy of an airship hovering some distance below the edge of the cliff. She tried instinctively to spread her arms to break her fall, but with them still bound behind her, the best she could do was try to go limp and hope her captor didn't land on her.

She slammed into the fabric of the canopy hard enough to knock the breath out of her, her nose stinging; she tasted blood as she slid wildly down the canopy's slope. There was no way to get any purchase on the rough fabric, and she figured this had only postponed the inevitable; it was still a long way down, and any moment she'd go tumbling off the canopy and start falling again.

Instead she was jerked to a stop by something that twisted and rocked under her thrashing weight; it took her a moment to realize she was hanging in a net extended out beyond the airship's canopy, and that hands were dragging her in.

"Let me go!" she demanded as she was roughly dumped onto the airship's deck. She rolled over and sat up, bracing herself on her hands.

The first thing she could see was that two more men were dragging Jack down out of the same net she'd landed in. He sprawled unmoving next to her, but he was breathing. In fact, he didn't look like the fall had done any worse to him than made him lose his hat, which she supposed was currently floating down to the distant ground below.

"Sir?" she tried, but he didn't open his eyes. She looked around, trying to readjust to a situation that, however bad it might be, was an infinite improvement over falling to her death.

There were at least half a dozen men moving purposely about the open deck, which had only a thin brass rail running around it to keep anyone on it from tumbling over the side. Ladders ran up from either side of the deck, probably to a catwalk above, and she could see an open hatch that must go down into the gondola below.

Toward the front of the deck, brass controls were set on a central pillar and surrounding consoles, broad levers and wheels and dials that must have been instruments of some kind. Two men were stationed there, one adjusting the levers, the other leaning over the rail to see ahead of them and making what Sam could tell were some kind of hand signals, even if she couldn't interpret them.

The propellers had to be aft and underneath them. She couldn't see the curve of their housing, but she could feel a mechanical hum through the metal deck. There were large swiveling brass devices mounted on the sides of the deck that might have been weapons, although from here she couldn't see them well enough to be sure they weren't telescopes of some kind instead.

She was currently being ignored. That rankled, after having been unceremoniously thrown off a cliff. The least they could do was talk to her.

"Hey!" she called. "This is all a big mistake."

"You may be right," one of the men said, leaning out precariously over the rail as if looking at something Sam couldn't see herself. He wore a heavy leather coat that fit stiffly enough in front that she thought it might be armored somehow, and had long dark hair caught back in a rough tail that whipped in the wind.

He turned to a stocky man who Sam recognized as her original captor, scowling. "Get us out of the Gap," he said. "They'll be down on our heads any moment."

"It's going to be a close thing already," the man said.

"So move!"

The stocky man scrambled off, shouting orders to the rest of the crew, while the other man stood looking down at Sam. "If Reba didn't get what we were after, you'd better be worth something yourselves."

"We're away, Keret," someone called across the deck. She could feel as much, the propellers thrumming under the deck, and the man — Keret — also seemed to think it too obvious to require a reply. "The *Heart's Desire* is already away as well."

"Of course she is," Keret said. "Trust Reba to be ready to cast off at the first sign things are going wrong. Who's missing?"

"We lost three at least," the man said. "Hemi, Bet, and Seneb. And Dayse — no, there he is. Arbel, though, I saw him go down. The Tau'ri had thunderbolts —"

"I noticed," Keret said, and glared down at Sam. "Where did you get the thunderbolts? Did your god give them to you?"

"I don't know what you're talking about."

"Thunderbolts," Keret said, drawing his zat by way of illustration and then pointing it at her.

Sam tried to hold perfectly still. It was probably still too soon for her to be able to survive another shot from a zat, especially at point-blank range. "We found them."

"Of course you did."

"It's the truth," Sam said.

"Search them," Keret said. "Make sure they've got no more weapons. Then get them below decks. I'll deal with them after we make the rendezvous."

He leaned over the rail again, peering behind them as the other man began searching Sam more thoroughly than she would have put up with if she'd had any other alternative.

Sam could see a flash of white against the blue sky, probably the canopy of a pursuing airship, but it was farther away than she'd hoped.

Then their own airship made one of those improbably sharp turns, angling out from the cliff and sweeping out into the Gap, the deck tilting as it climbed, and she could see the big airship that had been hovering over the ceremony now moored at the edge of the courtyard where the ceremony had been held. She could just make out guards climbing down from the airship and joining the others trying to clear the courtyard of spectators.

So much for their imminent rescue. They must have decided that protecting the king and figuring out what to do with the unconscious attackers was more important than pursuing them. Past the moored airship, she could see another smaller ship, its canopy the same dull gray as the ship she was currently aboard, sailing off into the Gap some distance away, trailing a streak of steam.

"Keret," the other man said, in a tone that suggested he was about to say something Keret wouldn't like.

"I see it," he said. He grimaced at the other, smaller airship, which was definitely setting a course of its own, aiming for one of the more distant passes. One of the royal ships was now clear of the hangars and moving off in pursuit, but Sam couldn't see that it had a chance of reaching the smaller pirate ship before it could lose itself in ravines too narrow for a larger airship to follow. She also suspected that bright crimson canopies and crimson and gold banners would make it a lot easier for the pirates to see the royal ships coming than the other way around.

"Do we still make for the rendezvous?"

"We do," Keret said. "It could be they're just taking the scenic route."

"You think so?"

"I think it doesn't matter," Keret said. "We got away with

enough ourselves to make the raid worthwhile."

"You mean us?" Sam said. She probably ought to stay quiet, but she couldn't help herself.

"I mean you," Keret said, and she didn't at all like his smile.

Hammond hung onto his pistol as he was manhandled away from the center of the courtyard, firmly resisting the tugging hands that wanted to take it from him but unwilling to shoot into the largely innocent crowd. By the time he managed to shake off his would-be rescuers well enough to move, none of the pirates were still standing. A few lay sprawled on the courtyard stones, downed by zat fire or knocked down by the guards, but most were simply gone.

"The pirates have returned to their ships, Great General," one of the High King's servants said insistently. "You must put your weapon away."

"All right," Hammond said shortly, tucking his pistol back into his jacket. He'd lost his improvised skirt at some point in the melee, which was the only bright spot at the moment. "What's happened to my people?" He couldn't see any of the members of SG-1, and he'd last seen Carter struggling dangerously close to the edge of the cliff.

"They have been taken as prisoners by the pirates," Walat said, pushing his way through the crowd to his side. He looked bruised, and the hem of his robes were torn, but he was straightening them as he walked. "There is no great cause for alarm."

"No cause for alarm? They were being dragged off a cliff by armed men, which your 'guards' did nothing to prevent—"

"It is forbidden to bring weapons into a holy place," Walat said. "The evil men who have dared to do such a thing will be struck down by Her hand."

"I didn't notice much striking down happening just now."

"The Queen of Heaven is far away," the High King said, brushing off servants who were clustering nervously around him. "When she returns, she will be told of these crimes so that her favor may pass from the evildoers all the rest of their days."

Hammond tried not to sound too impatient. "I'm more concerned about what may be happening to my people right now."

The High King shook his head, frowning. "Perhaps Asherah will be merciful to your servants, and not turn her face from them, since they are strangers and must not have understood that they stood on sacred ground."

"I'm very sorry that we offended you — and your goddess — by using weapons in a holy place," Hammond said, as diplomatically as he felt was humanly possible. "It's not the custom of our people to let ourselves be attacked without putting up a fight."

The High King nodded, his expression lightening. "We have heard you are great warriors. It is one reason we thought you would make valuable trade partners. I hope this small disturbance will not be a distraction from the many profits to be gained from an agreement between our people."

Hammond tried again, using very small words. "Where are my people?" He could see two small airships steaming away at a furious pace in different directions, the sun gleaming off their brass fittings. Both were too far away already for him to make out the tiny figures moving on their decks. "I take it you think they're aboard those pirate ships, or whatever they may be."

"They are the ships of pirates, wicked men who prey upon the righteous, and your servants have surely been taken aboard as prisoners," Walat said. "We will hear from the men who have done this soon enough. I am sure they will be eager to begin negotiating for your servants' timely and safe return."

"You mean ransom," Hammond said. "Is that what all this was about?"

Walat nodded. "It is fortunate that they were not able to capture a more valuable person."

"My team is valuable to me, and I want them back," Hammond said firmly. "I suggest you send some of your airships after those pirates rather than waiting around for them to send us a ransom note."

"I am sure their demands will not be unreasonable," Walat said. "This is a common enough misfortune."

"And you didn't feel you should mention that?" Hammond scowled at Walat, all too aware that he wasn't making any headway by simply making demands. "All right," he said after a moment. "What kind of a message are we supposed to get?"

"They will send word to us through one of the villages when one of our grain ships stops to collect the harvest," the High King said. "We will tell you of their demands when we hear of them." He looked around. "Where are the tablets?"

"They're gone," Walat said. "The pirates must have thought they were of some value if the Tau'ri desired them so greatly."

"Then send for some other token for the Great General of the Tau'ri," the High King said. "The tablets from near the Hall of Bulls that Dr. Jackson first took an interest in." He glanced back mildly at Hammond. "Will those serve?"

"I'm sorry," Hammond said as calmly as he could. "I don't think we can discuss any kind of trade agreement until my people are returned."

The High King shrugged. "Very well," he said. "Then you will want to return through the Stargate in the mean time. Walat, have the things brought by the Tau'ri carried down from the guesthouse and loaded aboard the *Ram of the Sun*."

"Wait just a minute," Hammond said. "I'm not about to just pack up and go home until I find out what's happened to my team."

"It may be some time," the High King said. "These men will wait to send their demands to us until they reach some safe harbor, and by then it will be the time of the Festival." He shook his head. "We will hear nothing from them while the Festival is under way. It is a time of worship and celebration when matters of commerce are put aside."

"With all due respect, Your Majesty, that's unacceptable," Hammond said. "If it's going to take a considerable length of time for them to make any demands, we're going to have to conduct some kind of search for them. You must understand that."

"We will search," the High King said. "But we are unlikely to find them. These men are skilled at hiding their craft within ravines and narrow passes. And tonight we must return our airships to the palace for the beginning of the Festival."

"We can bring our own aircraft through the gate if need be," Hammond said. "Even if your people will be busy celebrating this festival tomorrow, that doesn't mean we can't keep looking."

"That is impossible," Walat said, glancing at the High King as if unsure whether to add something more. "You must leave before the Festival."

"And why exactly is that?" Hammond asked, his voice rising in frustration.

It was the High King who answered. "Because at the Festival the goddess Asherah will come among us so that we may worship her at her temples and provide her with our offerings," he said. "She has no interest in the trade agreements we have made in her absence, but if she sees the Great General of the Tau'ri standing here among us, I fear that she will be inspired to ask for you as one of our tribute gifts."

"Obviously that's not acceptable either," Hammond said after a moment.

"It was never our intent. We would have returned you to the Stargate well before she arrived."

"You might have told us about this before now."

"As you might have told us that your servants planned to carry weapons onto our sacred ground during the ceremony," the High King said. "But perfect trust is a rare thing even between trading partners. Don't you think?"

Hammond let out a frustrated breath, for the moment unable to think of a suitable reply.

Jack opened his eyes, immediately aware of several things: he was in a dark, small room with a metal floor, he could feel some kind of mechanical vibration through the floor and the wall to his back, and he ached from head to foot. The last wasn't surprising for having been zatted, although his right knee protested when he moved it.

"Sir?" Carter said, close by. She was sitting against the opposite wall of the little room, which was really more of a large box. He could only just make out her outline in the dim light that was filtering in from some kind of hatch in the ceiling.

"This can't be good," he said.

"We were captured by pirates, sir," she said. "I think they're planning on holding us for ransom."

"I knew it wasn't going to be good." He glanced up at the hatch overhead.

"Locked," Carter said. "Or else there's something heavy over it. This wall has some small holes punched in it, and I do mean small — I can't get my fingers through. But I think enough air's getting in that we'll be able to breathe."

"Considerate of them," Jack said. "What about Daniel and Teal'c?"

"I saw Daniel go down," Carter said. "I think he was just stunned. I don't know what happened to Teal'c. They might be on the other pirate ship. Apparently Keret — that's the captain of this ship — is working with someone else, someone he doesn't entirely trust."

"Funny how pirates can be untrustworthy." Jack stretched his leg experimentally, and was glad it was too dark for Carter to see him wince. He thought he could smell blood over the more pervasive smell of sweat, and frowned. "You all right?"

"Just got a bloody nose," Carter said. "I don't think it's broken."

"I bet I should see the other guy."

"I wish. In this case the other guy was the canopy of the airship. You missed the part where they basically threw us off a cliff."

"And that's the best part," Jack said. "I'm definitely asking for my money back."

He couldn't see if she was smiling or not, but he suspected she was. "So now what?"

Jack felt for his pistol and was unsurprised to find it gone. He was equally unsurprised if slightly more disappointed that they'd apparently found his knife too, as well as most of the contents of his pockets. They'd left him his boots, though, which could be useful. "Did they leave you with anything?"

"You mean that seems useful for breaking out of here?"

"I mean anything besides your clothes."

"No," Carter said after what sounded like a brief exploration of her own pockets. "No, wait, I have a pencil. And a piece of paper. I think it's the receipt from when I stopped for breakfast on the way to work before we started this mission."

"What'd you get?"

"An Egg McMuffin."

"A fine choice."

"I'm glad you approve," Carter said. "How about you?"

He'd been doing his own inventory as they talked. "I have some duct tape." He frowned. "They took my sunglasses. And my hat."

"Actually I think you lost your hat when you were falling off the cliff," Carter said.

"And my sunglasses?"

"No, Keret took those. He seems to like them."

Jack shook his head. "Got any more bad news?"

"Only questions," Carter said. "Where do you suppose they got the zats?"

"The Goa'uld who runs this place?"

"I can't imagine she'd have a reason to arm these guys. But

maybe some of her Jaffa are dealing arms on the side."

"That's a hell of a risk," Jack said. "And given that this place doesn't have any actual resources that are interesting to anybody but archaeology geeks, why would they take it?"

"I don't know," Carter said. "Why *would* somebody be that interested in making a deal with these people when they clearly don't have much to offer in return?"

That sounded pointed. He chose not to take up the thrown gauntlet. "I can't see the Jaffa being interested in some old stone tablets, so... I don't know. We need more information."

"Yes, sir."

"What did you tell them?"

"Very little," Carter said. "We didn't exactly have a long conversation, just 'you're my prisoners and you're worth a lot to me' and then he threw us down here."

"So we'll probably have company soon. Hard to ransom someone if you don't know what they're worth to who."

"There's something to look forward to," Carter said. The note of unease in her voice was faint enough that he thought someone who didn't know her well would have missed it completely.

"Daniel and Teal'c are probably already looking for us," Jack said. "We just need to sit tight and wait for the chance to improve the situation." He hadn't expected to need to tell her that; after two and a half years in the field, she knew it well enough.

"Right," Carter said, and he could hear her taking deep breaths, calming herself down. He nodded approvingly, although he knew she probably couldn't see it.

"You did say you wanted to get a closer look at the airships," he said.

"There is that," she said, and it was more like what he expected from her that she sounded like that might actually make it all worthwhile.

CHAPTER SIX

DANIEL opened his eyes, blinking in the dim light. Next to his head was a fold of fabric, which turned out to be part of a stack of bolts of heavy woven cloth when he managed to focus on it more clearly. He was still wearing his glasses, and they seemed to be unbroken, which was a good thing. He looked past the bolts of cloth and saw bars. Probably not such a good thing.

"Daniel Jackson. Are you injured?"

Teal'c. That was a good thing, except in the sense that if he was in a cell of some kind, and Teal'c was in it with him, then Teal'c wouldn't be arriving to rescue him. Which was more of a bad thing.

He abandoned that particular exercise in mental arithmetic and sat up. Everything seemed to work properly. "I'm fine," he said, although he felt that he'd acquired a new collection of bruises. "You?"

"I am uninjured," Teal'c said.

"What happened?"

"I believe we have been captured by the men who attacked the ceremony," Teal'c said.

"Great," Daniel said, getting to his feet. "I saw Jack go down, I don't know about Sam—"

"She was still fighting when I was rendered unconscious," Teal'c said. "I have heard nothing so far that suggests that they are also prisoners aboard this vessel."

Once on his feet, Daniel could see that the barred walls formed three sides of some kind of large cell or cage. The fourth was a wall of solid metal. Most of the space was filled by bolts of cloth and sacks that might be filled with grain. There was a door in the wall opposite the solid one, fitted with a large and complicated-looking lock.

He hadn't thought until Teal'c spoke that they might be on a vessel, but when he thought about it he could hear the drone of what might be propellers, and feel a faint vibration under him that suggested some kind of engine in use somewhere nearby. There was no sensation of motion, but there wouldn't be unless they happened to be accelerating or turning.

Outside the bars, they seemed to be in some kind of bigger room, or maybe compartment was the word if they were on a ship. There was light filtering in from windows set deeply into two of the walls, and when he paced the length of the cage, he could see flashes of blue sky and wisps of cloud out the windows. No one was watching or guarding them, although he thought he heard the sound of footsteps overhead.

The immediate problem was being in this cell. He felt their options would be increased by being out of it. "I take it that door is locked?"

"It is."

"The bars?"

"A possibility," Teal'c said, inclining his head in a nod. "I did not wish to take the risk while you were unconscious and unable to aid in our escape."

"I'm up," Daniel said. "Let's see if we can get out of here."

His part in that consisted mainly of standing back out of the way as Teal'c wrestled with the bars, straining to bend them enough for them to be able to slip free. He'd been spending a lot of time in the gym since he joined SG-1, but Teal'c still sometimes made him feel like the 'before' picture in an advertisement for someone's patented workout routine.

Daniel had thought he was in reasonably good shape before he joined the team; scrambling through ruins and carrying around excavation equipment wasn't exactly a sedentary activity. Then he'd started working with Jack and Teal'c — and for that matter Sam — and discovered their definition of 'a nice little stroll.' Between not wanting their nice little strolls to be an exercise in suffering and being highly invested in running faster than their pursuers when they had to sprint for the Stargate, he hadn't needed much encouragement to make the most of the SGC's workout facilities.

Which still didn't make bending metal bars with his bare hands his job. He took the opportunity to take stock of their surroundings instead. A spiral staircase made out of what looked like bamboo ran up and down from one corner of the compartment. Several of its stairs seemed to have been mended and patched, suggesting frequent use.

Most of the space on all sides seemed taken up with shelves and doorways into smaller compartments. He could see coils of rope and a couple of coats and loose wool wraps hanging on hooks, but nothing that looked like an obvious weapon. Many of the shelves held what looked like machine parts of various kinds, though, which suggested he could at least find something heavy to hit people with.

Teal'c's shoulders strained as he tugged on the bars. It looked like he was actually getting somewhere, albeit slowly. Hopefully the bars wouldn't be solid iron, not given the need to reduce the airship's weight.

"I wouldn't do that if I were you," a woman said from behind them. Daniel turned, inwardly wincing.

The speaker was standing outside the bars on the other side of the cell, considering them. She was a handsome woman, tall and boyishly built, with dark hair that fell in long curls nearly to her waist. An affectation, he thought, one that didn't match her practical clothes, a dark leather coat and dark wool trousers tucked into the tops of her stained leather boots.

"Do what?" Daniel said, turning with his hands open. Beside him, Teal'c abandoned his attempts to bend the cell bars and turned reluctantly as well.

"Try to escape," she said. "This ship is crawling with my men, and unless you can grow wings and fly, I don't know where you'd be planning to go."

"I hadn't gotten that far," Daniel admitted.

"I see that." She turned her attention to Teal'c, looking him over with an expression of interest that Daniel didn't much like.

"You should release us," Teal'c said. "Our friends will be looking for us, and it will be unfortunate for you if they find us."

"Also unlikely," the woman said. "But believe me, I have no plans to hold onto you any longer than it takes for me to get a good price for you. You may as well get comfortable in there in the mean time, because I'm not about to let you run around loose as long as I have you aboard."

"I think we've gotten off on the wrong foot here," Daniel said. "Let's start over. I'm Daniel Jackson. This is Teal'c. Whatever you're trying to accomplish here, there must be a better way of doing it than kidnapping us."

"My name is Reba," the woman said. "You're aboard my ship, the *Heart's Desire*."

"Pleased to meet you." He couldn't entirely keep the note of sarcasm out of his voice. "So, were we just in the wrong place at the wrong time, or what?"

"More or less," Reba said matter-of-factly. "I was actually after the metal tablets with the writings of the Ancients."

Daniel blinked. "You know what they are?"

"Better than you do, I think," Reba said. "There are other copies of the texts. Incomplete copies. The ones I saw were hidden away in one of the temples of Asherah, high in the mountains."

"Aren't we high in the mountains?"

"Higher," she said, looking unimpressed. "When I worked out what they were describing, and figured out that the copies were incomplete, I knew I had to find the original tablets. We were hoping to find a less dramatic way of getting our hands on them, but when we heard the High King was planning to trade them to the Tau'ri, we went for dramatic."

"What's so valuable about the tablets?"

She shook her head a little. "And why would I possibly want to tell you that?"

Daniel repressed the urge to say *Actually, I have no idea.* "I might be able to help you interpret them. You said yourself you haven't seen the full inscriptions before. As far as I can tell from just a couple of looks, they're using a very abbreviated form of the Ancient language, almost a code, but I'm sure I can work it out."

"I'll work it out myself when I have the time," she said, which suggested that she expected it to be a challenging task herself. While that was disappointing in the sense that he would have liked to meet someone who was more fluent in Ancient than he was, it did suggest that his help really would be of value to her. "I ended up getting my hands on something better."

"And what would that be?" Daniel asked. He had a sudden sinking feeling that she meant them, and considered how best to tread the path between raising unreasonable expectations and making them sound expendable. "Our people will be willing to make some kind of reasonable deal for our safe return, it's true, but I don't want you to get the idea—"

"I'm not interested in dealing with the Tau'ri," Reba said. "All I've heard about your people is that they have a reputation for being unpredictable. I like known quantities."

Daniel felt he had to ask, even though he was pretty sure he wouldn't like the answer. "Who's the known quantity?"

"Our beloved goddess Asherah, of course," Reba said. "I intend to offer to sell her the *shol'va* Teal'c, the troublesome Jaffa who's been inciting rebellion against the gods. I think she'll find him a very marketable property."

The hatch in the top of the small metal compartment rattled, and Sam looked up sharply toward the ceiling, and then at Jack. It was too dark to see his face, but she could see the sharp shake of his head, and his 'hold-up' gesture.

She wasn't particularly enthusiastic about the idea of trying to jump whoever was up there when they were probably armed and she wasn't, so that was just as well. She leaned back against the wall of the compartment instead, shielding her eyes with her hand against the light as the hatch opened.

"Get them out," Keret said from above, and rough hands reached in to drag her up and onto the deck. As she tried to shake them off, to no avail, she could see stone rather than sky through the small windows set in the walls. They were flying low, then, through mountain passes, probably trying to lose their pursuers that way.

The compartment they'd been dragged out of had to be near the front of the airship, she thought, quickly trying to judge its size; most of the deck was taken up with some kind of barred cage stacked high with cargo, with doors leading through a bulkhead to some kind of closed compartment to the stern.

She saw Jack glancing around as well, marking the two spiral staircases to port and starboard not far away from where they stood. It might have been worth making a break for one if there were any way of freeing herself from the grip of the two men who held her. Still, she watched Jack, not wanting to miss his signal if he was planning on making a move.

"I thought we'd be having this little chat soon," Jack said, smiling at Keret in a way she didn't think Keret was stupid enough to interpret as friendly. He looked entirely at ease, not struggling against the men who held him, just waiting to hear what Keret had to say. She wished she thought she looked half as relaxed. "Let me guess. This is the part where you ask if there's anyone who's willing to ransom us."

"And is there?" Keret said. He was wearing Jack's sunglasses pushed up on his forehead like aviator's goggles, which Sam could see Jack take note of even if he kept quiet about it.

"There might be," Jack said. "If you'll give us back our

radios so that we can get in touch with our people, we can probably work something out."

"You mean you can signal someone to rescue you," Keret said. "I'm not that stupid."

"I'm sorry to hear that," Jack said.

"Let me make this very simple," Keret said. "If no one's going to ransom you, then I might as well dump you over the side right now."

"You don't want to do that," Sam said quickly.

Jack just shook his head, as if he'd heard it all before. "What happened to the rest of my team?"

"They're probably locked up in Reba's hold right now," Keret said.

"'Probably,'" Sam said. "He didn't make the rendezvous, did he?"

"No, *she* didn't," Keret said. "It hardly matters to me. I wasn't planning to waste my time chasing her imaginary treasure, anyway. You're worth more to me than some useless old tablets."

Sam frowned. "The ones being presented at the ceremony? What have they got to do with treasure?"

"Reba's got it through her head that they tell the location of a fabulous treasure," Keret said. "Probably a bunch of old pots and more useless carved rocks, but... there's a story told to children about a cave up in the mountains somewhere that hides a treasure greater than any man could possibly desire. Supposedly it can only be found if you know the way to the mountain's true heart."

"Open, Sesame," Jack said. Keret looked blank.

"You think it's just a story?" Sam said.

Keret shrugged. "I think there's no such thing as more treasure than any man could desire. I expect Reba's on her way to go wander around old ruins right now, and I say let her go." Jack glanced at the men holding Sam, as if reading something in their expressions that Sam couldn't see, and

Sam realized that this little speech might be as much for the benefit of Keret's crew as anything else. "We'll turn a profit off the two of you in the mean time, and be waiting to have a word with her when she heads back this way."

"Then I suppose you'd better find some way of letting General Hammond know where we are so you can ransom us," Jack said.

"I'll handle that part," Keret said. "I'm just wondering whether it would be more effective to return you both unharmed, or to use one of you as an example to make it clear that the ransom for the other had better be generous and prompt."

"You really don't want to do that," Jack said. There was a dangerous note in his voice, although he still stood easy, not making any move that would inspire them to wrestle him into submission. She wondered about that, wondering whether he'd been hurt in the fight or in his fall from the cliff and hadn't bothered to mention it, but there wasn't any way of finding out, so she filed that.

"We'll see, won't we?" Keret said. "Better hope your Great General makes a good first offer. In the mean time..." He gestured to his men, and they started to manhandle Sam back toward the hatch in the deck they'd been dragged out of.

"Hey," Jack said. "How about some water, and a chance to stretch our legs a little, if you know what I mean?"

"Later," Keret said. "Right now we're a little busy flying, unless you like smashing into mountainsides."

One of the men kicked the hatch open, and at the same time she felt the ship pitch, correcting course; she could see a sliver of blue sky come into view through one of the windows. There was something about that momentary stomach-dropping pitch that felt familiar to her, all wrong for an airship, more like something she couldn't quite put a name to.

"Move," one of the men holding her said, shoving her back, and she scrambled back into the small compartment, since there didn't seem to be any better options. Jack was shoved in beside her, trying to catch himself as he landed but still wincing visibly in the light from above.

"I'll be back," Keret said, and the hatch slammed shut.

"Okay, now what?" Sam said after the footsteps from above had all retreated. She could hear the hum of the motors, loud enough that they could probably talk without being overheard.

"We have some problems," Jack said. "Even if these clowns manage to get in touch with Hammond, I'm betting that whatever he has to say isn't going to make them very happy."

"At which point they start 'making an example' of one of us," Sam said. She knew as well as Jack did that Hammond wasn't going to give into a ransom demand without looking for other options first, especially not if Keret asked for weapons. It wouldn't be a particularly good idea if he did, given that they didn't want it to get around that kidnapping SG teams was profitable, but it put them in a dangerous position right now.

"Or, worst-case, they can't get in touch with Hammond, because he also got kidnapped by this guy's friend, the one who apparently just screwed him over. So he gets in touch with the folks back in the capital, and they contact the SGC, and we see how long it takes whoever's in charge back there to make a decision with Hammond gone."

"I'm betting a while," Sam said.

"Probably long enough for these guys to decide we're more trouble than we're worth." He shook his head. "Also, I should probably tell you that my right leg may be a problem. Walking and standing are fine. How climbing and sprinting go remains to be seen."

Sam let out a breath. "Okay. Do we have any good news?"

"I was going to ask you that."

"Not really," Sam said. "Although I think I know why these airships can fly even though they're really too heavy for the size of the canopy."

"Is it relevant?"

"Actually, it might be," Sam said. "I think they're using Goa'uld anti-gravity technology. When they changed course, just now, it felt a lot like changing direction quickly in a tel'tak."

"I would say that's pretty unlikely at their general level of technology, but given the zats…"

"I think they've gotten their hands on more Goa'uld technology than we thought at first," Sam said. "I'd be really interested in seeing whether this ship is actually using the drive out of a tel'tak, or a glider — if so, I'm not sure why they need the propellers, unless they aren't able to fully power it, which is certainly a possibility — or whether they've got some kind of stripped-down version."

"That *would* be interesting," Jack said. She was never entirely sure whether he was being sarcastic or not when he said things like that, but she'd learned that taking the words at face value was usually more productive than arguing about it.

"It really would. The only thing is, I think they're probably going to kill us first."

"I think you're right," Jack said. "We're going to have to escape."

"There is the slight problem that it's a long way down," Sam pointed out.

"So it is," Jack said. "That's why we're going to hijack the ship."

CHAPTER SEVEN

"SO, THIS isn't good."

Teal'c inclined his head in agreement. "It is not."

Daniel Jackson was pacing, as was his habit when confronted with problems that did not admit of immediate solution. He claimed that it helped him think, and as Teal'c had never yet been able to think of a way of disproving this, he once again repressed the urge to insist that he stop. "The Goa'uld weren't supposed to visit this planet often."

"The frequency of their visits is immaterial..." Teal'c began.

"As long as one of the visits is happening right now, yes, I see that."

"Our prospects for escape seem limited."

"They do at that. I just wish I could talk to Reba again and see if I can convince her —" He broke off as one of the crew came stomping down the stairs, a skinny man in dirty woolen clothes who gave them a scornful glance as he went by.

"Excuse me," Daniel Jackson said. "We really need to talk to Reba. Can you tell her that there's something very important we need to discuss with her as soon as..." He trailed off as the man stomped by in the other direction and headed back up the stairs. "As soon as she has a chance."

"Do you believe she will be amenable to persuasion?"

"Well, if she wants those tablets translated, it's worth a try. The other option is that we break out of this cell, fight a bunch of pirates who are armed when we're not, and then after we somehow defeat them all — and I'm just going to gloss over that part — we either learn how to fly this ship extremely fast, or we get off the ship somehow without falling to our deaths. And then all we have to do is climb back down a mountain and walk home."

"When you put it that way, it does not sound promising," Teal'c said.

"I'm thinking talking to Reba is a better place to start."

"Perhaps if you tell her that you are of little value to the Goa'uld, but of great value to General Hammond, she will see the value in attempting to ransom you."

Daniel Jackson looked at him as if he felt it was an unhelpful suggestion. "After she hands you over to the Goa'uld? That's not an okay solution here."

"I would prefer to avoid it," Teal'c said. "However, if one of us can return and tell General Hammond what has transpired, it will give the other a chance of rescue. I am the one Reba considers to be of value."

"Which is why she wants to sell you to Asherah, so she can make an example of you or trade you to someone who's more interested in doing that." He frowned. "You do know that I'm not okay with that happening, right?"

"I am aware that you are not," Teal'c said after only a moment's hesitation.

"Okay," Daniel Jackson said, although he still did not look entirely happy. "Because I would hate to think that you…"

He broke off again at the sound of footsteps descending the stairs. "Hey!" he called. "Do you think you could tell Reba —"

"Tell me what?" the woman said, coming into view as she swung herself briskly down the last few steps. "It had better be interesting."

Daniel Jackson considered her. "How's it coming with translating those tablets?"

"I told you, I'll work on it when I have time."

"I could help. They must be worth something to you, or you wouldn't have gone to all that trouble storming the ceremony. By the way, how *did* you know that those particular tablets would be brought out for the ceremony?" He spread his hands at her sharp look. "Just curious."

It would indeed be useful to know whether the High King

had been complicit in their capture, but Teal'c thought that Daniel Jackson's motivation was mainly to get her to begin talking. He knew well that it would be harder for her to conceal all useful information from them while speaking than if she simply remained silent in their presence. It had occurred to him more than once that his friend's talents would have made him particularly skilled at the interrogation of prisoners, had he served the Goa'uld.

Reba looked as though she were considering whether the answer to the question would be of value to them. "Anath is Keret's sister," she said after a moment, with a shrug. "She tells him anything interesting she hears in the palace, which he finds very useful. Which might have something to do with why he's never yet gotten around to paying off her indentures for her."

"Wonderful guy."

Reba smiled, a hard expression. "Yes, we're a virtuous lot. Did you have a point?"

"Let me see the tablets. Maybe I can translate them for you, and then you can..."

"Find a treasure greater than you could imagine," Reba said.

"And then you might not need to sell us to Asherah."

"Maybe I'll sell you to Asherah first and then go look for the treasure."

"Maybe you will," Daniel Jackson said evenly. "So there's no risk to you, is there? The tablets are metal, it's not like I can destroy them, and if you're worried that we're going to try to hit somebody over the head with them, you can stand there holding a zat on us."

"'Zat?'" Reba asked, and then looked a little amused. "Oh, a zat'ni'ktel, yes. Most people around here call them thunderbolts."

"But you knew what I meant."

"I know a little of the language of the gods," Reba said.

"May I ask why?"

"No." She considered him through the bars, her hands on her hips. "How do I know this isn't a trick?"

"You said yourself you'd already translated part of the inscription. You can check my translation against what you already have."

After a moment longer she shrugged. "Why not. You may as well make yourselves useful while I have you aboard. I'll even feed you a free meal for your trouble."

"That's nice," Daniel Jackson said. "Some people do consider feeding prisoners the humane thing to do anyway."

"Virtuous and humane," Reba said. "That's us for certain." She smiled sharply. "Just remember that you're worth a lot less to me than the Jaffa. If you try to cross me, I'll hang you from a rope and use you for target practice."

"We get the picture."

She walked away and made her way down the stairs, presumably to fetch the tablets from some lower compartment.

"If you translate the tablets for her accurately —" Teal'c began in a low voice.

"Then she may decide she doesn't need to keep me around after that, yes, I know. But let's start by seeing what they actually say."

"I have no better plan," Teal'c admitted, and took up a position by the bars where he could keep watch as they waited.

"Hijack the airship," Carter said. Jack couldn't make out her expression, but she sounded a little skeptical.

"Yep."

"And how are we planning to do this?"

"We get out of here, we find somebody with a zat and take it away from them, and then we take out the rest of the crew. After that we put the ship down somewhere, kick these guys off it, and fly it back to the palace. Piece of cake."

"Do you know how to fly an airship? I don't think they actually covered that when I was at the Academy. Although, you know, maybe in your day…"

"We were up to biplanes by then," Jack said. "Seriously, you can figure out how this thing works, right?"

"Probably," Carter said. "You know, one of these days we're *not* actually going to be able to learn to fly something in a crisis situation where failure means we crash and die."

"Today is not that day," Jack said. "Come on, Carter."

"Yes, sir," she said. "I think we can figure out how to fly the airship."

"We should wait until it quiets down for the night. Then we can figure out a way to get out of here without attracting a lot of attention."

"I'll think about that," Carter said. "I don't suppose you have a hacksaw blade in the sole of your shoe or anything?"

"I left my hacksaw in my other shoes," he said. "Which is to say, no. I don't know how long we were out—"

"I make it late afternoon," she said. "Local time. I'm not even sure anymore what time it is back home."

"So let's try and get some sleep," Jack said. "It's likely to be a busy night."

He stretched out as well as he could and closed his eyes.

"I still don't know how you manage that," Carter said after a while, cutting through his drifting thoughts and jerking him back from the edge of sleep.

"What?"

"Napping while we're stuck in a prison cell."

"Practice," Jack said without opening his eyes. "It helps not to talk."

"Right," she said a little ruefully. "Sorry, sir."

He opened his eyes some time later at the rattle of the overhead hatch. It opened, but the light from above was faint. He raised a hand to fend off several unidentified objects that were tossed down, and then the hatch was slammed shut.

"A canteen of water, some kind of bread — at least, I think that's what it's supposed to be — and a bucket," Carter said. "Wonderful."

"I knew we should have paid for the first class upgrade," Jack said. He waited while she drank, and then drank thirstily himself, trying to make out the sound of footsteps above over the drone of the propellers. They waited a while longer, until it had been some time since he'd heard any sound he could identify as other than mechanical. "All right," he said. "What do we do?"

"I've been thinking about that," Carter said. "These walls are sheet metal, and they're not that thick. If they're something with a low tensile strength like aluminum, which is possible if they're trying to keep the weight down, we might actually be able to cut through if we had a knife."

"Maybe," Jack said. "Would you build cell walls somebody could just cut through? You can figure somebody's always got a knife."

"I'm not sure this was actually built as a cell," Carter said. "It looks more like some kind of cargo compartment. Besides, we *don't* have a knife."

"Somebody's always got something," Jack said, prying the rubber silencer off one of his dog tags and carefully finding the edge he kept sharpened. He tried it on the wall, but the line it scored in the metal felt like only a faint depression, and it came away significantly duller. He tossed her the tags, and heard her catch them. "Try the wall on your side."

"No joy," she said after a moment. "Maybe if we used the bucket as a hammer —"

Jack shook his head. "Too much noise."

There was the sound of Velcro, presumably Carter searching her pockets again. "I still have a magnesium firestarter," she said after a while. "We could maybe burn through with that in one spot, but that's not going to get us out. There are already holes in this wall."

"Not to mention that smoke is going to attract attention fast with a big flammable balloon up there." He looked up at the very faint light filtering in through the cracks around the hatch. "The hatch closes with a bolt, right?"

"Looked like it," Carter said.

Jack stood up, reaching up to feel around the edges. "Hand me back my tags."

Carter pressed them into his hand, and he wedged one into the crack, sliding it along the side where he thought the bolt must be until he met resistance. "Yeah, right here," he said. He couldn't get enough play to budge the bolt, though, even with the sharp edge of the tag. He closed his eyes, trying to visualize how the bolt lay. "What I really need is a stiff piece of wire, something to catch the end of the bolt. I don't suppose you've got that in your shoe?"

"Umm," Carter said.

"'Umm'?"

"Yes, actually, I do have a stiff piece of wire that might work," she said a little reluctantly. "You just have to promise not to look while I… cut it out of my underwear."

"Right," Jack said, doing his best to sound perfectly casual. "It's dark anyway."

"And you're still not looking, right? Hand me those tags back. I need something with a sharp edge."

Jack held them out with his eyes closed, and kept them closed while trying hard not to imagine anything he shouldn't be imagining.

"All right," Carter said after a minute. "I'm decent."

She handed him a piece of flat wire bent into a double curve. He tested it, slipping it through the crack around the hatch, and pulled it back out to bend it into something more like the right shape. "I think this may do it," he said, slipping the end back through.

"Practical uses for underwires in survival situations," Carter said. "I should write a memo. You know, most of them are also conductive, and in a real pinch you could probably improvise some kind of weapon out of one, although that's more of a stretch."

"We're not there yet, but I'll keep that in mind," Jack said. The end of the wire caught the bolt and then skittered off its end. "Almost."

"Duct tape?"

"Duct tape," Jack said. He wrapped the end of the wire with the sticky side of the tape out and then tried again. He felt it catch and stick this time, and levered it carefully, feeling the bolt start to give. "Come on, you…"

The bolt gave suddenly, sliding easily now as he pulled the hooked wire back through the crack. He tested the hatch cover and felt it lift as he pressed up with his fingertips.

"We're in business," he said. He wasn't sure what to do with the piece of wire. "I'm not sure this is going back where it came from."

"That's all right," Carter said. "Let's just move on."

"Now comes the interesting part," Jack said.

CHAPTER EIGHT

DANIEL tilted the metal tablet, angling it to catch the dim light. It was dark now outside the porthole windows, dark enough that he couldn't tell whether they would have showed stone or sky, but one of the crew had lit a couple of fine-meshed lamps as the light faded. Safety lamps, he supposed, which accounted for why they hadn't all been blown up yet. Or set on fire.

He wasn't clear which was more likely, only that it was hard to keep visions of the Hindenburg out of his head as he bent close to the tablets. They were definitely Ancient, but in an abbreviated form he'd only seen references to before. Making sense of them meant interpolating vowels and in some places whole words, but he was beginning to think he had the trick of it.

Nearby, Teal'c sat cross-legged, eyes closed in kel'no'reem. It made sense for him to restore himself now so that he could watch while Daniel eventually slept, but Daniel was also aware that watching him work out translations in a language Teal'c didn't read was probably intensely boring.

He was anything but bored himself. If it weren't for his awareness of the danger they were in, he would have been thrilled; they had so few texts in Ancient, and this one used several words that were new to him but that he could guess at from context. He wished he had something to write with.

And then there was what the tablets actually said, which if he could possibly be right...

The last part was the most straight-forward, and probably the part that had been missing from other copies, the latitude and longitude of a particular point on the planet's surface. It was probably too much to hope that whatever system of longitude was still in use there could be matched to the Ancients' in any meaningful way, but given a general area to search, the latitude should narrow it down. Given that she'd studied other inscriptions left by the Ancients, Reba might even have worked out the longitude problem; it would only take having the Ancient coordinates for a single known point to do it.

The part before that was a set of directions leading to a particular point through what sounded like a maze of streets and pathways. Apparently there had been a complex of buildings laid out in a grid, although it wasn't clear to Daniel whether it had been a city or some kind of temple complex. Either way, it had been a special place, and the reason for that was what its innermost chamber held.

That was the part that Daniel had spent the last hour checking and double-checking, wracking his brain to remember every scrap of the language of the gate builders that they had found so far. He'd wondered if he was making some kind of elementary error at first, but now he felt confident in his translation, and suspected that he knew where Reba had gone wrong with hers. He could feel his heart beating faster, and told himself firmly to keep his expectations reasonable, but he couldn't entirely repress his excitement.

"Daniel Jackson," Teal'c said, opening his eyes. "Have you made progress in translating the tablets?"

"Actually, yes," Daniel said. "I see why Reba was interested. It's this part, here — it's very easy to mistranslate it as *a treasure greater than the heart's desire*. 'Treasure' should be, umm, not 'thesaurus'… 'thessera,' right, but here it's 'artefacta.' It doesn't mean something found, it means something made by a skilled creator, a… look here, it's clear from the rest of the context that whoever wrote this was talking about a device."

Teal'c looked as directed, although his expression made it clear that the words carried no meaning for him. "A device greater than the heart's desire?"

"Not quite. A device for *finding* 'whatever your heart desires most.' It sounds to me like the Ancients built a device that was intended to let them find anything they wanted to find. Some kind of... super-scanner that works at immense distances, from world to world or maybe even throughout the entire galaxy."

Teal'c raised an eyebrow skeptically, and Daniel held up a hand. "All right, I know how it sounds, but we're talking about the *Ancients* here. They built the Stargates, they obviously had access to knowledge and a level of technology that we can't even begin to understand. Is it that much more of a stretch that they could have had a way of finding things that we don't understand either? I mean, think about it, they must have had some way of finding uninhabited planets where they could put the Stargates, right?"

"You have said before that you believed them to have explored the galaxy in ships," Teal'c said.

"We don't *know*," Daniel said. "We still have no idea how the Ancients did most of what they did, and we can count the number of original Ancient artifacts — in the modern sense of the word — that we've ever found on the fingers of... well, not many hands. An actual functional Ancient device for locating things..."

Teal'c frowned. "You cannot be certain whether the device is functional, or indeed whether it is actual."

"Well, no, of course not," Daniel said. He felt that wasn't the point. "But it might be. And if it is, I think we may be able to find it." Teal'c still looked as though he disapproved. "All right, what?"

"Surely most people's greatest desire is not for a physical object, but for some event or state of being."

"Well, that depends, doesn't it?" Daniel said, trying to keep his voice even. "Anyway, that part is probably just a poetic way of saying it'll find whatever it is you particularly want to find. You have to admit that would be a huge discovery."

"If it is real."

"Which I think it very well could be," Daniel said. "The

tricky part is going to be getting Reba to believe me and go look for the thing without handing us over to the Goa'uld first."

Teal'c still looked deeply skeptical. "If you are successful in locating this... device... what is to prevent her from taking it from us and using it for her own personal gain?"

"We'll have to make some kind of deal, obviously. I hadn't gotten that far, all right?"

Teal'c shook his head. "If the device works as you describe, it would be of great value to someone in search of wealth. Do you truly believe Reba will keep any bargain you attempt to make with her and allow you to take it away with you?"

Daniel shrugged. "I'm not even sure it's something that we can take with us. For all we know, it could be the size of a building or hooked up to an Ancient power source that we have no way of moving without an engineering team."

"In which case, its potential benefit to us seems slim."

"Oh, come on," Daniel said. "There are all kinds of things we could find out even if we can't take it away with us. Where to find more sources of naquadah, or planets that have advanced civilizations that haven't been enslaved by the Goa'uld, or..."

"Are those things truly your heart's desire?"

"I told you, I think that part is poetic license." He felt the mood could use a little lightening. "I'm pretty sure that finding more advanced weaponry is Jack's heart's desire, anyway."

"I am not as certain of that," Teal'c said, unsmiling.

"All right," Daniel said. He was going to have to come out and say it. "Fine. What if we could use this device, whatever it is, to find Sha're's son?"

It had been her dying wish, communicated to him through an effort no one had thought possible as Amonet wracked him with the ribbon device. She had wanted him to find her son, hidden away by Amonet to prevent him from being destroyed because he possessed the genetic memory of the Goa'uld. And so far they'd found nothing, only dead end after dead end.

It was a while before Teal'c answered. "The possibility seems remote."

"You can't say that. We haven't even seen what exactly this thing is or what it does. Until we do, we don't know if we'd be passing up our only chance to… I mean, right now we have no idea where to even start looking. All we have is the name of a place that could be anywhere in a very big galaxy."

"I understand your desire to find the child," Teal'c said, "but —"

"Do you?" He couldn't bite back the words in time, although he knew as soon as he spoke them that they were unfair. Teal'c had a son of his own, and must have held him as a baby the way Daniel had held Sha're's child so briefly. He had barely paid attention at the time, his heart still sick at losing Sha're again to Amonet mere moments after the birth, her look of desperation transforming into the haughty glare of a hateful stranger wearing his wife's face.

"You must believe that I do," Teal'c said evenly. "I am not questioning your motivations, but I am starting to wonder if I should question your judgment."

"Sometimes we have to take risks," Daniel said, stung by the implication behind the words. "If we aren't going to —" He broke off as one of Reba's men came down the stairs from above, throwing them a disinterested glance and starting on down to the deck below. "Hey," Daniel said. "Excuse me. Please tell Reba I have some very interesting information for her."

The man shrugged in what might be assent and continued down.

Teal'c looked at him. "You mean to tell her what you believe you have discovered?"

"The way I figure it, we have two choices," Daniel said, talking fast. "One, we try to stall until somebody rescues us, and hope that happens before Reba can make a deal with Asherah. If it doesn't, we get handed over to the Goa'uld. Or, two, I tell her what I've figured out, and see if we can make a deal to go check out these coordinates together. Even assuming — no, wait, hear me out. Even assuming there's absolutely nothing there, that buys us a lot more time. Jack and Sam are going to be looking for us, but we have to give them time to find us."

"What is to prevent her from taking the information and then dispensing with us as no longer needed?"

"I'll give her the coordinates but not the directions for how to find the exact spot where the thing is located. We'll go from there. Come on, it has to be better than being sold to a Goa'uld who's going to take us offworld and put us somewhere where nobody's going to be this willing to talk to us."

"Very well," Teal'c said after a moment. "Perhaps the search for this device will present us with an opportunity to escape."

"Maybe so," Daniel said. He tried to push away unwanted emotions, to focus clearly on finding the right words to persuade Reba that a deal would be to her advantage. There was no point in thinking about the last time he'd seen the baby, nestled in Kasuf's arms with the man's hand cupped wonderingly over the fine fuzz of his grandson's hair.

"You'd better have something for me," Reba said, coming upstairs with a cup of something steaming in her hand. He let himself wonder where hot water came from on an airship for a moment, appreciating the distraction, and then looked her calmly in the eye.

"I think I know how to find whatever it is you're looking for," he said.

Sam watched as Jack carefully pushed open the hatch in the compartment's roof, to no immediate outcry. He nodded to her and then boosted her up. She braced herself on her elbows, hanging onto the hatch cover awkwardly for a moment until she could open it the rest of the way without letting it fall noisily.

She scrambled up, and Jack followed, pushing himself

up easily without making a sound. He glanced at the stairs, clearly weighing going up or down versus staying on this deck, and then turned away from them and started very cautiously working his way toward the stern of the ship.

In the middle of the deck, a large cage was stacked with cargo. She couldn't make out more than dark shapes in the moonlight that spilled in through the small windows set into the airship's hull. Jack peered in through the bars and then turned his attention to a small compartment set against the hull just aft of the stairs.

Storage, maybe, which meant there was some chance of weapons. He opened the door, moving very slowly. She couldn't hear any creak from the door's hinges as he opened it, which was a good sign; the hum of the motors below them was probably covering their footsteps.

She couldn't see his expression, but she could see him shake his head and push the door equally slowly closed again. She could also smell well enough to get the picture that they probably hadn't discovered a weapons locker. Well, finding the latrines was useful in the long run.

Jack moved slowly along the hull of the airship, making his way back toward the stern. She didn't see whatever it was he saw, only saw him freeze and flattened herself against the hull beside him. It was dark, but surely anyone coming would be able to see their shapes in the dim light, and probably take a closer look.

It was the door to the stern compartment opening, a man stumbling out sleepily, heading in their direction. Probably heading for the latrine, which meant he'd have to pass them, which meant there was no way he wouldn't see them.

She stepped out from the shelter of the wall just before she thought he'd have to see her. "Hey," she said softly. It shouldn't have worked, but his eyes went to her face for a moment as he opened his mouth to speak, and that was all it took. Jack was already moving, wrapping his arm around the man's neck in a chokehold and then lowering him carefully to the deck once he went limp.

Sam went down on one knee, pressing her fingers to the man's throat long enough to determine that a pulse was still beating there and then rifling quickly through his clothes. She found a knife first, handing it up to Jack, and then finally a zat, tucked in an inner pocket in his reeking coat.

She held it up as the man began to stir. Jack nodded, and she fired at the man as he opened his eyes. The man jerked under the zat's blast and then went limp again. Sam winced, sure that someone must have heard the zat discharge, but she couldn't hear an alarm being raised.

Jack moved fast all the same, making for the door, which was still open a crack. He flattened himself against the bulkhead and peered in, then shut it as carefully as if he were trying not to wake a sleeping child. He thrust the knife into the crack just below one of the hinges, jamming it in tightly.

Sam shook her head. "That's not going to hold," she whispered.

He spread his hands, looking around for something better. Sam investigated the cargo that was dimly visible through the nearby bars of the cage, hoping he didn't expect her to produce any more solutions out of her underwear.

Wool, more wool, a sack of something that felt like grain, another sack, but filled with the hard shapes of something definitely not grain. She reached inside and had to repress a noise of triumph, pulling out a handful of nails and holding them up.

He nodded appreciation and waved her toward the door, taking the zat from her and covering her as she spiked the door as quietly as she could. "Sleeping quarters," he mouthed when she glanced at him, and she nodded. If they could keep most of the crew contained for the moment, this might actually work.

Jack tensed, and she looked up to see someone coming up

the stairs from below. She could only make out their outline in the shadows, and Jack must have had the same thought, because he strode easily toward the stairs, as if he were someone who belonged there, and made it nearly to the man's side before he fired. The man went down, and Jack beckoned her over, handing her the man's zat.

He jerked his head questioningly toward the door, and she shrugged. It had better hold, because she couldn't jam the door any more securely without making an unholy racket. He nodded, started for the stairs, and then hesitated, his shoulders tightening.

She leaned in to whisper. "What?"

"You go first," he said, not sounding happy about it. Which suggested he was going to be working just to get down the stairs, and that jumping off them or scrambling back up them under fire was probably right out. Right, then.

She took a deep breath and then took the stairs fast, zat at the ready, trying to take in the scene below in the split second she might have before someone saw her. Aft was probably the storage compartment they'd been trapped in, and directly in front of her was some larger compartment that thankfully shielded the stairs from most of the deck.

Forward around its corner she could see a jumble of machinery, some of it moving in a clockwork tangle of gears and pistons, and in the middle of the deck the shapes of two long tables, with low chairs like overturned baskets scattered around them. There was a yellowish glow coming from above the tables that she was pretty sure... She leaned out as far as she dared. Yes, it was some kind of light bulb, bulky and odd-looking but bright enough behind its thick glass that they weren't going to be able to sneak around in the shadows.

There was one man sitting at one of the tables, drinking out of a steaming mug, and she thought she could make out two more tending the engines. They hadn't seen her yet. She motioned Jack down behind her, and waited for him to make it down to move. He was moving carefully but quickly enough, although she noticed that he braced himself on the stair rail as he crouched, zat raised.

He pointed out targets with his free hand, and then fired, her own first shot a heartbeat behind his. She thought she saw the man at the table go down, but he was Jack's to worry about, and she was already moving, scrambling forward toward the machinery of the engines.

"What in the name —" someone growled, close by, and she fired again, hoping the zat bolts didn't hit anything vital in the airship's machinery. She could feel the heat coming from what must be the top of the main engines, and from the small metal stove on which a kettle was steaming, probably warmed by the heat of the engines rather than an actual open flame.

She could hear Jack firing behind her, and see someone ducking down across the deck from her, disappearing behind a bank of spidery levers. She eased out from behind the minimal cover she had, waiting for a flash of movement that she could fire at.

She saw it closer than she expected, someone moving behind the stove, and she hesitated. If the stove was resting right up against the engines—

Jack fired before she could warn him, blue fire crackling over the man's body and across the surface of the stove, and the man fell, luckily for him not onto the stove but back to sprawl on the deck. The kettle skittered across the surface of the stove and fell clattering to the deck.

Sam waited for a moment, but nothing else happened except that Jack put his foot on the kettle to stop it rolling. She stood up cautiously. "Is that it?"

"Looks like," Jack said. He looked a little annoyed. "Didn't you see that guy?"

"I saw him," Sam said. "I just wasn't sure what would happen if I shot something conductive that's connected to an engine burning explosive gas."

"Right," Jack said after a moment. "Well, now we know."

"Now we do."

She saw over his shoulder the door in the compartment to the stern opening, saw the metallic glint of a zat's muzzle, and motioned him sharply down; he dropped to one knee, and she fired over his shoulder. The man on the other side of the door yelled, the zat clattering to the deck, and the door swung open just long enough for her to fire again.

It was Keret, she saw when she got close enough. Behind where he was lying she could see through the door into what must be his cabin. Against one wall, a low box bed was piled high with crumpled wool blankets, and a clutter of cups and clothing was strewn around the room. Along the walls, rimmed shelves held a magpie collection of everything from decorated pottery to small clockwork machines that at a glance might have been anything from models of the planets to mousetraps.

Jack came up behind her. "He alive?"

"Looks like," Sam said. Jack rifled through the man's clothes while Sam worked on finding something to tie the man up with. She settled for slicing a strip from one of the blankets with the knife Jack handed her. Jack pocketed the man's zat, and with a look of satisfaction returned his own sunglasses to his pocket as well.

"One more deck to go," Jack said. "The one where they're steering the ship. You're sure you can fly this thing?"

She looked up at him. "What if I said no?"

"You'll be fine," Jack said after a moment. "Let's go."

CHAPTER NINE

"I WOULD very much prefer to stay until we find Colonel O'Neill and his team," Hammond said, for what was probably the hundredth time. He was aware that he wasn't in much of a position to make demands. He'd already been escorted back to the Stargate over his strong protests, apologetically but firmly. Behind Walat, SG-1's packs and equipment were now being offloaded from the airship and stacked next to Hammond on the Stargate steps, where their weapons already rested.

Walat shook his head firmly. "It is too great a risk to the High King," he said. "You must understand." Behind him the banners of the High King's airship fluttered in the wind, gold fringe trailing from every window. In front of the Stargate, several servants were laying down heavy wool carpets and strewing them with flower petals, most of which promptly whipped away in the breeze. Presumably this was for Asherah's benefit and not for Hammond's own.

"What I understand is that you've concealed some fairly important facts from us from the beginning," Hammond said. He held up a hand as Walat seemed about to mention the incident with the weapons again. "I'm not saying there haven't been mistakes on both sides, but it's my people who are out there in the hands of criminals."

"It is highly unlikely that they will be harmed," Walat said. "They will be in much greater danger if you attract Asherah's attention to them by your presence here when she arrives."

That was unfortunately hard to argue with. "That's assuming the pirates don't think along the same lines and tell her themselves."

Walat shook his head. "Such impious men would never dream of approaching Asherah or her servants during the festival. She would sense their evil at once and blast them from the sky with her thunderbolts."

Hammond wasn't sure if Walat actually believed that, or if he was just determined to get the Tau'ri off his porch before the Goa'uld arrived, and was willing to say whatever he thought would accomplish that. Either way, he wasn't making any headway.

He glanced down at the packs. He didn't much like the idea of bringing them back instead of SG-1, and then stacking them in a storeroom somewhere until he knew whether he'd need to unpack them. If he did, it would be to file the videos and the notes away for future study, and to pack up Sam's effects so he could hand them to her father and say *Jacob, you know how sorry I am*. He didn't want to even start down that road yet, but Walat had been firm that none of the gear brought by the Tau'ri could remain for Asherah to see.

He looked over the pile of packs and weapons again, and then back up at the airship. The crew were climbing back aboard, clearly finished with their unloading. They'd forgotten one thing, though, and he forced himself to keep a poker face, hoping they wouldn't remember it before they were safely away. Walat had been entirely absorbed in the trade negotiations and the preparations for the ceremony, as far as Hammond could tell, and with any luck he hadn't been paying much attention to anything else.

"I expect you to let us know if you hear anything," Hammond said grimly.

"Of course, Great General," Walat said. "If we hear any word of your people, we will contact you as soon as we can."

"You mean as soon as you can after the festival."

"Just as I said, as soon as it is possible for us to do so."

"It's much appreciated," Hammond said, dialing the gate.

The wrenching pull of the wormhole was still enough of a novelty to take his breath away for a moment as he stepped out of the gate onto the ramp. Luckily it wasn't too long a moment, because he had to step smartly out of the way of SG-1's packs as they came tumbling through behind him. The rifles and Teal'c's staff weapon clattered out behind them, thankfully pushed through the gate rather than thrown, accompanied by a swirl of flower petals that were still settling to the ramp when the wormhole shut down.

"General Hammond," Dr. Janet Fraiser said, coming down the stairs into the gateroom. "We were starting to worry." At the end of the ramp, several airmen were moving the MALP he'd sent back ahead of him out of the way. A medical team was standing by near the entrance to the gateroom, but Janet shook her head at them as she saw that they weren't apparently needed.

"And well you might," Hammond said. "SG-1's gone missing."

Her eyebrows went up. "From a treaty signing?"

"They've apparently been kidnapped by pirates, if you can believe that." Hammond said. "And better yet, the Goa'uld who controls this planet will be showing up at any minute for a week-long festival, and the local government has thrown us out for the duration."

"I can see why they might not want us around if the Goa'uld are visiting, but what do we do now?"

"I don't think there was going to be much I could do on that side to find SG-1, anyway," Hammond said. "I'm hoping we'll have better luck from this side."

Janet looked puzzled for a moment, and then smiled slowly. "Major Carter was doing weather surveys with a UAV, wasn't she? It hasn't come back through."

"And I'm pretty sure the High King and his people have forgotten all about it. I expect Major Carter set it down somewhere out of the way. With any luck, we can get it up in the air again and use it to find the airships that took SG-1. That way as soon as this festival is over, we can send a rescue party through."

"We'd better hurry," Janet said. "The more of a head start they have —"

"I wish it were that simple," Hammond said reluctantly. "But the Goa'uld party may arrive at any minute. We need to give them at least enough time to get clear of the Stargate so that we don't attract attention when we dial in ourselves." He shook his head. "They're resourceful people," he said. "I'm sure they can stay safe until we can send someone to get them."

"Yes, sir," Janet said. "They're probably fine."

"That's the spirit," Hammond said. "We'll give it eight hours before we dial in."

Hammond turned to take another look at the gate before starting up the stairs to his office. He told himself that SG-1 probably was fine, at least in the sense of being alive and maybe even more or less unhurt. SG-1 had a remarkable way of turning up in one piece despite going through the most harrowing experiences.

He tried not to think about the times recently when they'd come back in somewhat less than one piece, and hoped that this wouldn't be another one.

"Let's move," Jack said, motioning Carter ahead of him. She scrambled up the stairs, crouching cautiously to scan the deck above before she straightened and stood to cover him as he climbed the stairs himself.

The man Carter had zatted was still sprawled unmoving, and the door at the far end of the corridor didn't look to have been opened, but he wished he had handcuffs and a more secure lock for the door. Nothing for it but to move fast.

"The upper deck is open, just a rail on the sides," Carter said. "The controls look to be forward."

He nodded and motioned her up the stairs. They ended in a hatch, which she pushed up. He took the last few stairs at as close to a run as he could manage, zat in hand, and came out onto the open deck.

It was shockingly cold, the wind whipping across the deck hard enough to rock him back as he stood. Beyond the rail, he could see mountain peaks and open sky beyond them, going by fast enough that they were clearly making good time. Carter was already moving forward, where two men stood over a bank of controls. One of them turned, and she fired.

The second man turned zat in hand, and Carter ducked as he fired, the blast crackling down the rail behind her. Jack scanned the deck, waiting for someone else to move. Carter dropped the second man and sprinted forward toward the controls. Jack could feel a slight change in the angle of the deck, some control pitching them downward, and he took a moment to find his footing securely.

They were high above what had to be an open plain or plateau, with the nearest visible mountain peaks some distance away, which was a very good thing in terms of not immediately running into anything dangerous. On the other hand, they could still run into the ground. The nose pitched farther downward, the wind whipping off the canopy with a noise like enormous sails shuddering.

"Carter!" he called.

"I know!" she said. "I'm on it!"

He saw the movement out of the corner of his eye and swung around, raising his zat as someone hit him hard, knocking him to the deck and rolling him over. He jammed his zat against the man's stomach and fired, too close for the zat's energy not to arc through him as well.

He gritted his teeth at the pain and tried not to black out. The world grayed for a moment, and then swam back into view. He managed to shove the other man off him and roll to his feet, or at least stagger to his feet.

The deck still felt anything but level. "Carter!"

"I think we have a problem!" she called.

He climbed the deck to her side, and it was definitely climbing. Something felt very wrong about it, every step taking too much effort. He leaned out over the rail to see if they were really diving at that steep an angle to the ground, and shook his head when they barely seemed to be descending at all. "Carter, what the hell?"

"It's the Goa'uld gravity drive they're using," she said. "It's creating an artificial gravity field that's affecting the entire ship. I'm guessing it's some kind of failsafe when the controls aren't manned. The good news is, we're descending very slowly, so we're not actually about to crash into the ground. It just feels like it."

"Good to hear."

"The bad news is, we are still descending."

"This might not be a bad place for that," Jack said, leaning out over the rail again. Some distance below he could see a rocky plateau patched with scrubby trees and undergrowth, rising in the distance to a higher wall of mountains some miles ahead of them. "Setting down somewhere flat could be good."

"We don't have any way of tying down," Carter said. "In this wind, we'd just skate across the rock until we hit something. Like those cliffs up there. And we'd probably take the bottom of the hull off in the process."

The few spindly trees below them wouldn't help; the weight of the airship would snap one of them like a matchstick if they tried to moor the ship to it. "So, what?"

"So, I need to figure out how to engage the gravity generator at maximum strength so that it'll anchor the ship to the ground. That may make it a little uncomfortable for us, but I'm not sure we've got much choice."

"Then do that," Jack said.

"I have to go below," Carter said. "I'd have to do that anyway to stop the engines. You're going to have to fly this thing."

"Great," Jack said after a moment. He frowned at the controls. "Okay, these are probably the rudders."

"Which would make these the elevators. Probably. See what you can do to keep us level. Your perception of the horizontal is going to be off, so you're going to have to go by eye."

"I can do that," Jack said.

"Hopefully with the controls active, the ship will stop whatever automatic routine is kicking in."

Jack played with the controls tentatively, feeling the airship shudder but not able to tell whether he'd made much difference to its attitude. The weird pitch of the deck abruptly leveled, and he caught at the rail to steady himself.

"Are you going to be okay?" Carter said.

"Go," he said. "Do what you can to secure these guys so they aren't going to give us problems when they wake up."

There was a coil of rope with one end tied to the rail, and he cut it loose and used it to tie up the two pilots, leaving them behind the minimal shelter of the bank of controls. They were in his way, there, but they were also out of the wind.

He was already wishing for gloves, the wind whipping across his knuckles, although the controls themselves were warm, as if conducting heat from somewhere below. He held out for a few minutes, and then let go the controls just long enough to crouch, wincing, and strip the leather gloves from one of the pilots.

With gloves, the wind was bearable, although he wished he had his hat back. He could see the shadow of the airship running along the floor of the plateau, a crisp black shape floating across the rocks far below.

And now slightly less far below. He pulled back on the elevator controls, but the airship shuddered rather than perceptibly responding. He tried the other direction, experimentally, and winced at the sound of grinding metal.

"Okay," he said. "Any time, now, Carter."

CHAPTER TEN

SAM dragged the last of the airship's engineering crew out of her way and handcuffed him to something she hoped wasn't a vital mechanism. She was glad she'd found several pairs of metal handcuffs in her hurried searches of unconscious crew members. Before that she'd been very near running out of both rope and patience for tying people up.

She should have asked Jack for the duct tape, because at this rate she was going to run out of handcuffs. She'd used one pair to fasten the door to the crew quarters more securely closed, apparently without waking anyone inside, which was a small mercy. She didn't think it would be easy to take the door apart from the inside, but she wasn't sure how long it would withstand being battered at or zatted.

Next problem, that was the next problem. The first problem was figuring out the engines, and then how they were going to land. The engine controls were a maze of levers and dials, and for a moment it seemed hopeless. She ran her fingers over the levers, trying to trace their connections to the systems they controlled, and slowly their configuration began to make a certain kind of sense.

That dial had to be measuring propeller RPM — at least, she wasn't sure what else it could be measuring — and that was probably a throttle control. She traced the Rube Goldberg tangle of levers and gears with her fingers. She could shut the engines down, probably. She wasn't at all confident of her ability to start them again, especially safely, but she'd have plenty of time to figure that out if they could manage to put down somewhere.

She mentally crossed her fingers and began what she sincerely hoped was a reasonable shutdown procedure. She was rewarded by hearing the engine's dull roar quiet, its numbing shuddering under her feet going still.

That would surely not escape the attention of the sleeping crew. She searched the machinery, hoping that the gravity drive would be obvious. None of the rest of what she saw bore any resemblance to Goa'uld technology, and so it should be clear enough when she stumbled on it—

She nearly stumbled into it, backing up against a metal pillar that rose between the engines and the more open galley area of the deck. It was engraved with lines and whorls that suggested the shape of a tree trunk, with stylized leaves near the ceiling. Another Asherah, maybe, some kind of symbol of the goddess or of fertility that these people used as a good-luck charm, like the figurehead of a sailing ship on Earth.

It was warm to the touch, warmer than she expected. She looked closer, and saw the outline of a separate metal panel set into the center of the pillar. She felt around its edges until she found a catch, and the entire metal panel slid outward to reveal a bank of crystals that she could definitely recognize as Goa'uld.

The problem was that they weren't connected to anything she could recognize as a Goa'uld interface. She'd learned some common labels in Goa'uld by now, things like 'on' and 'off' and 'danger: electrical hazard,' but here they'd apparently cobbled together an interface out of electric wires and manually flipped switches. It looked like a remarkably bad idea in action, and made her wish for rubber gloves, but she thought she could see how flipping the switches would direct power to one subset of the board's crystals or another.

That would have been great if she'd had any idea which ones she needed to power at what levels. She considered experimenting, but hesitated. She didn't like either the prospect of sending herself suddenly slamming to the deck as the ship plunged downward under several g's or of overloading one of the crystals and having it blow up in her face. Both seemed like definite possibilities.

She bit her lip, aware that the knowledge was probably there in her head somewhere. Jolinar had spent her very long life working with Tok'ra and Goa'uld technology, and she'd left a lot of her memories behind. The trick was actually getting at those memories. Sam had been fighting off unwanted flashes of Jolinar's past ever since Martouf had used the memory recall device on her, and now when she tried to conjure them up at will, any relevant memories that might be in there stubbornly refused to surface.

"Come on, help me out here," she muttered. Not that Jolinar could hear her. Jolinar was dead, and the blending process that might have made it possible for her to make more sense of her memories had never really been completed. She could hear the sounds of footsteps overhead, now, a dull clang that might have been someone putting his shoulder to the crew quarters door, and she could feel her heart pounding.

She tried to relax, trying to deliberately summon the memories, the disorienting feeling of being in a different body, the shape of her hands different as she looked down at them. That felt like exactly what she'd been trying to avoid doing since she left Ne'tu, though. She'd told herself over and over again that Jolinar's experiences hadn't actually happened to her. Those weren't her hands, they were Jolinar's host Rosha's hands, the hands of a stranger she'd never met—

A stranger. Jolinar was staring down at her hands, the hands of a strange man, larger and more awkward than the hands she was used to. Not Rosha's hands, because Rosha was gone, and Jolinar would never see those familiar hands again.

This man was a stranger, and would stay one. She refused to think of him as anything but a refuge, a temporary necessity. It was wrong, she knew that, but hiding within him was her only chance to survive. In time she'd make her way back to the Tok'ra, free this man to go back to his family, and find a new host for herself.

It just wouldn't be Rosha. The aching grief tangled with a gnawing guilt that made her long to cry, but she couldn't even do that. Without coming forward to take control of the body she had no tears.

Rosha would have shaken her head and asked her what she expected, taking an unwilling host? She would have been so angry, demanding control of their body so that she could throw up her hands and storm at Jolinar out loud. She'd say she couldn't believe Jolinar had done this, and that she didn't know why she put up with her. And Jolinar would have happily let her, if only Rosha were there.

If Rosha were there, she would want me to live, she told herself. The water in the pond was clearing, and she stared down at the face that looked up at her, a strange man's face that seemed to reproach her with its eyes. She fought the urge to come forward long enough to smash her foot down and shatter the reflection —

That was Jolinar, Sam told herself fiercely, shaking herself out of the memory with her stomach twisting with guilt and grief. It was Jolinar who'd taken that man as her unwilling host after her longtime host Rosha was killed, Jolinar who had been desperate enough to do anything to survive. It wasn't her.

She wasn't Jolinar or Rosha or the unlucky man Jolinar had used as a hiding place when she was being hunted by Goa'uld assassins, she was Samantha Carter. All she wanted to know right now was how to direct power to the crystals safely to adjust the gravitational force affecting the ship. She wasn't interested in anybody else's feelings right now, or for that matter in her own.

She stared at the crystals, willing them to make sense to her, and had almost given up when finally there it was, the memory suddenly coming clear as easily as if it were her own. She could name each crystal and explain its use, and could see at once how to cut the power completely. She hesitated, though, not sure that the craft would actually handle properly in the air if she did, given the weight of the gondola.

She ought to be able to bring it down to the ground by adjusting the strength and direction of the gravitational force affecting the hull. That was how Goa'uld ships landed, and they seemed to survive the process. She experimented, and felt her stomach drop as the tug of gravity abruptly grew perceptibly stronger. The effects should be confined to the external hull, but clearly they weren't, not entirely.

Still, it was tolerable. She'd have to find their radios, and coordinate the landing with Jack at the controls above. But then the crew of the ship would have the same problem, wouldn't they? They wouldn't have radio, but it was possible… She hunted quickly around, flipping the covers off various controls and dials until she found one that looked like it at least might be a voice-pipe.

She flipped off the cover. "Sir? Sir, can you hear me?" There was a bell and a lever next to it; she pulled the lever, hoping there was an identical bell above that might draw Jack's attention to the voice-pipe. "Sir! It's Carter!"

"Carter!" Jack said, his voice distant and hollow from the other end of the long speaking tube but still comprehensible. "Is that you, Carter?"

"Yes, sir!" she called. "Sir, I've shut down the engines, and I think I can bring us down using the gravity generator. But I'm afraid we may not have enough time to do that before somebody gets out of the crew quarters and tries to take back the ship!"

She could see one of the stunned engineers already beginning to stir, mumbling a protest as he tried to move his cuffed hand. She was pretty sure that if she were handcuffed to the airship's machinery, she could do a fair amount of damage to it without being able to free her hand. She hoped this man wasn't planning to try.

"If I come down, will the ship crash?"

She winced, wishing she didn't have to make that call. "If

we have sufficient altitude and we're not in danger yet of running up against the cliffs —"

"Carter!" he interrupted tinnily.

"Not immediately!"

"All right," he said after a moment. "I'm coming down! Try to find our stuff!"

They'd lost a wide variety of gear when they were captured, including stun grenades, which would make dealing with the guys currently pounding on the door of the crew quarters a lot easier. Some of it had probably been divided up among the crew, but Sam thought she knew where to start looking. Keret seemed like the type who'd keep the best of it for himself.

"Hopefully not immediately," Sam said under her breath, and headed for Keret's cabin.

He was conscious already, but still securely bound, sitting up against one wall and apparently trying to loosen his bonds against a corner of a shelf. He looked up at her as she came in.

"Good try," he said. "You won't get away with it."

"Watch us," Sam said. She looked around, and saw the familiar shape of a penlight resting on the top of a small cabinet. She reached for it and pocketed it, and opened the cabinet it had been resting on, revealing a welcome assortment of their belongings.

"Let me go, and I'll put you off the ship right now."

"I bet you will," Sam said. There was a hard, cold knot in her stomach, some part of her that urged her to zat the man again to silence him, and didn't care whether it had been long enough since the first shot for him to survive. Or maybe not a part of her. It felt a lot like Jolinar, which meant it wasn't anything she needed to think about at the moment.

"On the ground, I mean. There's a town not far from here. As long as you don't mind a hike." He was smiling, and Sam had to fight the urge to kick him. That wasn't her, she told herself. At least, she was pretty sure it wasn't her.

"Sorry, this isn't my stop," Sam said. She tucked as many useful things as she could into her jacket and headed for the door.

"Let me go, you—"

She slammed the cabin door on the words, and then staggered as she felt the airship gondola rock, the wind catching at it now that the controls were unmanned. She steadied herself against the cabin wall and headed for the stairs at a run.

Daniel Jackson stood at the bars of the cage that imprisoned them, the tablets tucked carefully in one arm, his eyes on Reba. Teal'c was still less than confident that his approach to dealing with her was wise, but he could say nothing now to make the woman suspect as much.

"I have good news and bad news," his friend said.

"That's bad news for you," Reba said. "If you can't translate the tablets—"

"Oh, I can. I mean, I've already done that. No, the bad news is that they aren't referring to a treasure in the sense of ordinary valuables. They're instructions for finding a device, something created by the Ancients that's supposed to have the power to *find* a fabulous treasure. Or whatever it is you desire most."

Reba let out a breath. "If you're lying—"

Daniel Jackson spread his hands. "Why would I do that? If it really were a literal treasure, that would probably be more motivational."

"Yes, it would," Reba said. "Apparently I'd be better off selling you to Asherah."

"Wait!" Although Reba had begun to turn away, she hesitated and then turned back, still listening. "This could still be incredibly valuable to you. If you had a way to find all the treasure you wanted—"

"There can't be that much treasure on this planet."

"You don't know," Daniel Jackson said. "From the number

of tablets in the High King's collection, there must have been extensive Ancient settlements on this world once. There may be storehouses of technology that could be of tremendous value, here or any other world. Not to mention precious metals, or whatever it is you're looking for."

"Mainly metals," Reba acknowledged.

"You could find those."

"Could. May. You don't know anything."

"I know you believe these tablets reproduce the authentic writings of the Ancients, and so do I. In fact, I suspect these may be originals, actually left by the Ancients as some kind of signpost to help people who came later find this device of theirs."

"Why would they do that?"

"Maybe they wanted it to be used. Maybe they were trying to be helpful. Maybe... I don't know, but you believe there's something there, and so do I, and I know exactly where you can find it."

Reba shook her head, her long hair brushing her waist, her fingers brushing a leather sheath where a long knife lay against her thigh. "And then you'll just walk away and hand it over to me, because you like to be helpful too, is that right?"

"We're *your* prisoners. And I like surviving. I'll help you find the device, you can use it to find whatever you want, and you can still ransom us back to our people. Just don't hand us over to Asherah."

Reba looked tempted for a moment, seeming as if she would agree, and then she shook her head, her expression hardening. "Sorry," she said. "I like long chances, but that's too much of one for me. I'd rather stick with a sure thing."

"No deal with the Goa'uld is a sure thing," Teal'c said.

Daniel Jackson nodded. "He's right. If you try to trade us to Asherah, there's no guarantee that she'll hold up her end of the deal. She's more likely to take us and send you away with nothing, if she lets you go at all. Believe me, it would be a very bad idea for you to trust —"

"You think you know so much," Reba said, her expression suddenly stormy. "What do you know of the gods?"

"I know they can't be trusted," he began, but she was already stalking off toward the stairs, swinging herself down the staircase and out of sight. "Great." Sitting down next to the bars he settled the tablets down carefully. "That really went well, don't you think?"

"I do not," Teal'c said. "But perhaps you can persuade her to reconsider."

"If I can get another chance to talk to her before she turns us over to the Goa'uld." Daniel Jackson let out a frustrated breath. "They really have a racket," he said. "'Trust me, I'm a god.' Sometimes I wonder why we don't try that."

"Because it would be wrong," Teal'c said calmly.

"I mean, other than that."

"Because one day the slaves of the Goa'uld will rise up and destroy them all."

"Yeah, that's nice to think." He leaned back against the bars. "There's no point in hoping that Asherah won't realize how much you're worth, is there?"

"She is unlikely to be unaware of the fact," Teal'c said. "Before his death, Apophis offered a sizeable reward for our capture. It is likely that any of the system lords would pay an equally high sum for the traitor who helped to kill Apophis." It might not be equal to the value Apophis would have placed on him in his rage at his First Prime's betrayal, but there were many Goa'uld who would take pleasure in providing an object lesson to their Jaffa in the price of rebellion.

"Which is true whether or not they know that Apophis didn't actually die when he tried to invade Earth, because we just killed him again."

"Indeed," Teal'c said. "The best that we could hope for is that she intends to drive a hard bargain."

"While we sit around in prison."

"It is more likely that we will be interrogated for the knowledge we possess."

"And there's a cheery thought," Daniel Jackson said. "Right, so, we have to sell Reba on taking us to find this artifact. There's no other good way out of this."

"We could attempt to escape this cell."

"I still don't know how to fly this ship. Do you?"

"It is nothing like any Goa'uld vessel I have ever flown. Still, if the alternative were being handed over to the system lords to suffer perpetual torment at their hands, I believe I would be willing to make the attempt."

"Maybe that should be plan B. If we can't talk her around..."

"How long are you intending to wait?"

"I think we should have a little time. She surely can't fly this ship straight back to the capital, not without tangling with the king's airships. She's going to have to wait until Asherah starts her tour of temples, and try to meet with her somewhere along the way."

"It will be harder to escape this cell in the daytime," Teal'c said.

"It probably will, but on the other hand, do you really want to try to fly this thing for the first time at night?" He pressed on, seemingly encouraged by Teal'c's lack of an immediate reply. "Just give me a few more hours to see if I can talk Reba around," he said. "If not... then I guess we go with plan B. Break out of here and either learn to fly this thing fast or start looking for parachutes."

"I would prefer not to jump from this airship, even equipped with a parachute," Teal'c said. He had pointed out to O'Neill on more than one occasion that the entire purpose of aircraft was negated if one left them in mid-flight.

"Me, too," Daniel Jackson said. "That's why I'm still hoping plan A will work out."

CHAPTER ELEVEN

IT WAS still quiet in the cell, from which Daniel guessed it was still some time before dawn, although between getting zatted and the time difference between wherever they were and Colorado Springs, he'd lost any internal sense of time. Jack and Teal'c always seemed to be able to keep track of local time effortlessly; he never had figured out how they did it, one of many mysteries about the two of them that still eluded him.

Teal'c had offered to keep watch while he slept, but he didn't feel tired, running on adrenaline and probably thoroughly jet-lagged to boot. It was a familiar problem, one that he'd gotten used to in the days after he first returned from Abydos. For a while, every time he lay down to sleep knowing that Sha're was in the hands of Apophis and that the sun was still high on Abydos, getting up and drinking more coffee had seemed infinitely more attractive.

Thinking about that made it hard not to think about his more recent return from Abydos, after Sha're's funeral. He'd come home and found a bed in one of the guest rooms and closed his eyes and slept. He wasn't sure if that was a sign that he'd changed, gotten so used to horrible tragedy that it no longer kept him awake staring at the ceiling. Possibly it was just that it had finally been an ending. Never one he would have wanted, and one he still wasn't sure how to live with. But an ending.

That was the point of funeral rites, of course, to bring some kind of closure to the grieving friends and family, to delimit the boundary of a life… He shook his head and tried not to let his mind wander along those lines. Composing academic essays in his head was his usual refuge from thinking too much about Sha're, even if he was fairly sure that since her death he hadn't had a single original idea worth ever writing down. It wasn't one he could indulge in here in the field, though, not when they had more pressing problems to worry about.

He tried to keep his mind on the present. Teal'c had stretched out to sleep, sensibly resting while he could. The moonlight came in patchily through the small windows set in the hull, fading and strengthening as distant clouds slid across the yellowish moon.

He looked up sharply at the sound of footsteps coming up the stairs. They were light, hesitant, not someone stomping on their way to some necessary task. Maybe someone who also couldn't sleep. It was Reba, as he'd hoped, and she stepped off the stairs and crossed the deck to stand on the other side of the bars, looking at him as if trying to see within him.

"I'm telling you the truth about my translation of the tablets," he said quietly.

"You may be," she said. "But what if the Ancients lied?"

"I can't see any reason for them to do that," Daniel said. "The only question is whether the device is still there, and I can't make any promises, but I think it's worth finding out."

She shook her head. "Now you're an expert on the Ancients, too."

"Not an expert," Daniel said. "A student of their language, and I've learned a few things about them, but... no." He considered her, and decided it was worth playing a hunch. "You asked me what I knew of the gods," he said. "What do you know of them yourself?"

"More than you," Reba said. She hesitated, and then shrugged. "My father was an unlucky farmer, just like Keret's, but a more pious one. Or maybe it was just that he couldn't afford to raise me until I was old enough for anyone to want to pay for my bond. He gave me to the temple of Asherah when I was practically a baby."

"You were raised in a temple?"

"Brought up to serve the Queen of the High Places and to love her with all my heart," Reba said. "Her temples here are kept by humans, you understand. Her Jaffa can't be bothered to keep temples in such an out of the way place as this. But we loved her as well as any Jaffa priestess ever could."

Daniel nodded, choosing his words carefully. "I'm sure you did."

"I had a friend, Saba, and we hoped Asherah would choose one of us to serve at her side one day. We were children, what did we know? We wore our best clothes for the festival and trembled when she came near us. I learned to read the ancient writings that talked of ships bigger than these, ships that could sail the stars." She looked at him, a question in her eyes that she wasn't willing to ask, and he nodded.

"The Goa'uld have ships that can travel in space. I've been on one of them."

"So. Well, we were always told so. We promised each other that if she chose one of us to be her slave, whichever she chose would ask for the other to come as well. We would be together on Asherah's great ship, and serve her all our lives, and see the stars. We used to lie awake in the dormitory talking about it when we were supposed to be asleep. Making plans." Her eyes were far away, and he recognized the softening in her voice, the sound of someone talking about a time she had been happy.

He could imagine it too clearly, little girls raised to dream of their future enslavement the way some girls played at weddings. The Goa'uld could twist anything to their own ends, any impulse of friendship or faith. He knew that, and knew that he couldn't afford to let his feelings about it show. He was an anthropologist here, he told himself, and these were just the interesting customs of the local people. It had nothing to do with him.

"We were little fools," Reba said.

"What happened?" he asked as gently as he could when she

didn't immediately go on.

Reba's expression hardened. "She wanted a new host, and she took Saba. And then she went away without saying a word to me. I never saw Saba again. I ran from the temple before the next festival. I didn't want to see her and know she wouldn't speak to me. That she'd look at me as if she didn't know me."

"I'm sorry," Daniel said after a moment. It felt inadequate, especially when he knew that his next words had to take the hurt he saw in Reba's eyes and drive it home like a knife. "After that, do you really want to trust her to make a fair bargain with you?"

Reba let out a breath. "Never mind being sorry," she said. "And never mind Asherah. You believe this thing, this device of the Ancients, could be real?"

"I do," Daniel said. "The Ancients built amazing things. The Stargates. Repositories of information that we could never begin to understand if we had a hundred years to explore them. I don't know how I would construct a device that can find whatever a person using it wants to find, but I don't know how to do a lot of things that the Ancients could do. For that matter, I don't even know how to build this airship."

Reba put her head to one side. "And what is it that you want so badly to find?"

"I didn't say there was anything I wanted to find for myself."

"You didn't have to."

He shook his head. "That doesn't matter."

"It might."

Daniel hesitated, but he couldn't think of a reason not to tell her some part of the truth, except that it still felt like something he wanted to clutch painfully tight to his chest. Apophis already knew he was searching for the Harcesis child. He'd pried into Daniel's mind when he had him captive at Ne'tu, asking him in Jack's voice where the child was, twisting words of comfort and encouragement in hopes that they would lead Daniel to tell him everything he knew.

It was probably a good thing he wasn't that easily comforted. He shook his head, dismissing the memory. It took an effort to focus on what he needed to say, and he began to wonder just how long it actually had been since he'd last slept.

"My wife is dead," he said abruptly, the words hanging bare between them. "Before she died, I have reason to believe that she sent her son... away to a safe place, but I don't know where that place actually is. I need to find it. To find him."

Reba considered him, as if trying to decide whether she believed him. "If you find this thing for me, and it does what it says, I'll let you use it to find the boy," she said. "If you can do that without taking it away with you. The device stays with me, and you're still mine to ransom back to your friends."

"And we don't get sold to Asherah." She nodded. "That works for me," Daniel said. "I'd also like to get out of this cell."

Reba shook her head. "What do you expect, a palace guesthouse? You won't find better accommodations on the ship, except my own quarters, and I don't like you that much." She looked amused despite herself. "I expect I could find you a pair of hammocks to sling, and give you some time to take the air, although I won't be to blame if you let the wind sweep you overboard."

"That sounds good," Daniel said. "I'm sure we can manage."

"Just you," Reba said, all amusement gone. "The Jaffa stays locked up nice and safe until you keep your part of the bargain."

Daniel turned to look at Teal'c, who he couldn't imagine was actually still asleep.

"We have little choice," Teal'c said, climbing to his feet as he spoke. "It seems the best of our alternatives."

"I'm glad you see it that way," Reba said. She drew her zat and held it on Teal'c as she opened the cell door. Daniel met Teal'c's eyes for a moment, hesitating. They could probably overpower Reba and take her weapon if they moved fast, but they'd still have the problem of how to get down.

Teal'c nodded, turning up his hands in an almost imperceptible gesture of acceptance. He didn't look happy, but then Daniel didn't expect that he would be.

"How about returning our belongings?" Daniel said.

"Don't push your luck," Reba said, and then sighed. "If there's anything no one had a use for, you can have it back."

"That's very generous of you," Daniel said dryly.

"I know," Reba said, and locked the cage behind him.

Jack made his way carefully down to the middle deck. Now that he was out of the wind, feeling was returning painfully to his face. He dropped to one knee, zat leveled, as he heard footsteps coming up from below, and then relaxed as he saw it was Carter.

"I got back a lot of our stuff," she said. He stood, trying to ignore the way his knee protested the movement, and held out a hand to catch the stun grenade she tossed him. He tucked it away in his jacket, along with various other gear she handed over. He still wished they'd insisted that tac vests counted as appropriate ceremonial dress for the treaty signing, but this was an improvement.

"Nice," he said. He glanced in the direction of the door to the sleeping quarters, which someone was now banging on. They'd had time to get good and mad by now, and if they had any sense they were currently planning to jump him and Carter the moment they opened the compartment door. "Everything under control below?"

"Pretty much," Carter said. She considered the door. "So…"

"We zat the door just to knock anybody behind it back, open it, toss in the flashbang, and then…" He mimed repeatedly firing his zat.

"Open it, right," Carter said. She looked at the handcuffs that were snapped through the door's handle, holding it closed. "I probably should mention I don't have the keys to those."

Jack drew out a concussion grenade and considered it, and then the door.

"In an airship?" Carter said, her eyes going wide.

He spread his hands. "I don't suppose you have a pair of metal cutters on you?"

"Actually, I might," Carter said, rifling through her own pockets until she found them. "They were with the other stuff. They're not very big."

He took them from her. "Haven't you ever heard it's not the size?"

"I don't think that's true of levers."

"They're metal cutters, not levers."

"Anything that works on a scissors principle is a lever. Well, actually, a pair of wedges connected to a lever…" She trailed off. "Probably not relevant."

"Probably not," Jack said. He moved in and cut the handcuffs free of the door, although the grinding noise of protest the tool in his hand made suggested he'd be buying Carter a new pair of metal cutters when they got home. He nodded to Carter, and she flanked the door on the other side.

Jack shot the door with the zat, its energy crawling across the metal, and was rewarded by hearing at least one unlucky person hit the ground on the other side. He waited until he was sure he wasn't going to give himself a jolt by touching the door, and pried out the nails jamming it shut.

He put his shoulder to it, just barely fast enough, as someone thudded against it almost immediately from the other side. He glanced at Carter to be sure that she was ready and then pulled the pin on the stun grenade.

Jack stepped away from the door and let it swing open, zatted the guy who came stumbling through it when it abruptly gave, and tossed the stun grenade in, ducking back against the wall and covering his ears against its piercing thunderclap, his eyes firmly shut against its flash. It was loud anyway, a crash he could feel through the soles of his feet. He moved in behind it, zatting anything that moved, with Carter backing him up.

One guy jumped Carter, knocking her to the deck, but she elbowed him in the face and then rolled free as he reached reflexively to shield his broken nose, zatting him as soon as she was clear. Jack let her be and concentrated on firing. In a matter of seconds, no one was moving but them.

Jack swept the room with his gaze, zat at the ready. Carter had her back to him doing the same. He didn't see anywhere for anyone to hide. It was a metal box with hammocks hung from rings in the ceiling, and they were loose folds of cloth that would have clearly showed it if anyone were still in them. The small metal lockers that lined one wall from floor to ceiling might have concealed a cat, but not a man.

"I should probably go fly the ship now," Jack said, as the deck rocked alarmingly under his feet.

"Probably," Carter said. "I'm going to try to bring us down by manually adjusting the gravity drive. Right now, the drive is keeping us neutrally buoyant. I want you to try to keep us as level as possible, and let me know if we're about to run into anything."

"Other than the ground?"

"I think I can make this more of a landing than a crash."

"That's what I like to hear," Jack said, and headed back above.

They were still a comfortable distance from the cliffs, although they'd drifted closer to the western edge of the plateau, where the flat plain turned into a series of rocky cliffs and precarious hillside drops. That was not where they wanted to land. He wrestled with one of the rudders, and was rewarded by seeing their drift slow, although the airship rocked and shuddered as it fought the wind.

"All right," Carter said, her voice tinny and distant through the speaking tube. "I'm going to start bringing her down."

He could feel the shift in gravity, like stepping out of the water onto dry land and feeling his full weight suddenly returning. And then some.

"Am I supposed to be able to feel that up here?"

"No!"

"Well, okay, then," Jack said. He shook his head. Off to the east, the sky was beginning to shade from black to blue, which at least meant that it ought to be getting warmer in the foreseeable future. They were sinking fast, still kiting westward in the wind. "Slow it down!"

"What's our altitude?"

Jack glanced down at the controls under his hands. One of the dials was undoubtedly an altimeter; he could barely see them in the faint pre-dawn light, and he was willing to bet that the numbering on them was at best in Goa'uld, which meant that given that best-case scenario he could probably recognize them as numbers.

He watched the ground rising toward them, trying to judge scale. "Maybe 500 feet," he said. "You said you weren't going to crash this thing!"

"Just keep us level!"

"I'm more worried about keeping us going in a straight line," Jack said, still fighting with the rudder. He put his shoulder to it to keep it from kicking back, at which point it whined alarmingly. He hoped those weren't important gears of some kind.

"Are we going in a straight line?"

"No! We're still pulling to starboard."

"I can fix that, just let me..."

The deck tilted, and Jack swore and threw himself against the rudder before he realized that the deck wasn't tilting; he was tilting, fighting not to slide down the deck as if on a steep slope, but the deck was still parallel to the ground.

"Carter, this is weird!"

"Sorry, sir! I'm trying to dump speed!"

It was working, he had to give her that. They were slowing, although the levers under his hands were shuddering, the canopy snapping like an enormous sail where the wind caught at it. He could hear something creaking, could do nothing but hope it was something that was supposed to be creaking, and risked leaning over the rail again.

"A hundred feet!"

"Hang onto something! This may get a little rough!"

Rough wasn't the word for it, Jack thought as the deck pitched and then dropped abruptly out from under his feet. Weird was definitely it. He had just enough presence of mind to hang on as his feet left the deck and he started to fall upward toward the undersurface of the canopy above, and then was just as abruptly dropped back on his feet.

His right knee buckled under his weight, but luckily he was already hanging onto something. "Are we done?"

"You tell me!" Carter said.

He looked cautiously over the rail. The airship was hovering an arm's length above the ground, drifting very slowly to starboard.

"What's our altitude?" Carter called.

"About three feet!"

"Well, here goes nothing," she said, and the airship dropped to the ground.

It sounded about like Jack imagined dropping a metal cargo container three feet might sound, a resounding clang that jolted through his bones. Nothing audibly crunched or screamed — either metal or any part of him — and after a moment, he let out his breath in relief.

He still felt strangely heavy, and the deck under his feet felt once again like it was tilting. He kept a careful grip on the railing, but although the airship shuddered in the gusting wind, it wasn't either dragging across the rocky ground or tipping over as the wind battered the canopy. That was a good thing.

After a minute, Carter came up the stairs, making her way cautiously across the deck. "Sorry," she said. "That wasn't the world's smoothest landing."

"It works for me," Jack said. "Let's get these guys off the ship and figure out which way is back to the Stargate."

Carter leaned over the rail, her eyes on the sky. "What about Daniel and Teal'c?"

"One problem at a time," Jack said, but he followed her gaze for a moment, wishing he could make out the shape of another ship against the lightening sky.

CHAPTER TWELVE

TEAL'C was not surprised when Daniel Jackson did not return promptly. It would be to their advantage for him to attempt to learn more of the pirates, and it was characteristic of him to do so by making an effort to engage them in lengthy conversation. Besides, he felt that he himself would not have voluntarily returned to the cell in which they were confined any sooner than was strictly necessary.

He had to admit it was a comfortable enough captivity as such things went. One of Reba's men had come down and tossed things through the bars at him, first hard bread and a warm metal bottle that proved to contain a salty soup, and then lengths of woolen cloth that the man had grudgingly pointed out could be hooked to rings set in the underside of the deck above as slings for sleeping.

Still, it did little to ease the frustration of being once again a prisoner. Since joining SG-1, he had spent more time than he cared for being imprisoned, detained, and otherwise not free to leave, starting with his arrival at the SGC. It was a part of his job, and one he accepted, but not one that he was becoming any more fond of.

As Apophis's First Prime, he had led troops into battle many times, and carried out many missions. The threat of capture had always been something he took for granted. The reality of capture had not. He had always returned from battle, and if he had not, he was aware that Apophis would not have taken many pains to retrieve him. Had he been captured by the forces of a rival system lord, it was unlikely that he would have survived the experience.

At least, he had thought so at the time. Since joining the Tau'ri, he had learned not to underestimate the chances of surviving what seemed like impossible situations. The prison of Ne'tu should have been one of them. It was widely known that no one had ever escaped its confines and lived to tell of it, and even Martouf's assurance that Jolinar of Malkshur had once done so had not appreciably increased their odds.

And yet when Major Carter had insisted they attempt to rescue her father from Ne'tu, he had actually believed O'Neill when he said that if they could find a way in, they would find a way out. He had been pleased but not as surprised as perhaps he should have been to see them when they ringed aboard the transport ship. Their clothes had been scorched and stinking of sulfur, and they had been exhausted and battered but very much alive, smiling as he pressed water on them and assured himself that they were not in imminent danger of expiring.

His own current captivity was at least less unpleasant than being confined on a volcanic prison world run by a Goa'uld who imagined himself the incarnation of evil. He hung the cloth sling and climbed into it, finding it more comfortable than the floor for resting. It was certainly no worse than the quarters aboard a ha'tak, where he had slept for so many years.

He shook his head, remembering that time in his life. He had been so proud when he had first come aboard one of Apophis's ships as Bra'tac's young apprentice, even if his duties had been limited to guarding things that were unlikely to be attacked and reporting that there was nothing to report. His doubts had been fewer, then, and he had taken great pride in victories that now he thought of with regret.

One of the airship's crew came stomping up the stairs and gave Teal'c a curious look. Teal'c met his gaze impassively.

"You're Jaffa," the man said after a moment. He was a tall man with a face that might have been handsome without the scars that raked across it from forehead to cheek.

"That is true," Teal'c said.

The man came closer, although he stayed a cautious distance back from the bars, like a man used to dealing with prisoners. "What is it like, serving the gods?"

"I no longer serve the Goa'uld," Teal'c said. "And they are not gods."

The man shook his head. "If your god comes to strike you down for blasphemy, we'll put you over the side."

"The false god I once served is dead," Teal'c said. "Asherah will not strike you down either, unless she learns of your actions from some human who has reason to tell her of them."

"She's got no reason to blast us," the man said. "We give our share to the temple and leave her priests alone. Reba's nearly as good as a temple priestess, anyway."

"Do you not feel that it is wrong to kidnap people and hold them for ransom? Or to steal from farmers who have little to spare?"

The man's eyes shifted away from his, but he sounded defiant when he spoke. "The High King does as much, doesn't he? And as to kidnapping, if your people didn't have the ransom to spare, they wouldn't pay."

"And then you would drop me from a great height."

"I never said we were as holy as all that."

"Do you have a name?"

"Yassi," the man said. "I don't suppose it'll do me any harm to be known to the goddess for bringing her a blasphemer and traitor. If it comes to that."

"We will find the device of which Daniel Jackson speaks," Teal'c said. "His profession is finding relics of past civilizations that have been lost."

"A treasure hunter?"

"Of a sort," Teal'c said.

"Good luck with that." Yassi shook his head. "If there were a way to get rich by digging scraps out of the ground, somebody would have done it by now." He turned away, pulling down a coat that was hanging from a rusting hook and shrugging into it. "Filthy wind, but at least we're running ahead of the bad weather."

He headed up the stairs toward the upper deck, leaving Teal'c wondering if it would do any good to say that the only way that these people would ever be prosperous was to stop paying tribute to the Goa'uld. Not likely. They would only say that even if they were to do such a blasphemous thing in defiance of their gods, they would surely be struck down by their wrath.

And if there were any way to overthrow the gods and be free of them forever, someone else would have done it by now. That was surely what these people would say, even if he were able to persuade them it was a desirable goal. It was what he had heard from all too many of his own people since he began trying to raise them against the Goa'uld. *Who are you to tell us we can do what has never been done, Teal'c? Who do you think you are?*

It had been done at least once, on Abydos if nowhere else. The people of Abydos were free of Ra, but it was hard to point to them as an example without acknowledging that their future was uncertain. One of the other system lords would surely eventually attempt to claim a world rich with minerals that could be mined, especially one where the people needed to be taught a lesson in obedience. It was only Apophis's desire to hide Amonet on Abydos during her pregnancy that had protected the insignificant world and its people so far, but now that time was over.

But that was a problem for another day. For now, he comforted himself with the thought that even confined behind these bars, he was finally free of Apophis. Apophis's death in the destruction of Ne'tu was worth all the risks that SG-1 had run while imprisoned there, many times over. Apophis's *final* death, Teal'c hoped, although he would have felt even more certain if they had witnessed the death of Apophis with their own eyes. But surely even a Goa'uld could not have survived the massive explosions that had claimed the planet, triggered by the Tok'ra attack. There would have been nothing left for a sarcophagus to revive.

He looked up at footsteps coming down the stairs, and reached out a hand to catch the bundle that Yassi tossed him from halfway down. "Reba says you can have all this back," Yassi said. "Nobody wanted it."

Teal'c bent his head in a gesture somewhere short of actual thanks, and Yassi disappeared up the stairs again. He unwrapped the bundle, which contained mainly items of no obvious use. Among them were Daniel Jackson's notebook and a rubber eraser but no writing implements of any kind, his friend's flimsy cloth hat, apparently not considered attractive enough or warm enough to be of value, and a paper-thin metallic survival blanket, which had clearly been unfolded before being discarded.

He lifted the survival blanket to refold it, and when he saw what was under it his heart lifted. Reba had returned their radios. She must not have recognized them for what they were; he had seen no sign that these people used radio technology, or had any means of communication at a distance beside signals from banners observed by the eye. That meant their chances of rescue had just significantly improved.

He turned on one of the radios, but at the sound of footsteps coming back down the stairs, he silenced it immediately and thrust it under the edge of a bolt of heavy cloth where he hoped it would be effectively concealed.

The portly man who had come down from the upper deck glared at him. "What are you about? You leave the cargo be, Jaffa."

"I am preparing to sleep," Teal'c said calmly, unfolding the survival blanket.

"That's a poor enough excuse for a blanket, sure enough, but don't go thinking you can use our cloth to make up for it. You've got a hammock, and that's more than good enough for the likes of you." The man shook his head. "Reba's a fool not to keep you both in chains."

Teal'c let a little of his frustration show on his face. "On the contrary, I think her decision is wise. Were she to keep us in chains, she would eventually regret that decision."

"You stay out of the cargo," the man said, muttering an oath and heading down the stairs.

By the time they'd dragged a dozen unconscious people up the stairs, Jack was limping with every step. Sam's own legs were aching; she estimated the current subjective gravity at significantly higher than 1G, and every step felt like she was hauling an enormous pack on her shoulders. Jack looked ready to abandon the whole idea of lowering crew members down the side with rope in favor of just rolling them off the upper deck.

"We really could have just blown a hole in the crew compartment hull," he said.

"I think that would affect its aerodynamic properties," Sam said.

"Unfortunately, I think you're right."

"There's just Keret left," Sam said.

Jack frowned, leaning back on the rail, or maybe that was just the only expression he could manage at the moment. "Yeah, I've been thinking about that," he said. "It might be a good idea to keep somebody aboard who knows how this thing works."

"Do we really want a hostage?"

"Better than being hostages, right?" Jack shrugged. "Who knows, we might even be able to trade him to the High King for some really nice sheep."

Sam couldn't repress a laugh. "Yeah, I think we can live without the sheep," she said. "I think I can figure out how to fly this thing back the way we came. Probably. And I don't imagine Keret's going to be in the mood to help."

"Maybe not, but I like having a fallback plan," Jack said.

There was a sharp crackling from Sam's pocket, and both

she and Jack stared at it for a moment before she pulled out her radio and thumbed it on. "Daniel? Teal'c? Do you read me? This is Major Carter." She waited, and then shook her head. "Okay, nothing, but I'm definitely picking up a signal."

Jack tilted his head a little to one side. "Have we seen anything to indicate that these people have radio?"

"Nothing, and if they did, I expect they'd be using it," Sam said. "It would make a big difference in terms of coordinating the movements of these airships."

"So that's our people out there."

"Or at least their radio." Sam gazed out over the rail, but there was nothing moving against the morning sky but a few swift clouds. "If we head back to the gate, we can come back with a rescue team and track them by their radio signal."

"As soon as we can get home and then talk those yahoos back in the capital into letting us come back. And if there's a Goa'uld hanging out in the capital who would probably be pretty unhappy to learn that we're here…"

"We might not get back very soon." It was hard to drag her gaze away from the sky. "What did you have in mind?"

"You can track their radio signal too, right?"

"Sure, although if we're planning to be a rapidly-moving object trying to track another rapidly-moving object, some kind of bigger directional antenna would help. I should be able to rig that up easily enough, though," Sam said.

Jack fished his sunglasses out of his pocket, made a show of cleaning fingerprints off them, and then put them on, adjusting them in the slanting sunlight. "Then we can go after Daniel and Teal'c."

Sam wished she felt as confident. "Even assuming we can go after anybody in a ship we really don't know how to fly…"

"If we can fly back to the capital, we can fly in another direction just as easily," Jack said. "Right?"

"It probably depends on the winds," Sam said. "But, okay, even granting that we can do that, what happens when we find them if they're on another airship that's just as big as this one but fully manned? I don't even know what kind of weapons these people use to fight ship-to-ship, but do we really want to find out?"

"If Daniel and Teal'c have their radios, they'll get in contact with us," Jack said. "If not, we need to get close enough that we can figure out what their situation is. Keret said that the captain of the other ship was likely to run off chasing some kind of treasure. They'll have to tie up somewhere to check it out if they actually find it."

"Keret said he didn't think the treasure really existed."

"He could be right, but we haven't got much else to go on. And there's another thing. You haven't been able to pick up any radio transmissions from the MALP, have you? Or from anybody back at the gate?"

"There may not be anybody back at the gate, if Hammond was captured along with Daniel and Teal'c and we haven't been able to send a rescue team through yet."

"Maybe," Jack said. "Or maybe we're out of radio range of the gate. I think that's pretty likely. Which means that if we head back, we're going to give up any chance of getting in touch with Daniel and Teal'c."

"All right," Sam said after a moment. "What do we do first?"

"We get Keret put somewhere safe," Jack said. "Then we get this thing back in the air and put some distance between us and the rest of these goons. And then you can rig up that antenna."

CHAPTER THIRTEEN

IT WAS tempting to dump Keret back in the compartment they'd been locked in and nail down the door — Sam wasn't sure whether she wanted to believe that impulse was Jolinar's or not — but they settled for putting him in the large cargo cage in the center of the middle deck. That way they could keep an eye on him and talk to him without having to open the door, although at the moment Keret wasn't making any visible efforts to escape.

"We could make a deal," Keret said. "There must be something you want."

"Some Percocet and a cheeseburger," Jack said. "Oh, wait, did you mean things I want that I'm likely to get? I'd like to find my teammates." He was sitting on a container near the cargo cage, taping his knee.

"Do you want me to help with that?" Sam asked.

"No offense, Carter, but I think I'll pass on your first aid for now."

"None taken, I guess," Sam said.

Keret shook his head. "How do you expect to take them back from Reba?" He'd made himself comfortable, stretched out on a pallet of sheepskins with his ankles crossed. Just looking at it was enough to make Sam wish she'd taken the opportunity to sleep when she had the chance.

"We'll cross that bridge when we come to it," Jack said.

"I might be able to negotiate their release. For a percentage of the fee, and of course getting my ship back." His lazy expression didn't change, but his voice was sharp on the last words.

"I'll keep that in mind," Jack said. "Let's get this show on the road." He took the stairs to the upper deck deliberately, as Sam headed for the ones down to the engine room. She leaned toward the speaking tube once she reached the controls.

"I'm going to adjust the gravity drive for neutral buoyancy," she said. "I think if I play around with the settings, I may be able to actually increase our top speed significantly, but I don't want to experiment while we're on the ground."

"Fair enough," Jack said. "Fire up the engines!"

"Actually, sir, I think that's a bad idea while we're on the ground, too," Sam said. "Normally we'd be starting from a mooring mast, or from the rails that guide the airships in and out of the big hangars back in the capital. We're going to have to get airborne before we start up the propellers."

"So, what, you turn down the gravity and we lift off like a kite?"

"Not so much turn down as, um, direct up," Sam said. "You should probably hold onto something."

"Oh, jeez, Carter..."

Sam ignored him and slid one of the switches wired into the crystal array slowly from closed to nearly fully open. It spat sparks, and she yelped and sucked at her hand where one of them had scorched her. There was a moment when she wondered if the connection was shorting out, and then her stomach dropped. She bounced experimentally on the soles of her feet and had to grab for the table edge not to go flying. Only 0.25 G, if that.

She found a convenient handhold bolted to the side of the pillar — clearly she was not the first one to try this trick — and held on tight. "Here goes nothing," she said, and pushed another switch open.

It was as if the room had suddenly pitched upside down. She was being pulled toward the ceiling, not violently but strongly enough that she had to twist in midair to hang onto her handhold and catch at the underside of a nearby bench for balance. A number of small objects were rattling across the underside of the deck above, although most things thankfully seemed to be bolted down.

"That's enough!" Jack shouted. She hoped that was his judgment of their altitude and not just disapproval at weird Goa'uld technology.

"All right!" she called, and then realized she couldn't reach the switch that needed to be flipped to return the direction of subjective gravity to something more normal. She gritted her teeth, hauling herself up, and finally managed to slide it back to its original position. The room flipped again, and she landed more or less on her feet.

"I'm going to fire up the engines!" she called.

"Can we not do that again?" Jack said after a minute.

"Yes, sir! If we try not to land again, sir!"

She began starting up the engines, hoping she wasn't neglecting some essential step in the start-up procedure. They started with a sputter that turned into a steady growl, and she glanced at the gas tanks that were presumably fueling them. They were nearly full, although she had no idea how long they were intended to last.

"One more bridge to cross when we come to it," she muttered, and engaged the propeller. "All right! You should have steering!"

"We're away," Jack said. "Come take a look." He sounded more cheerful than Sam thought was called for under the circumstances.

"Yes, sir," Sam said, and headed back up the stairs. On the deck above, she felt some of her normal weight returning. Keret considered her through the bars, and then shook his head.

"You must have ships like these at home, or else a lot of sheer dumb luck. You know messing around with the box of winds like that is dangerous, don't you?"

"Box of... oh, the gravity drive. The box with the crystals, the one that controls the ship's weight and which direction it... well, wants to fall?" Keret nodded grudgingly. "I've seen technology something like it before."

"It's the gods' work," Keret said. "You're no priestess."

"Not hardly," Sam said. The last thing she wanted was to talk about Jolinar. "We've captured a few Goa'uld ships, gliders. One of them had a partly-intact drive that we've been studying. I wouldn't have thought there was any way to safely interface it with the rest of your technology, though."

Keret shrugged. "Sometimes ships do explode."

"Right," Sam said after a moment. "We'll try to avoid that."

"Carter!" Jack called.

"Coming!"

The wind was chilly but no longer bitterly cold when she came out onto the upper deck. Sunlight slanted in from one side, illuminating half the deck, while the rest was shaded by the canopy above.

"Come take a look at this," Jack said.

She came to his side at the rail and looked out. Her breath caught at the sight. They'd cleared the edge of the plateau, and were turning to follow the course of a wide gap between towering mountain peaks. Behind her, she could see the crewmen they'd left behind starting to make their way down a trail that wound down to the barely visible shapes of rooftops halfway down the hill.

Ahead of them, the sky opened up brilliant blue between the dark crags of stone. Higher up the mountains, sun glittered off snow carved into jagged points by the relentless wind. A flock of dark birds arrowed into sight and then slid by below them, unable to match their speed. Far below, the valley twisted and turned, following the shape of a river far below.

"It's beautiful," she said.

"Isn't it?" He was smiling, his hands confident now on the controls.

"You really like flying, don't you?"

She expected a flip answer, but instead he nodded. "We cover a lot of ground in this job, but we don't get to spend a lot of time in the air."

"I wanted to be a fighter pilot for a while," she said. "Back when it seemed like they were going to lift the ban on women in combat positions any minute." She shrugged. "By the time they decided women could fly combat missions, I'd already decided that science was a better bet."

"And that kept you out of combat positions, right?" He smiled sideways, like he appreciated the absurdity of defining SG-1 as a non-combat assignment. It was, of course, technically, because otherwise it would presumably have been a ground combat unit, which would have meant no female troops could be assigned to it.

"Right, totally." There were memories trying to intrude, hers or Jolinar's, she couldn't be sure, choking sulfuric smoke and burning heat on her skin, the crackle of a staff weapon being charged and leveled at her chest—

She dug her fingernails into her palms, insisting on the reality of the present moment, standing at the rail of the airship sailing briskly through the clear cold sky with Jack watching her a little too sharply.

"See if you can rig that antenna," he said. "And then you can get some rest for a little while. We can trade off taking the helm."

"I guess we're going to have to," Sam said. "It would be better to have one of us monitoring the engines, but…"

"You can sack out down there if you want," Jack said. "But I need you at your best."

"All right. After I set up the antenna," Sam said. "Have you had a chance to check out these instruments?"

"I've checked them out, but I don't have any idea what most of them are," Jack said. "I'm betting the thing that looks like a compass is a compass, and beyond that, you've got me."

"Let me know if you find anything that looks like a barometer," Sam said. "The last UAV survey I did showed a storm system forming off to the south. I don't know if we're anywhere in its path at this point, but it would be nice to have some warning if a storm's blowing up."

"It looks clear enough right now," Jack said, but he kept his eyes on the horizon.

Daniel clung to the rail of the airship's upper deck as the wind buffeted him. The view was spectacular, the golden sun slanting through deep canyons shadowed by the mountain crags. Even with the distant hum of the engines it was quiet compared to flying, more like being in a ship in space.

And when had that started being a familiar metaphor drawn from daily life?

"It's beautiful," he said, as Reba glanced at the ship's instruments over the shoulder of one of the men at the helm. He thought her expression softened a little at that, although she shrugged elaborately.

"If you like rocks," she said. "Personally I prefer fields of grain and storehouses groaning with tax goods just begging to be taken off the High King's hands."

"Actually I like ancient artifacts and interesting inscriptions," Daniel said. "But this is a change from the usual trees."

"Trees are worth more than rocks," Reba said. "What are your people doing out here? We hear the strangest things about the Tau'ri."

"Strange how?" He edged into the minimal shelter from the wind provided by the bank of controls, hoping that if he let go of the rail, he wouldn't regret it in the next hard gust of wind.

"Nobody's sure what you're up to," she said. "You visit worlds and do strange things and go away again. You trade generously for practically useless goods, and never enough in any one place to be making you rich. Unless your people aren't used to getting anything at all from offworld?"

"We're not out here to make a profit," Daniel said. "Although we are interested in technology that could be useful to us. Mainly we're out here to learn about other cultures and build relationships with the people on other planets."

"You're just... what, curious?"

"It's important to us to understand other people, and it helps us understand ourselves as well. The history of humans in this galaxy — where we came from, and how the Goa'uld and the Ancients and the Asgard have all interfered with human development in various ways — is important to understanding everybody's situation now." He considered her. "You've learned to read some Ancient. You must have been at least a little curious about what you could learn."

"The location of valuables."

"Come on, though, there are plenty of easier ways of making money than hunting down relics of the Ancients."

"Oh, surely," Reba said. "Stealing grain and selling it in the villages to people who are starving on the High King's grain ration after most of their own crops have gone in taxes. That's a quick way to riches, right there. After you've paid the crew and taken on supplies and bribed the miners for lifting gas, you can build a fine house and retire there. One of these days."

"There must be other options besides piracy."

Reba leaned back against the rail, her eyes on the sky, seeming unconcerned about the long drop to the rocks below. "Maybe on your world," she said. "Here you can be a farmer and go hungry a year or two out of every five, and watch your babies too young to sell off into indenture starve. Or you can be a miner and break your back to feed your family, or sell yourself into indenture and sweep some lord's floor. Do any of those sound particularly attractive to you?"

"Not particularly," he said. "Have you ever considered that the real problem here is the amount of what you produce you're handing over to the Goa'uld in tribute?"

Reba shook her head. "Asherah takes her due, and that's the way it is," she said.

"Not everywhere," Daniel said. "It's true that my people are comparatively wealthy, but that's because for the last couple of thousand years, we haven't had the Goa'uld exploiting our natural resources and taking our people as slaves. If your people didn't have to pay tribute—"

"Yes, I've heard that about the Tau'ri, too," Reba said. "You're troublemakers, stirring up people to defy the gods."

"Isn't that what you're doing, when you get right down to it? The things you're stealing aren't delivered to the capital, so they aren't turned over as tribute, which from a certain point of view could be considered defying Asherah's rule over this planet already."

"There's a difference between being wicked and being troublemakers," Reba said. "If your people haven't found out the difference yet, you may well find it out soon. Asherah has better things to do than bicker with the High King over a few sacks of grain. But if you spread that kind of talk around the villages…"

Daniel spread his hands innocently, wondering if he'd pressed the point too far. "I'm hardly in a position to do that, am I? Not while I'm a prisoner aboard your ship, and one you're going to trade back to the Tau'ri as soon as possible."

"I'm really starting to wonder if pushing you over the side wouldn't be a better idea," Reba said.

"It wouldn't. You said it yourself, how many ways are there to gain everything you could possibly desire?"

She shook her head, her hair flying in the whipping wind. "You'd better hope the answer is at least one. And I think that's enough fresh air for you. Down you go."

He took the stairs slowly, considering whether there was any point in trying to make a break for it. There really wasn't, although he found himself thinking through whether he could do it. It shouldn't be that hard to reach back and catch hold of her arm, flip her over his shoulder and send her tumbling down the steps.

Assuming she wasn't already holding the zat on him behind his back where he couldn't see. It was an academic exercise, really, since he still thought negotiation was the best strategy.

He stepped back into the cage as she opened it for him. Teal'c stepped aside wordlessly, and watched the door as it closed.

Daniel glanced at him, feeling a little bad about his brief unshared freedom, and frowned when Teal'c immediately looked away. Then he followed Teal'c's gaze to the corner of one of their radios, tucked nearly out of sight under a bolt of cloth.

Almost immediately, two of the crew came up the stairs from below, tramping past their cell on their way to the aft storeroom. Pulling out the radio and trying to reach Jack and Sam was only going to get it taken away. They'd have to wait until the ship quieted down overnight.

"Your notebook," Teal'c said, and handed it back to him. Daniel dug in his pockets and found a stub of a pencil, sharp enough to write with. He flipped the notebook open and began sketching the deck above as he remembered it.

Teal'c raised an eyebrow, and Daniel shrugged. "I left my camera back in the capital," he said.

Teal'c waited a moment until the two crewmen were out of sight, and then said in a low voice, "Were you able to determine how this vessel is armed?"

"I think there may be some kind of weapons mounted on the top deck," Daniel said.

"What kind of weapons?"

"They were just some big mechanical things that looked like they might be a way to aim weapons. Although really they could be anything, I don't know. I was talking to Reba, trying to get her to open up a little. I'm not sure how well that worked, though."

"I see," Teal'c said, not particularly patiently.

"We're not planning to shoot it out with anybody else up here, right?"

Teal'c raised an eyebrow. "Are you certain?"

"I'm certain that's not my *plan*," Daniel said. As was unfortunately usual in his life these days, that was about the best he could say.

CHAPTER FOURTEEN

CARTER came up on deck to set up her makeshift tracking device; she'd rigged a looped antenna that could be angled to test the signal strength from different directions and what she said was the local equivalent of a light bulb that brightened as the signal strengthened, so that he didn't have to strain to hear a crackle over the gusting wind.

"There," she said with satisfaction once she'd lashed the whole assembly to the panel that held the airship's instruments. She pushed her hair out of her eyes wearily, looking very nearly dead on her feet to Jack.

"Go sleep," he said.

"You want something to eat?"

He brandished an energy bar at her, one of the items of their personal property that she'd liberated from Keret. "Off with you."

It was quiet on deck once Carter had descended to sleep in the engine room, presumably so that if alarms went off she could do something about it, or maybe just because it was the warmest place on the ship. He didn't really mind the chill. The air was crisp and clean, without the lingering taste of smog that hung in the air even in Colorado Springs. He bet that when the sun set, the night sky would be amazing.

Of course, when the sun set, it would be bitterly cold on deck even in gloves and wearing a wool hat he'd found below decks pulled down over his ears. They'd have to take short watches overnight and take turns warming themselves below. One more reason for Carter to sleep while she had the chance.

She emerged in what he judged by the slant of the sunlight to be mid-afternoon; if one of the dials on the ship's instrument panel was a clock, he hadn't found it yet. She looked a little better rested, and was carrying steaming cups of something.

He took one gratefully and let her take the controls. The drink proved to be salty rather than sweet, some kind of broth or soup, but the main thing was that it was hot. "I take it you've figured out how to work the stove."

"If you put a kettle on it, it boils," she said. "I think this stuff is some kind of fermented grain paste, sort of like miso. At least I hope this is what it's supposed to taste like."

"Works for me," Jack said. He took the opportunity to lean over the rail, watching the ship's shadow chase them across the rocks far below. "The signal's been getting stronger," he said. "I think we may be gaining on them."

"I hope so," Carter said. "I've been trying to get as much speed as I can out of this thing without using the gravity drive too much. We could probably go faster if we were willing to fall straight forward, but…"

"But that would be exceedingly strange, so let's not do that unless we have to."

"That was my thought," Carter said.

"What happened to sleeping?"

"I slept for a while," she said. She smiled a little. "But I've got a new toy to play with, here, so you can't expect me to leave it alone for long."

Squinting down at the nearest rocky slope, Jack could just see the tiny shapes of some kind of sheep-like animals — probably sheep — scattering for cover as the airship's shadow passed over them. "You know, if we hadn't been kidnapped, this would be fun," he said after a while.

"It would," Carter said. "Kind of like a vacation."

"Well, that was the theory," Jack said. "We sure can pick them."

"What was the theory?"

"That we could all use a softball mission this time," Jack said. "You know, sitting around, drinking tea…"

"*That's* what we were doing here? All that time you were insisting that we should keep looking for something useful to trade for —"

"We found something," Jack pointed out, although he was beginning to suspect that mentioning his intentions might have been a tactical error.

"Only by Daniel accidentally tripping over it."

"He does that," Jack said. "We needed some light duty."

"If your leg was still bothering you —"

"It was fine for drinking tea," Jack said. "Daniel's still off his game after losing his wife." He hesitated, but went on, "And it's not like you had much fun on Ne'tu."

"I'm fine, sir," Carter said, every syllable clipped.

"I'm not saying you're not," Jack said evenly.

"With all due respect, sir, that is exactly what you're saying. I assure you, I'm every bit as capable of handling this kind of thing as any other member of the team. I'm an Air Force officer. Sir."

"I know you are," Jack said. He gazed out over the rail again, searching for the words that would convince her this wasn't about her being a woman, because it wasn't. It was about the dark circles under her eyes, which she'd damn well earned the right to have at this point. "You always planned on going into the service, right?"

Carter looked at him for a moment like she was trying to figure out where he was going with that, and then nodded. "That's right."

"But not in a combat unit on the ground."

"That wasn't an option," Carter said. "It still technically isn't."

"You're not in a combat unit, you just shoot people," Jack said. "We all know how that works. What if it had been?"

"It wasn't an option," Carter said. "When I joined the Air Force, I wanted to be an astronaut, or maybe a fighter pilot. But the kind of things you spent most of your career doing, special ops work... I honestly never thought about it."

"It's a rough job," Jack said.

"I know that, sir."

"You're learning that. You have to do the job to really understand the kind of things it does to you. The kind of things it requires from you. The deal you make with the Air Force is that you give it everything, and make no mistake, the kind of work we're doing will take things from you. Do you understand what I'm saying?"

"I know we can get hurt out here," Carter said. "I've always known that."

"What I'm saying is that we're *going* to get hurt out here. There's no way to avoid that. The best you can do is take care of yourself when something comes along that really shakes you up."

"I thought 'just deal with it' was the Air Force motto."

"It's 'Aim High.' I see how those two are easy to confuse."

Carter looked down at the instrument panel and smiled a little. "Actually, sir, the Air Force doesn't have an official motto."

"I thought we got a memo about the 'Aim High' thing."

"It's our unofficial motto."

"That figures," Jack said. "We could suggest 'just deal with it,' if you want."

"Seriously, sir, I'm okay," Carter said. "It's just that when Martouf used the Tok'ra memory recall device on me, it made me remember a lot of things that Jolinar went through while she was on Ne'tu that... weren't very pleasant."

"Prisons aren't fun places," Jack said. "You can trust me on that one."

"Yes, sir," Carter said.

"I trust you to handle this," he said, waiting until she looked up and catching her eye to let her know that he meant it. "I'm not going to think you've lost your edge if you say you could really use some time sitting around drinking tea."

"I don't think that's in the cards right now," Carter said.

"We might have some tea aboard."

"We probably do. It's the sitting around that I'm not so sure about. I did find a barometer, and it's been falling pretty sharply."

"You think we're in for some rough weather?"

"I'm afraid so," Carter said. "You should probably go get some sleep yourself while you can. I'm going to have to wake you if the weather gets really bad."

"Do that," Jack said.

He left her at the helm and walked the length of the ship back to the aft rail, leaning on it to examine the sky. It definitely seemed to be darkening on the horizon. "Hey, Carter," he said on his way back, before heading down the lower deck. "What happens if we get hit by lightning in this thing?"

"We probably have lightning rods to help channel and discharge the electrical energy," Carter said.

He raised his eyebrows at her. "Probably?"

She looked up at the bottom of the canopy, which it wasn't exactly possible to see around from where they stood. "You want to climb up there and check?"

"I'll live with 'probably,'" he said.

"I thought you might, sir."

Teal'c woke at the crack of thunder, aware at once that the ship was being buffeted by turbulence in the air. He climbed cautiously out of his swinging hammock and shook Daniel Jackson's shoulder to wake him.

"What?" He protested, flinging an arm over his eyes, and then lowering it, frowning. "This ride's a little rough, don't you think?"

"We seem to be experiencing inclement weather," Teal'c said.

"That would be my guess, too." Clambering down out of his own hammock, he made his way cautiously to the bars, hanging onto them as the ship shuddered and rocked. "Hello?"

he called. "Anyone? Hello?"

Teal'c had grown used to Daniel Jackson's assumption that everyone he met would be willing to talk to him, even people who had begun their first encounter by taking SG-1 prisoner or announcing that SG-1 would make an ideal sacrifice to their vengeful gods. It was true surprisingly often.

In this case, a man eventually tramped down from the upper deck, looking half-frozen even wrapped in a thick wool coat, his hair wild.

"What's your problem, then?" he said.

"Should we be flying in this weather?"

"It does seem unwise," Teal'c said. He was not certain what would happen should lightning strike the craft in the air, but he did not much want to find out.

The man snorted. "We're running well ahead of the storm," he said. "You may want to stay tucked into your hammocks, though. Don't want to knock your brains out if down doesn't stay down all night."

Daniel Jackson turned to Teal'c as the man went off, raising inquisitive eyebrows. "What do you suppose...?"

Teal'c had also grown used to the tendency of the Tau'ri to ask for opinions when given their lack of reliable information, any opinion could be no more than a guess. He still found it unsettling. Apophis had little patience with speculation. Anything his First Prime thought important enough information to report had best be correct, or the consequences would not be pleasant.

"I suppose nothing," he said, but just then the ground seemed to shift under his feet, tugging him inexplicably toward the bars on one side of the cell. The sensation ended as abruptly as it had begun.

"Whoa," Daniel Jackson said, catching at the bars for balance. "What was that?"

"Did not Major Carter say she believed these craft were too heavy to remain in the air unassisted?"

"You think they have some kind of anti-gravity technology?"

"It would explain their ability to function beyond the capabilities of most aircraft of this type."

"Well, I suppose that's good. I'd like to think that Reba knows what she's doing flying in this weather."

"I do not believe that pirates are generally known for their caution and good judgment," Teal'c said.

"Yeah, unlike us, right?" There was a bitter note to the words that Teal'c did not remember often hearing in his friend's voice before Sha're's death. Before Teal'c had killed Sha're, because Daniel Jackson would not have. He would have trusted to his last breath that Sha're could somehow break free of Amonet's control over her body and save him from Amonet's murderous attack, and Teal'c had not wished to watch him breathe his last.

"We take necessary risks," Teal'c said.

"I just wonder sometimes how much we've actually gained from being out here, as opposed to..." He spread his hands wearily. "I mean, do you ever wonder how many people we've actually helped, in the long run, compared to the people whose lives we've just screwed up one way or another?"

"Many," Teal'c said. "And there can be no freedom from the Goa'uld without sacrifices."

"We're good at sacrificing things to get what we want. Just not ourselves."

"We have been willing to sacrifice ourselves many times."

"But it never seems to happen. It's always somebody else."

"If it had not been, we could not be having this conversation," Teal'c pointed out. "That proves nothing but that the dead are not in a position to regret."

"Lucky them." He seemed to see something in Teal'c's expression that made him relent. "No, you know I don't mean that. I'm just..."

"You are still in mourning."

He shook his head. "We don't really have those customs anymore. Not in any kind of formal way, not after the funeral and... There used to be more elaborate customs about mourning, but I suppose people decided they didn't really need them anymore."

"Perhaps that was unwise," Teal'c said carefully.

"I don't know. I think it's good to get back to work and try to just... put things behind you. When... you know my parents died when I was a child, right?"

Teal'c nodded. He had spoken of it very briefly after their experience with the alien caretaker who had forced them to relive their worst memories for the entertainment of his charges. Teal'c had not seen Daniel Jackson's memory for himself, having instead watched O'Neill live out a failed mission over and over, fighting vainly to save a dead friend, but he knew he had watched his parents die, crushed by a falling stone before his eyes.

"So, after that things were... complicated for a while, getting settled in a foster home, and really the thing that helped most was going back to school and having things to do that took my mind off everything. You never want to hear 'it's time for your life to get back to normal,' but at a certain point it is."

Teal'c could not help thinking of the weeks after his own father's death. It had meant leaving his home for Chulak, then a strange world full of people who served a strange god, and had shaken the certainties of his young life up to that point: that his father was a great warrior, that his mother would not lie when she said his father's final battle had been unwinnable, and that Cronos could do no wrong. It was the last belief that he had abandoned, in what he now recognized was his first tentative childish step toward freedom.

There had been no return to normal, no going back to the life he had led before his father's death, when he had trusted in his god without any doubt. He did not believe there had been one for Daniel Jackson, either, but Teal'c could see that he wished to believe that his life would once again be what it was before Sha're's death, or perhaps before their marriage, if he only waited long enough.

"Perhaps you are right," Teal'c said.

"I wish there were something we could do for these people,"

he said in frustration. "But Reba may be right that anything we do is going to make things worse for them. And yet if we just sit around and do nothing…"

"We must wait for a chance to escape and return to the Stargate," Teal'c said. He felt it was best that they kept their mind on the things that were in fact their responsibilities at the moment.

"Right," Daniel Jackson said, but he still seemed distracted. He looked as though he had slept little, his eyes shadowed in the dim lantern light.

I am sorry, Teal'c was tempted to say, although he had said it before and knew another apology would not be welcome. It was not only Sha're's death that he regretted, while knowing that he would make the same choice again, but the death of the young man who had stubbornly believed that she would someday return to him. These last weeks had aged his friend, and set his face into harder lines that Teal'c doubted would ever entirely fade.

He sat down instead, to avoid having to fight to keep his balance on the swaying deck, and risked edging the radio out from under the folds of cloth that concealed it. He turned the volume up and spoke softly. "O'Neill, Major Carter, do you —"

He broke off at footsteps coming down the stairs, and quickly muted the volume before hiding the radio again. If the storm kept up, the crew was likely to be active through the night. It would give them little chance to attempt to reach the rest of the team. They could only hope that Major Carter could track them despite their silence.

The deck seemed to pitch again, the pull of gravity shifting oddly, making Daniel Jackson clutch at the bars of the cage so as not to stagger into the wall. "Looks like we're in for a long night."

Teal'c nodded. "Indeed."

CHAPTER FIFTEEN

SAM wrenched the valve she was working on closed, wiping it clean to test the seal. It stayed dry, to her satisfaction. The engine was well-built, although various systems had clearly been jerry-rigged over the years.

Jack was at the helm again, while she thawed out. The temperature had dropped sharply after sundown, and the wind was picking up, the gondola rocking as they were buffeted by the storm. She'd have to spell him again before long, as cold as it was, although she thought they both felt better having the more experienced pilot at the helm in winds like these.

She was running out of obvious improvements that wouldn't mean dismantling the gravity drive, which she still wasn't sure she felt like doing. The patchwork interface was frankly a bad idea to start with, and although she thought she might be able to build something more suitable given enough time, she'd need Jolinar's memories of Tok'ra technology to do it. She wasn't sure she wanted to open that box any further.

She shook her head and tested the next valve. The point of working on the engine was to avoid unwelcome thoughts. It didn't seem to be working. Jack was right, their stay on Ne'tu had thrown her, and that was infuriating. She'd spent so much time proving that she had a right to be here. She couldn't afford to let things get to her.

It was all very well for Jack to say that the job got to everyone. Nobody was going to say that he ought to be in some nice safe support position where he wasn't ever going to get hurt. And, all right, he'd apparently had some personal problems after his son's death, to the point that it had been a black mark on his record, but no one had seemed to feel like bringing that up since the first time he'd saved the planet.

Sam was pretty sure that no matter how many times she saved the planet, she still couldn't afford to have nightmares about exactly what it felt like to be on her knees with a pain stick wracking her until she screamed, hoping that it wasn't hurting her symbiote too badly for it to heal—

Yes, because you need me to survive here, Jolinar couldn't help thinking.

Because I care about you, Rosha thought back just as sharply, trying to steady herself with her hands on her knees once the guard had moved on to punish one of the other unlucky prisoners. The thought seemed to strengthen her, as if it was easier for her to keep herself alive if she told herself it was for Jolinar's sake. *Of course it is*, Rosha replied as she caught the thought. *That way I don't have to think about whether it would be easier to just give up.*

We'll find a way out of here, Jolinar told her, but she wasn't sure her tone was reassuring. She didn't have the energy to spare to be reassuring, or to take care of Rosha beyond healing her body, mending her burns and easing the cramps in her muscles, improving the function of her lungs as much as she could so that they could breathe the hot, polluted air.

You don't have to take care of me, Rosha thought, forgiveness for the things Jolinar was too tired to even ask forgiveness for, her single-minded focus on her own survival and the things she'd need to do to ensure it. It was still hard not to just push the part of her that was Rosha down far enough that she wouldn't have to feel any of this, and where Jolinar wouldn't have to think of her until she found a way for them both to escape—

No, Rosha said firmly. *What if I'm the one who can find a way out of here?*

She didn't feel alarmed, just insistent, but Jolinar was distantly aware that this was an alarming train of thought. Maybe that was the way it had been for the first Goa'uld, maybe they had never intended to take over their hosts' bodies and minds entirely, but at some point it had just seemed so much easier...

Jolinar, Rosha said, and the tenderness in her mental voice made the back of Jolinar's throat ache treacherously. *Will it really be easier for you if I go to sleep until we can get out of this place?*

I'm afraid this is hurting you, Jolinar thought, keeping the thought as cool and dry as she could. At the same time, she started climbing unsteadily to her feet. They would be distributing water rations soon, and she could not keep them alive without water.

Of course it is, Rosha said calmly. *But I think you need me.*

Jolinar didn't answer at once. She was opening her canteen, keeping a tight grip on its lid so that she wouldn't drop it with weary hands.

I can't afford to, she said finally. The canteen still held a precious few drops of tepid water, and she tipped it up so that Rosha could drink.

Sam swore under her breath. Once again she'd gotten caught up in a memory that wasn't even hers. It wasn't real, she told herself, just a story about something that happened on television, or that happened to someone who lived a long time ago.

The ship rocked in the wind, and she realized she wasn't sure how long she'd been staring at her own hands holding the wrench. She looked up sharply at the warning dials at a low, ominous rumble, and then realized after a moment that it must have been thunder.

Sam made her way cautiously to the speaking tube, the deck still rocking, and raised her voice as she spoke. "Sir? How's the weather?"

"Not good!" he called down.

"Should we try to set down?"

"I don't think we can! You're going to have to come up, I can barely hear you."

She ran up the stairs, sparing a glance for Keret, who seemed to be sound asleep despite the weather. When she stepped out on deck, she caught her breath as the wind whipped snow into her face. There was another crack of thunder, and she could see the flash lighting part of the gray sky white.

She could immediately see the problem; the visibility was terrible, the sky in all directions turning into a featureless gray that obscured all but the faint dark outlines of the towering peaks. The wind whipped at her as she made her way across the deck, and Jack caught her arm when she came close enough, towing her close enough to the rail that she could grasp it gratefully.

"I don't see how we can set down," he said. "Not when we can't see a damn thing in this snow." He shook his head. "Better to get as much speed as we can out of this thing and try to run out of it."

"While avoiding running into the side of a mountain," Sam said.

"That would be the trick."

"It's getting too cold to stay on deck for long," Sam said. "We're going to have to trade off at the helm."

"We need more speed," Jack said.

"I can maybe get it, but I'm going to have to adjust the gravity drive—"

"So go do it."

The wind was punishingly cold, and even wrapped in a wool coat and hat over his uniform jacket, she didn't think Jack was dressed to spend all night in it. "If you get hypothermia, or frostbite—"

"Then that'll suck, but what else have we got?"

"There's Keret," she said.

"Sure, the guy who kidnapped us."

"That is why we brought him."

"I was thinking more that he could tell us how to keep that overgrown coffee maker these guys call an engine from blowing up."

"I can do that," Sam said. "I just can't do experimental modifications to the Goa'uld gravity drive interface and take a turn flying the ship at the same time."

"Remind me to requisition another one of you when we get home," Jack said.

She shook her head. "Yes, sir."

"All right, take the helm," Jack said.

"Hang on a minute," Sam said. "They've got a couple of staff weapons mounted up here on the rail. They're bolted in place, and they won't swivel to fire on the deck, but we probably shouldn't give Keret the chance to take them apart."

"Pull the power cells out of the staff weapons," Jack said. "Just in case. And then I'll go down and have a little talk with Keret about how helping us not crash the ship would be in his best interest."

"And not double-crossing us," Sam said.

"I'm going to make that clear, too," Jack said, drawing his pistol pointedly and bracing himself to make his way back to the hatch against the wind.

Jack descended the stairs as fast as he could manage, on the theory that stopping to think about whether he'd like to climb more stairs today wasn't going to help. He was developing a list of things that he was irritated at the people on this planet about, and 'not putting elevators on your airships in clear violation of the Don't Make Jack O'Neill's Day Worse Act' was starting to be high on the list.

"Wake up," he said, thumping the bars of the cargo cage for emphasis, since kicking them seemed like a bad idea.

"Who could sleep through this?" Keret said without opening his eyes or moving from where he was sprawled on his pallet.

Jack cocked the pistol, and then realized the noise was unlikely to be a meaningful threat on a world without firearms. He drew his zat left-handed and activated it. That did get Keret to open his eyes.

"Easy, there," the man said. "I don't see what I could have done to make you angry while I'm locked up in my own cargo hold."

"I don't really need new reasons," Jack said. "You may have noticed the weather."

"Not being stone deaf, yes," Keret said. "Regretting stealing my ship yet?"

"About as much as you regret kidnapping us. If I let you out of here, will you help us fly the ship?"

"It's my ship."

"Answer the question."

"What's in it for me?"

"We don't all crash and die."

"Besides that."

"You help us, and after we find our friends, you can have your ship back. You don't help us, and after we find our friends, we're handing you over to the local authorities so that they can throw the book at you."

"What book?"

"A really heavy one. You get my meaning."

"I think I do." Keret shook his head. "Fine."

"That's all you have to say? Fine?"

He shrugged. "You want me to say, no, I'll fight you with my dying breath? I know how to cut my losses. At this point, I just want my ship back."

"If you take one step out of line…" Jack held up both the pistol and the zat meaningfully.

Keret shook his head. "And Reba said the Tau'ri had a reputation for being agreeable people."

"I am being agreeable," Jack said. "You don't want to see me when I'm not being agreeable. Now get your ass out here and help fly this thing."

"I have a better idea," Keret said as Jack unlocked the cage door. "Why don't I go up and fly my airship, and you two go fix whatever you've done to the engines that's making them sound like they're about to burn out."

"It's cold outside," Jack said. "You'll need someone to spell you after a while."

"I've seen worse," Keret said, holding up one hand to show off frostbite scars across the back of his knuckles.

"Me, too," Jack said. "You want to have a pissing contest over who's been colder, or you want to trade off at the helm?"

"Do you have any idea what you're doing?"

"I've flown fixed-wing aircraft and helicopters, and I've flown second seat in a Goa'uld Death Glider," Jack said. "This is my first time flying an airship, and if you want to show me how the controls are actually supposed to work, feel free."

"You're going to crash my ship," Keret said.

"That's what you get when you kidnap people."

Keret shook his head. "Will you stop harping on it? It's a tradition in these parts."

"Where I come from, it's a crime."

"The two aren't mutually exclusive."

Jack gestured toward the stairs with his pistol. "Can we get on with this?"

"How about, as a little gesture of mutual trust, you stop pointing weapons at me?"

"I don't trust you," Jack said, but he holstered the pistol and put away the zat. "You go first up the stairs."

"Your friend isn't going to shoot me?"

"Probably not," Jack said. "I wouldn't make any sudden movements."

He followed Keret up the stairs. Surely at their level of technology it was ought to be possible for these people to have invented elevators. He'd have to ask Daniel when the elevator had been invented, once they found him, just to see his expression.

The weather hadn't improved when they came out on deck, the wind howling against the ship's struts. Carter was clinging to the controls as if worried that she'd be blown overboard if she let go. If the wind picked up any more, that would start to be a possibility. She didn't turn for a moment, clearly not able to hear them over the shriek of the wind.

"Carter!" he called, and she turned, and then drew her pistol. "It's all right. I think."

They made their way forward, Keret keeping his feet easily despite the shifting wind and the icy deck.

"I take it we've got a deal," Carter said when they got close enough to hear.

Keret ignored her, flipping open a panel below the controls and hauling out coils of rope. He tossed one at Carter, who managed to snag it before it was whipped away by the wind. "Clip onto something," he said, taking another coil of rope and fastening the carabiner at one end of it to a metal loop on his belt. He ran the rope around a nearby handhold and tied it swiftly, and then looked at Carter like she was a slow student. "Unless you'd like to find out how far it is down?"

"Hang on," Jack said. "You go see what you can do to get more speed out of this thing. I'm going to get some lessons in flying an airship." He took the rope from her and clipped it onto his own pants, tying it off nearby, although he didn't trust Keret not to cut the rope if he really went over the rail.

"It doesn't go *faster*," Keret said, sounding alarmed.

"I think it will," Carter said. "It's just a matter of making the right adjustments to the gravity drive."

"You people are insane."

"A lot of people say that," Jack said. "Carter, see what you can do." He squinted into the driving snow. "You show me how to keep this thing on course."

"We have a course?" Keret said as Carter started cautiously making her way across the deck. "Here, wait, you." Keret tossed her a rope, and she caught that as well, although she skidded off-balance in the process. "There's a ring next to the hatch. Fix the line!"

She did, and Jack secured the other end around the rail, making a guide rope that would make the trip from hatchway to controls at least a little less nervewracking. Carter nodded and disappeared below.

"We're following your friend's ship," Jack said. He pointed out Carter's tracking device. "Just keep us pointed so that the lights glow nice and bright."

"In a storm, threading our way through mountains you've never even seen before, with *your* friend doing the Queen of Heaven only knows what to our engines? You don't ask for much, do you?"

"Can you do it, or not?"

"Why not try?" Keret said, throwing his hands up. "The worst we can wind up is dead, and anyway I'd really like to have a talk with Reba about this really bad plan of hers."

The ship rocked in a particularly strong gust of wind, and at the same time, Jack could feel the deck tip dramatically under his feet, knocking him against the rail. He held on tight and tried not to look alarmed.

"That would be Carter," he said.

"She's crazy," Keret said again, and grappled desperately with the controls. "You have no idea how close we are to —"

He broke off as a dark shape loomed behind the snow, coming up way too fast and blocking out most of the sky. Jack recoiled, and then scrambled toward the speaking tube, as well as he could against the forward pull of gravity. "Carter! Slow us down!"

"That may take a minute!" Carter said.

Keret wasn't saying anything, his head bent over the controls in desperate concentration, wrestling the ship into a shuddering turn that seemed to violate a number of familiar laws of physics.

"We don't have a minute!" Jack said. "We need a hard starboard turn!"

"I can do that!" Carter said. "Hang on —"

Jack felt himself sliding to starboard, felt the deck seem to tip under his feet. Without being able to see the horizon, there was no point of reference to tell him that down wasn't somewhere toward the starboard rail, with the bulk of the ship looming above him, the huge rock outcropping above them like a black wave, blotting out the sky.

He braced himself for a crash that never came. Instead, the airship skimmed past the rock face with what looked like barely meters to spare. There was a crack of thunder, far too close for comfort, and lightning illuminated half the sky.

"Carter! We're clear!" He held on tight to the rail as the deck returned to its forward tilt. "See, piece of cake."

"Your god must love fools," Keret said grimly, easing them back into a more level course.

"You may be right," Jack said.

CHAPTER SIXTEEN

GENERAL HAMMOND stepped into the control room, glancing down at the blue shimmer of the active wormhole. Everyone always said it looked like a ring of water, but no water had ever shed that kind of rippling light from within. Hammond shook his head and glanced back at Walter Harriman, who had his head bent over his screen, apparently immune to the hypnotic appeal of watching the active gate.

"Any sign of SG-1?"

"I'm not sure, sir," Walter said, frowning at his screen. "We thought we picked up a radio signal a little while ago, but the weather's getting worse. We're getting gale-force winds across a wide area. If this keeps up, we're going to have to recall the UAV, or..." He broke off, wincing. "Sir, we've just lost contact with the UAV."

"Do we have a video feed?"

"Yes, sir." Walter's hands moved swiftly over the keyboard, playing back the last few seconds of the UAV's transmission. The image looked grainy at first, but as the UAV soared over a jagged spur of rock, it became clear that the blurriness of the picture was due to swirling snow. The UAV banked, too sharply as one wing caught the wind, and the dark shape of a cliff face loomed briefly into view before the picture cut off abruptly.

"Damn," Hammond said.

"Yes, sir," Walter said. "We could launch a second UAV."

"Not in this weather," Hammond said. "And we can't keep the gate open indefinitely. Especially not when we've been expressly forbidden by the local authorities to do exactly what we're doing right now." He shook his head. "Shut it down. We'll try again in a couple of hours."

"Shutting it down, sir," Walter said. The shimmering ring of light died out abruptly.

"You're sure you picked up a radio signal?"

"I think so, although the UAV was near its maximum transmission range at the time," Walter said. "It... yes, sir, it looks like the UAV did alter its course to track a moving radio signal."

"That would make sense if SG-1's still on one of the airships that attacked the treaty ceremony."

"I can project a course over the next couple of hours based on the data that the UAV sent back, although of course there's no way of knowing whether the ship will stay on the same heading."

"Do it," Hammond said. "At least that'll give us somewhere to start."

He'd only been back at his desk a few minutes before there was a knock at the door. "I have those budgetary forms for you," Janet said. "And I wanted to see..."

"If there's been any word about SG-1?" Hammond shook his head. "Not yet. We're going to keep looking."

"Of course," Janet said. He knew it had gotten harder for her in some ways since she'd developed personal friendships with the people she worked with. SG-1 spent a lot of time walking into danger and a lot of time in the infirmary. Not to mention that she'd be the one who'd have to explain it to Cassie if anything happened to Sam.

"I'm hoping we'll get authorization for the expansions to the medical department that you're requesting."

"So am I, but I'm also not holding my breath," Janet said.

"Well, in the past the idea that an undetected alien disease has the potential to wipe out this facility — or for that matter the planet — has been motivational."

"Understandably so, but what we really need isn't more emergency response capability, but more capacity to handle things that aren't crisis situations while still having the ability to deal with things that are. I'd like to have a physical therapist on staff, for instance, and another physician's assistant."

"Things that aren't crisis situations can be dealt with at Peterson or over at the Academy hospital," Hammond said.

"As long as they don't involve patients who aren't from this planet, or injuries that can't be adequately explained without endangering national security, yes, sir, they can. But seeing someone outside the SGC means losing half a day's work for some very busy people, and in actual practice, a lot of the time it doesn't really happen. The more we can do here, the more likely people are to actually comply with their physical therapy routines or get treatment for minor problems before they become major ones."

"Understood," Hammond said.

"I'd say we could also use another psychologist on staff, but the ones we have are already chronically underutilized."

"I take it that's your way of saying no one's willing to go see them unless they're under orders or plain out of their minds."

"I wouldn't say no one," Janet said. "But I'd like to see more people taking advantage of the resources that we provide to help them deal with some of the things they go through."

"I'll tell them you said so," Hammond said. "I don't expect that'll make very much difference, though."

"You'd be surprised," Janet said. "It can be very helpful for people to know that they won't get in trouble for admitting they're having problems. Or for taking the morning off to go to the dentist, if that's what they need to do. It's the least we can do, and when you think about all the health hazards our people face that we can't do a thing about…" She turned up her hands in frustration.

"Feeling discouraged?"

"Maybe just a little," Janet said. "I'd like to feel like my patients were at least fully recovered from one set of injuries before they go out there and start getting more."

"For all we know, SG-1 is perfectly fine," Hammond said,

as reassuringly as he could manage.

"Yes, sir," Janet said, turning to go.

"Dr. Fraiser? For what it's worth, I'd like that too."

Sam looked up from wrestling wearily with one of the engine's valves at the sound of footsteps coming down the stairs. "Good timing, sir, you can help me —" She broke off when she saw that it was Keret, and let go of the valve wheel to draw her zat.

"If you strike me with the thunderbolt again, I won't be much good at the helm," Keret said. Snow was melting in his hair, and his cheeks were red with the cold. He moved stiffly, like it was hard for him to feel his feet.

"I'm sorry," Sam said, although she wasn't, particularly. "It seemed like a good idea at the time."

Keret came to stand over the stove, unfolding his hands over it painfully. "Can't we make some kind of a deal, here?"

"I thought we had a deal," Sam said, going back to her efforts to wrench the valve closed. "You help us fly the ship and we give it back to you when we're done with it."

"Not much of a deal," Keret said.

"Having second thoughts already? That figures."

"Just pointing out that you could trust me better if you were offering me more than I'd get if I managed to get you both off my ship."

Sam shrugged. "If we find the fabulous treasure your friend was looking for, you can..." She was about to say *you can have it*, but was aware that wouldn't sound very plausible. "You can have a share of it."

"I doubt very much she's finding any treasure," Keret said, shaking his head. "Reba's stared at those old writings until they've made her crazy. But if there's anything there to find, she'll have found it and be long gone by the time we catch up."

"I wouldn't be so sure about that," Sam said. "We're making considerably better speed than we were to start with."

"I've noticed that," Keret said. "I'm just not sure how you've managed to keep from killing us all in the process."

"Part of it is the adjustments I've made to the gravity drive — I've had the opportunity to work with similar kinds of technology. I'm also working on getting more power to the drive without the kind of power spikes that could burn out the crystals."

"Here," Keret said, and came over to her side. She drew her zat again pointedly, but he merely rolled his eyes at her and put his shoulder to the jammed wheel. At first it wouldn't budge for him either, but eventually he managed to pry it loose and get it turning.

"Thanks," she said reluctantly.

"Will you show me what you've done to the crystals?"

Sam ran a grease-stained hand through her hair. "I swear, it's not going to explode."

"So you say," Keret said. "I was thinking more of a bargain. Show me what you know about the device of the gods, and I'll have a reason to keep faith with you even when you're not pointing a thunderbolt at me."

She looked at him skeptically. "You're really interested?"

"My ship is my life," he said. "The extra speed you say you can give us could be the difference between taking a fine prize and being left empty-handed."

"I can show you what I've done," Sam said slowly. She wasn't sure that helping pirates be better pirates was really the mission of SG-1, but if it kept Keret from trying to zat them in their sleep, that was probably for the best. She looked the man up and down as he checked the row of gauges in front of her, adjusting one with practiced fingers. "Where did you get this ship, anyway?"

Keret shrugged. "Won her in a fair fight with her last captain. Fair enough, anyhow. He'd crashed her trying to chase down one of the High King's tribute ships in a gale very much like this one, and I had to rebuild half her engine before me and the men who stuck with me could get her back in the air. So I figure I've worked for her."

"Is this really what you want to be doing with your life?"

Keret shook his head, looking more amused than offended. "You think I'd make a better herder of sheep? Well, too bad for me if I would, because I've got no farm and no sheep, and no skill at wringing a living from a rocky patch of upland soil that gets scoured by every gale."

"The High King must need men who understand how these airships are built."

"How often does he need that? When one of the old ones wears out or isn't fashionable enough to impress those herds of wastrels in the capital, and then it's mainly a matter of putting a new skin over the same old engines. If we had more boxes of winds, it might be a different matter, but there aren't more than a few dozen in the whole of the world."

A few dozen crystal arrays like the ones that powered the airship could have come from a handful of tel'taks, or maybe some shipment of Goa'uld starship parts that had once been intercepted. "You could build craft that would stay in the air without the gravity drive. We used to use similar airships on our world."

"But they wouldn't look as fine or carry as much, and that's what the High King cares about. Putting on a show to look grand for the Queen of Heaven, and no matter that the rest of us starve." He shook his head. "Anyhow, what's it to you?"

Sam shrugged. "I suppose I would just prefer not to be helping you carry on with a life of crime."

Keret grinned wolfishly. "You mean, unlike stealing other people's airships?"

"We're borrowing it," Sam said.

"Spoken like a pirate," Keret said.

By the time she'd finished working on the set of valves she'd been tightening and shown Keret the first of the adjustments she'd made to the gravity drive, she was beginning to feel a prickling sense of guilt about how long Jack had been out in the driving wind.

"I'm going above," she said. "But I'm wondering if I can trust you down here without me."

"I could use the box of winds to shake the ship so that the two of you might lose your footing," Keret said. "That wouldn't be wise in this storm. Or I might have a thunderbolt stashed away down here and shoot your friend when he comes down the stairs."

"That won't be so easy," Sam said.

"And then I'd have to spend all the rest of the night out in the storm myself, which isn't as appealing as all that. So you can probably go on up without bothering to handcuff me to anything. Unless that's your idea of fun."

"I'll pass," Sam said firmly.

She headed up, bracing herself at the top of the second flight of stairs as she opened the hatch. The wind still hit her hard, whipping her hair back and driving snow into her face.

She was glad of the rope they'd strung between the hatchway and the controls, gripping it tightly with hands made clumsy by the oversized gloves she was wearing. She didn't even try to speak to Jack over the howling wind before she was in arm's reach, and even then she had to thump him on the arm to get his attention.

"I'll take the helm!"

He nodded without arguing and let her slide into place where he'd been standing. The controls themselves broke some of the wind, but it was still painfully cold. Jack pulled off the wool cap he was wearing and handed it to her, and she nodded thanks as she put it on, tugging it down over her ears.

"Where's Keret?"

"At the engines," Sam said, raising her voice to carry over the wind. "He says he'll behave, but I'd watch yourself!"

"I always do!" Jack said, resting one hand on his holstered pistol pointedly before grabbing onto the rope to make his way back to the hatch.

Sam smiled a little and peered at the radio receiver. The light designed to show the signal strength abruptly strengthened, and she frowned, and then crouched quickly to put her ear close to the radio itself. Even with the volume all the way up, she wasn't sure at first that she was making out words.

"… O'Neill, please respond."

"Teal'c! Is that you?"

"Major Carter! We…" The signal faded abruptly, the wind dying down slightly as well, and she scrambled to her feet, leaning bodily on the controls to bank away from the cliff face looming in front of her.

They cleared the shelf of rock with bare meters to spare, the wind once again driving snow into her face, and it took her a minute to get the radio angled toward the handset's signal and get the ship more or less headed in that direction as well. When she thought she could without risking a collision, she crouched near the radio again.

"Teal'c! Is Daniel with you? Are you all right?"

There was no answer. She pressed her ear to the cold metal, but there was only a low static hum.

"Damn!" She straightened, not wanting to let go of the controls for long. She couldn't help feeling a surge of relief. At least Teal'c was alive, and he still had access to his radio. That was more than they'd known for sure a few minutes ago.

She pulled her coat more tightly around her, bracing herself against the persistent feeling that she was going to slide forward until she ended up plastered against the rail. It would be a relief to be back on solid ground with down staying under her feet. Or at least for the wind to slacken so that her face wasn't already going numb.

It wasn't as bad as Antarctica, she told herself, and wished that wasn't the kind of thing that passed for a comfort in her life these days.

CHAPTER SEVENTEEN

SOME hours later, the weather had only worsened, although Keret insisted that it should be better once they turned to the south and put the backbone of the ridge between them and the wind. Jack wrestled with the airship's rudders, hoping that the stiffness of their response was because the steering column was cold and not because the rudders themselves were jammed with ice. He wasn't sure what to do about that short of climbing over the side to try to knock it loose, which didn't appeal to him at the moment. Maybe Keret would volunteer for that. Or maybe Jack could volunteer him.

Keret had taken a turn at the helm, with a great many complaints that Jack was going to kill them with his reckless flying. Jack wished Teal'c were there, for a lot of reasons starting with the desire to have a third pilot he trusted implicitly and ending with the fact that Teal'c could probably wrench the damn rudder controls around without having to throw his shoulder against them bruisingly hard. Somewhere in the middle was the fact that Teal'c probably knew something about the Goa'uld technology this ship was using.

Carter seemed to have figured out what made it tick for the moment, and he trusted that she'd keep it running if anyone could, but he hated trusting himself to technology they barely understood. Of course, they did a lot of that. While a lot of Carter's explanations of wormhole physics went over his head, the ones that didn't had made it clear that every time they stepped through the Stargate, they were trusting themselves to a combination of unproven theory and luck.

The one mercy was that the gate builders had apparently wanted to make the Stargates idiot-proof, and most of the time they were. The times they weren't were the problem. Which he was probably thinking about because one of those times had left them stranded in an ice cave in Antarctica, and right now it felt about that cold.

A flash of lightning strobed across the sky, illuminating the driving snow and the dark shapes of mountains, and then a crack of thunder followed it far too quickly for comfort. He'd flown in worse, and for that matter parachuted in worse, but that wasn't any guarantee that this was going to end well.

He still felt a sneaking sense of exhilaration at their sheer speed, the wind whipping snow into his face. With the pull of gravity still making the deck seem to slant sharply down under his feet, it felt a little like sledding, although he was pretty sure he'd never gotten away with sledding in a driving storm with thunder crashing wildly around him as a kid.

He flipped open the cover of the speaking tube, hoping Carter would be able to hear him over the howling of the wind. "How's it going down there?"

"It's going!" she yelled. "The power interface is a little — whoa!"

He thought he heard an electrical snap in the background, but was distracted from it by his feet once again going out from under him as 'down' re-established itself as being somewhere in the direction of the airship's canopy. He let himself flip in the air, hanging onto the controls, and managed to wrestle himself into a position where he could still make himself heard below.

"Carter!"

"We lost one of the crystals! I'm trying to re-route power!"

"Now would be a good time!" Jack yelled. Snow swirled disorientingly around him, but as far as he could tell, the airship was rising sharply. He wasn't sure why it wasn't flipping in the air, its gondola tumbling below — or above — its canopy. For that matter, he wasn't sure why it wasn't just rising smoothly the way a Goa'uld ship would. The Goa'uld didn't usually make their passengers tumble around like loose socks in the dryer. "Any time!"

"I'm working on it!" Carter said. "Keret, get over here!"

"This is my ship you're wrecking!" Keret's voice carried clearly enough, although he was pretty sure Carter was object of his wrath. "I can't replace that crystal—"

"We don't have to replace it if we can work around it!"

"How?"

"I don't know!"

"Figure it out, kids!" Jack yelled. They were still gaining altitude, the dial that he guessed was an altimeter spinning wildly and the snow swirling and seeming to rise in driving sheets toward the sky. But that was really the ground, which they were rapidly leaving behind them.

That was good in the sense that they'd be less likely to run into anything. It was bad in that they were rising into the center of the storm, and if they couldn't check their ascent, the drop in pressure would eventually be a serious problem. Jack was betting the airship wasn't equipped with oxygen masks, and they were already pretty damn high.

"Carter!"

"I know!"

There was a sudden blinding flash, and a tearing crash split the sky. For one heart-stopping moment he could see the lightning arc somewhere below his feet, up near the top of the canopy, and then the world darkened abruptly in the aftermath of the brilliant light. The control column he was clinging to pitched wildly.

We've been hit, he thought, his eyes stinging. He braced himself for an explosion, or the roaring of igniting flame, but nothing happened except that they kept plunging upward, the air stinking of ozone for a few seconds before the driving wind whipped the smell away.

"What happened?" Carter called anxiously.

Jack squinted, blinking through watering eyes to try to see if there was any obvious damage. He couldn't see any, although the upper side of the canopy was out of view. Still, the canopy didn't seem to be deforming as he thought it would be if the lightning strike had ripped through its canvas.

"I think we just found out that we do have lightning rods!"

Carter's voice rose a notch. "Did we get hit by lightning?"

"Fix the drive!"

"I'm trying!"

Jack's numb hands were slipping on the steering column, the metal slick with ice. He spared a glance down under his feet, and then let himself slide, finding his footing on the underside of the canopy. He scrubbed snow out of his face with the back of his hand, but the icy glove wasn't much help.

Anywhere that isn't hot for our next mission, he'd said after Ne'tu. *Just send us anywhere that isn't hot.*

"I take it back!" he yelled, but the wind whipped the words away.

Sam scrambled up to reach the control panel, thinking furiously. The crystal that had shorted out was most likely burned out completely; she could see the dull gray scorch marks along its length. That meant she needed to rewire so that the ones around it were somehow bridging the gap and compensating for the missing crystal.

It would have been an easy problem given an hour. She glanced at the altimeter. She figured at their present rate of ascent, they had a few minutes.

"Give me a hand, here!" she snapped at Keret.

He was balancing easily on one strut of what had moments ago been the ceiling, watching her efforts to hang upside down on the pillar that housed the crystal with apparent amusement. "Where do you want it?"

"This is not the time," she snapped.

"We're probably about to die. When would be a better time?"

"I can fix it," Sam said. "Assuming I can reach it."

Keret got his hands under her, bracing her as she craned

her neck to see. She wrapped the rope she was still clipped to around the pillar and pulled it taut, hoping that if the gravity suddenly reversed itself again it would keep her from crashing to the floor. If she pulled that crystal...

She had a bad feeling about that, but one that stubbornly refused to crystallize into a clear idea of what she should do instead. She gritted her teeth in frustration. She was sure Jolinar could have fixed this. She'd been good with the tel'taks, patching their systems to keep them in use even when they should have long since been retired, because they couldn't afford to lose them even when they were battered and scarred.

She could feel the memory threatening to swim up into consciousness, and knew she had a choice in whether to let it.

"You have no idea how to fix this?" she demanded.

"You broke it," Keret said. "I don't even know what you did."

You knew, Sam thought, knowing at the same time that Jolinar couldn't hear her, because she was only a handful of memories left behind like shadows in Sam's mind. She let herself slip into one, seeing a similar tray of crystals pulled out for repair, her own hands moving over them, the knuckles still pink with healing burn scars —

"You should give yourself more time to recover," Martouf said, frowning at her in a way that made Jolinar turn her head so she wouldn't have to see. "You're not even completely healed."

"These are superficial injuries," Jolinar said.

"Which have taken this long to heal because of the damage to your lungs. The vapors on Ne'tu —"

"You weren't there," Jolinar snapped. "Don't lecture me about dangerous vapors."

"I know I wasn't there," Martouf said, and the regret in his voice made her chest ache treacherously. "You've said hardly anything about Ne'tu since you returned."

"There's nothing to say," Jolinar said, pulling out one of the crystals and stacking it neatly in a pile with the others that

were burned out. They didn't have enough replacements on hand, but she could bridge the gap with what they did have until they had the leisure to grow more. "I escaped."

"For which I'm grateful," Martouf said. "You've said hardly anything at all since you returned."

"I'm busy," Jolinar said.

"You could be resting."

"I am resting. And while I'm resting, these repairs still need to be done."

"Just tell me you'll wait until you're fully recovered before you go out again."

She looked up at that. "I'm fine," she said.

"Jolinar..."

"Is there anything else?"

Martouf bowed his head for a moment, his expression shifting from naked worry to a less easily readable one. "Martouf is worried about you," Lantash said. "So am I."

Let me talk to him, Rosha said. Jolinar threw up her hands in frustration and bent her own head. She didn't have anything to say to Martouf and Lantash right now, except that she wanted both of them to stay out of her way for a while.

"We're just tired," Rosha said.

"Which is why we were suggesting you rest."

"We will. But this does need to be done, and it doesn't hurt anything for us to do it. Don't mind Jolinar."

Jolinar didn't reply to that, working through the rest of the repairs in her head instead. There could be no privacy between symbiote and host, and she had learned long ago that it was better to let Rosha say what she would about her without protest, in return for the knowledge that in her turn, she could do the same.

"This isn't like her," Lantash said.

"Yes, it is," Rosha said. *She sat back on her heels, putting the crystals aside for a moment and rubbing absently at the half-healed burns on the back of her hand.* "You haven't spent as *much time with her in the field."*

Rosha, Jolinar thought warningly. They'd agreed that there were parts of their time on Ne'tu that they wouldn't speak of, not to Martouf and Lantash and not to anyone who might tell them. Lantash would probably understand, Jolinar thought, but Martouf was too soft-hearted. It would hurt him to know how she had made her escape, and she didn't want to see his pain when he realized what she had done, or see his eyes harden when he understood how she'd betrayed him.

It wasn't a betrayal, Rosha said. *And he's not like that.* Now that it was done and they were home, Jolinar was all too aware that right now Rosha was the stronger of the two of them. Rosha was patient with their healing when Jolinar wanted only to be done with the reminders of Ne'tu that were still written on her skin. Rosha was certain they had done the only possible thing when Jolinar felt only the sick sense that if she'd stayed in Ne'tu long enough, every one of her principles would have been stripped away, leaving only the animal urge to survive.

Even so.

"She stops thinking about anything but the mission, past a certain point," Rosha said aloud. "It's part of what makes her so good at surviving. But sometimes it's hard to put it down when the mission's over."

Lantash looked at her sideways. "You're certain that's all?"

"That's all," Rosha said. "We just need some time."

"We'll give it to you," Lantash said. He went out, leaving them in the quiet of the hangar.

I hate lying to him, Rosha said, as Jolinar came forward again, picking up the next crystal that she'd need to install.

We aren't lying, Jolinar said. *We're just not telling the whole truth.*

There's not that much difference right now, Rosha said.

Then why did you?

Because you're not ready to tell him yet, Rosha said. *And you come first.*

The mission comes first, Jolinar said.

Sometimes the mission is fixing what's broken, Rosha said. *Because we still need to use it.* Jolinar started to set the next crystal into place and then realized it was clouded, its depths streaked with burns. She reached for another one instead. It wouldn't fit as well, but she could make it serve—

"Hey, Tau'ri!" Keret said, shaking her. "What's the matter with you?"

"Nothing," Sam said, trying to clear her head. The memory had been so vivid. Including what she needed to do. "We need to re-route the power away from these three crystals, so that I can switch this one and this one without shorting anything else out. It looks like I'm going to need to disconnect this wire and reconnect it."

"Use the switches," Keret said. "Four open, six closed, nine open, eleven open."

Now that Sam looked closely, she could see the markings on the switches. "I can't read your numbers."

Keret swore under his breath. "Let me up there," he said, and Sam leaned heavily on her improvised rope harness as Keret scaled the pillar himself. He flipped switches swiftly. "Move them fast."

Sam didn't need to be told that twice. She switched out the crystals as fast as she dared with tired fingers. She could see how to construct the bridge, and as soon as she set the last crystal into place, she was sure it was working.

"Hang onto something," she said, and adjusted the power, the play of light through the crystals shifting as she did. She felt the momentary disorientation of weightlessness, and worked to get her feet under her as the gravity reversed itself.

The ropes binding her to the pillar jerked painfully as her weight returned, and she disentangled herself as fast as she could. She leaned across a bank of controls to shout into the mouthpiece of the speaking tube. "Sir! Are you all right?"

There was a pause long enough for her to start worrying, and then Jack said, more reflectively than anything else, "Ouch!"

"Sorry, sir!"

"I think we've leveled off," Jack said. "I'm going to try to bring us down using the elevators. If you're thinking about making us all weigh twice as much as we should right now, please just... don't, all right?"

"Understood, sir!"

"You're both madmen," Keret said.

"We're just doing our job," Sam said, and smiled when he shook his head in disbelief.

CHAPTER EIGHTEEN

"MAJOR Carter? Please respond."

Daniel waved Teal'c silent hurriedly at the sound of footsteps on the stairs. Teal'c silenced the radio immediately and thrust it back into its hiding place as Reba came clattering down the stairs from above. She pushed back a heavy wool hood, shaking snow from her hair, but she looked satisfied.

"The worst of the storm is going south of us," she said. "You'd best come up. If what the tablets say is true, we'll be coming in sight of the ruins soon."

Daniel waited while she unlocked the cargo cage door, slipping out with an apologetic shrug at Teal'c.

"Here," she said, thrusting a heavy woolen blanket at him. "You're no use to me if you freeze."

He wrapped the blanket around his shoulders like a serape and followed her up to the deck. It was bitingly cold above, the sun just barely up and still shaded from them by the highest peaks.

"The ruins will be fairly high up the mountainside," Daniel said, and hoped that he was right. He had felt sure of his translation at first, but an edge of doubt was beginning to creep in. He was all too aware that if he was back at the SGC, there were a number of words he would have wanted to compare to their use in other sources, just to see if in context —

"So you say," Reba said, but then she shrugged. "Well, at least that means there's less chance of them being somebody's farm by now."

"I haven't seen many settlements in this area," Daniel said.

"You've been all snug and warm below, so you haven't seen much," Reba said. "There are a few, sheep farmers and crop farmers. There's not such a thing as a town this side of the

High Ridge, though, and precious few trails that are passable most of the year. A lot of people think twice about a life where they've got no way on or off their farm other than when the High King bothers to send an airship."

"It sounds like it was a fairly big installation," Daniel said. He leaned out to see over the rail, and then snatched his hands back when the cold metal bit like ice. "I don't suppose I could have my gloves back?"

"I think Tami's using them. Aren't you?" she called cheerfully to the man at the helm, who turned to reveal a face blotched with what looked like burn scars. Frostbite, more likely, Daniel thought, and was glad they hadn't tried to escape the ship somewhere that would have meant a long hike in this weather.

"Sorry," the man said without sounding it, holding up one hand to show off one of Daniel's gloves. "But I suppose I could be making it a trade." He pulled a pair of rough woolen mittens from his pocket and tossed them in Daniel's direction, but Reba fielded them neatly out of the air.

"You're getting soft, Tami," Reba said, starting to pocket them herself.

"If you expect me to explore the ruins, it would help if I could take my hands out of my pockets," Daniel said.

Reba shook her head. "I'm still not running a guesthouse here," she said, but she handed the mittens over. They were threadbare and less than clean, but Daniel slipped them on anyway. He leaned out over the rail again. "How close are we?"

Reba strode forward, shouldering Tami aside to squint at the instruments. "Close," she said. She shaded her eyes with her hand as they turned east, sailing through the rocky gap between two towering peaks. "See there, that pass?"

"I wouldn't call that a pass," Daniel said. The peaks she was pointing out were joined by a rocky saddle of land higher than Daniel felt any reasonable person would want to climb to cross between them.

"Call it a ridge, then, or what you like, but that's where your ruins are supposed to sit." Reba frowned. "I can't see anything like buildings from here."

"We're still pretty far off. And they may well have been overgrown, or even covered over by earth and shifting rocks."

"In which case what are we supposed to do?"

Daniel couldn't help sounding a bit exasperated. "Dig. You'd be amazed how few fabulous ancient treasures are just sitting around in exposed buildings with nice wide doorways, waiting for people to walk in and pick them up."

"I suppose treasure hunting is your livelihood," Reba said.

"It used to be, anyway," Daniel said. "Not treasure hunting, exactly, but looking for the remains of past civilizations." He shook his head. "These days I spend more time fighting the Goa'uld."

"Fighting the gods seems a remarkably pointless effort," Reba said.

"I have days when I think so, too, but… okay, there, what is that?" He shaded his own eyes, trying to make sense of the shapes on the high ridge.

"Rock," Reba said. "Rock and more rock, it looks like to me."

They were drifting closer, slower now than any airplane would travel, and angling to come up parallel to the ridge. He could see how broken the ground was now, a series of deep ravines and sharp shelves of rock splitting the land into jagged stair-steps.

"It should be here," he said. The only growing things were some patches of low, tangled evergreen, not big enough to hide the shape of a building.

"Should isn't good enough," Reba said, drawing her zat. Daniel scoured the rock with his eyes, willing something other than broken rock to appear.

"Wait, there!"

Reba's mouth tightened as if she suspected him of stalling for time, but she followed his gaze to the unmistakably manmade curve of a tumbled stone wall. It was near the top of the ridge, shielding anything beyond it from view.

"Can you take us over the top?"

Reba frowned. "I could, but I won't. We're in the lee of the wind on this side, and we may as well stay here as cross the ridge and get battered against the rocks on the other side." She pointed to a broad shelf of rock some distance below the wall's curve. "We'll drive an anchor there and tie up."

"How are you planning to get up the ridge?"

Reba looked at him sideways. "Climb," she said.

To Daniel's relief, while it was a steep climb up the rocks, there were only a few places where he could find no obvious way upward. In several places, they found the remains of stairways cut into the rock, although they were broken and often led from one gaping crack in the rocks to another. Each time Daniel had to admit he saw no way up, Reba shook her head and took the lead, scrambling up sheer rock faces with no apparent concern for the possibility of falling and then tossing him down a rope.

By the time they reached the ruins of the wall, his shoulders were aching and he could feel the beginnings of a headache threatening from the exertion at this altitude. He was grateful that he'd spent the last couple of years in Colorado Springs, rather than somewhere nearer sea level. Like Sha're's home on Abydos, he caught himself thinking, and pushed the thought ruthlessly away. This was no time for distractions.

He hauled himself over the wall and sat down on it for a moment, considering the view beyond. There had clearly once been an extensive complex of buildings here, although many of them had been tumbled as the earth shifted. The smooth facades and the remains of sweeping pillars were nothing like the architecture he'd seen in the capital.

"This definitely looks Ancient," Daniel said.

Reba gave him an impatient look, coiling her rope and hooking it to her belt. "Find the device."

The tablets had implied that the temple complex was laid out in a grid, but it was hard to make out the original lines now. He slid down from the wall and started making his way down the steep hillside. Beyond the lowest wall of the complex, the ground dropped off precipitously, which made climbing downhill toward it a little dizzying even though it was a good distance below him.

"Do you know where it is, or not?"

"I'm looking," Daniel said. The wind was worse on this side of the ridge, scouring grains of blowing snow against his face, although at least now that he wasn't having to use both hands to climb, he could catch at the ends of the wool blanket he was wrapped in when they whipped loose and threatened to snatch the thing off him entirely.

"What are you looking for?"

He scuffed at the rock with his toe, trying to determine whether he was looking at a deliberately created path or simply the results of the fracturing of the rock. "I'm trying to see how this place was originally laid out."

"Because?"

"Because I need to know that to find what we're looking for. I don't tell you how to fly your ship." He scrambled down a little further, and then slid faster than he meant to down the steep slope, catching himself on the edge of a fallen slab.

Reba tossed him the end of her rope wordlessly, and he caught it and knotted it carefully around his waist. He'd gotten used to using his tac vest for that, which was strange when he thought about it. He felt naked now without the vest, and without the magpie collection of gear he packed for the field, an ultimately doomed but still often useful attempt to prepare for every possible circumstance.

"It should be…" He slid down another rocky slope, and caught himself before he toppled over the edge of a deep ravine that split what he thought had once been some kind of courtyard.

"Do we have to cross this?" Reba said, weighing the rope in her hand as if judging whether any of the rocks on the other side were solid enough to anchor it securely.

"I don't think so," Daniel said. "What we're looking for should be... well, I think right around here." He looked at what he'd caught himself against, the broken wall of a stone building with part of its low roof still intact. The orientation of the entrance seemed wrong, but it was the only structure still standing at the coordinates specified by the tablets. It was possible that he was looking at a side door, and that the main entrance had been on the wall that was worst damaged.

He reached for his flashlight, and then remembered it wasn't in its usual pocket. "I don't suppose you have my flashlight with you? The little..." He mimed sweeping a flashlight beam across the entrance.

"The small electric light," Reba said. "I liked that. I'm going to have to see if someone clever can make me more of them."

"You don't have it with you." She shook her head, and Daniel gritted his teeth and considered the building. The two pressing questions were whether he'd be able to see a thing once he was in the shadow of the intact roof, and whether the roof would collapse on his head if he brushed the wrong stone. He wasn't optimistic about either one.

"All right," he said. "We need to go back to the ship and get something to make a scaffolding, to shore up this roof. I'm also going to either need my light back or something fairly sizeable that's reflective, even if it's just a polished piece of metal, to use to get some light in there."

"No stalling," Reba said. She had her zat in her hand again, and Daniel fought the urge to roll his eyes. He was frankly getting really bored with the same old threats, but that didn't mean that if she zatted him he'd be any less unconscious. Or dead.

"This is a very old structure that's obviously sustained some damage from whatever geological activity did that,"

Daniel said as patiently as he could, nodding toward the gaping chasm a few feet from the building's most damaged wall. "It's not safe to go in there without providing some support for the roof and the uppermost wall."

"That's why you're going to do it," Reba said. She armed the zat pointedly. "It's cold out here, and you're running out of time to persuade me that there's anything here to find. Get to work."

"Right," Daniel said. He crouched in the entrance, trying to see if there was an intact interior wall. It looked like there might be, which at least meant more support for the roof, but which also meant that behind the wall, he'd have basically no light. "I'll just go see what I can find, which will probably be nothing, since I can't see a thing."

"You do complain," Reba said, and to his surprise extracted his flashlight from an internal pocket of her coat.

"Thanks," he said dryly.

"Don't break it. I want it back."

"I'll try not to let it get crushed by falling rocks," Daniel said. He thumbed on the flashlight and ducked inside the small building before he could talk himself out of it. He ignored the voice that screamed in his head that he ought to know better, especially after watching his own parents killed by a falling cover stone that they shouldn't have stood under while it was being moved. He'd gotten used to ignoring that voice lately, and had actually thought he might have shocked it into permanent muteness somewhere around the time he was letting himself be fired like a missile from orbit toward a volcanic prison planet.

Still, apparently he still had some kind of sense of self-preservation, because his neck prickled with tension as he worked his way further into the stone building. The outer room was largely featureless, a smooth stone façade still mainly intact over the rougher building stones that made up the walls. There was nothing here that could conceivably be an Ancient device, no writing to be interpreted, nothing.

The archway into the inner room was visibly cracked. He stood back and panned the light around the small inner room. It was nearly as featureless, but there was a niche or basin of some kind set in the opposite wall. He set his jaw and stepped forward, careful not to touch the wall on either side of the arch.

The alcove in the wall had a smooth, curved basin, and there was a hole in the back of it. Plumbing was the first thing that came to mind. If he was looking at a pipe, there was no way to follow it down without disturbing the stones of the wall.

If it wasn't a pipe, though... He considered it, wondering if it could possibly have been a socket of some kind. If something had been plugged in there, and rested in the niche in the wall...

He ran his fingers gingerly along the dry curve of the stone, hoping to find something that moved when pressed, or any unusual warmth that might suggest a hidden power supply. The stone remained cool and unyielding under his hand. If anything had rested there, it wasn't there now.

He retraced his steps with the same caution, taking a grateful breath of the cold air as he stepped outside.

"Well?" Reba demanded.

"It's not there," Daniel said. "There might have been something there in the past, but if so, it's not there now."

Her hand tightened on the zat, and Daniel braced himself for its painful blast. Instead, she jerked her head angrily back the way they had come.

"I don't want to have to drag you all the way back to the ship," she said. "You'd just better hope that my people can find your device when they search the place. If not, and you've been lying to me all this time..."

"It was here," Daniel said. "It may just take more work to find it." He was already glancing around, trying to see where he might have gone wrong in interpreting the coordinates from the tablet. "If you'd just let me —"

"Move," Reba said, leveling the zat at him. "And give me that light back. It's mine."

"You have an interesting definition of 'mine,'" Daniel said.

"It involves being the one holding the weapon," Reba said, and he had to admit she had a point.

CHAPTER NINETEEN

"I THINK we've got something, sir," Walter said, head bent over his computer terminal. Hammond leaned over his shoulder to see as the computer began reading out the data from the UAV. "That's definitely one of our radios it's picking up."

"Still moving?"

"Negative, sir. It's stationary, or close to it. Near this mountain ridge here."

"That's good enough for me," Hammond said. "How's the weather?"

"Clearing between the gate and the site of the radio signal," Walter said. "Let me see if I can get a visual. The UAV's right at the limits of its range."

The signal swam into view, grainy at first and then sharpening. Hammond could see the jagged peaks of mountains, the white flash of snow and the darker shapes of rocks. Near the bottom of the frame, he could just make out something brighter, an unnatural shape that caught the eye.

Walter's hands were already moving swiftly over his keyboard, sharpening the image and zooming in. As the UAV passed over the ridge, for several seconds its video transmission clearly showed the shape of an airship anchored at the ridge.

"It looks like there may be some kind of man-made structures in the area," Walter said.

It didn't look like the kind of place where there was any reason for people to live, Hammond thought. "Up there?"

"I don't know, sir."

"All right. The best information we have right now suggests that our people are up there. Let's go get them."

"Yes, sir," Walter said. "How, sir?"

"I've been thinking about that," Hammond said. As far as SG-1 was from the gate, he couldn't send in a rescue team on foot without it taking weeks for them to get there, and he wasn't betting on the local authorities being very cooperative. Besides, if the High King's airships weren't any faster than the pirate ships that had taken SG-1, they could wind up playing hide and seek for a long time. "Get Sgt. Siler up here for me, please."

Siler turned up promptly, still carrying a tool kit. "Yes, sir?"

"I've been thinking about how to extract SG-1," Hammond said. "I think we're going to have to do it by air."

Siler frowned at the gate, sizing up the problem immediately. "There's no way to get a light plane through without disassembling it completely. Putting it back together on the other side would take time. We could do it, but not quickly."

"I was thinking a helicopter," Hammond said.

Siler considered the gate again. "That could work, sir," he said. "We'd still have to break it down, or else use the crane to get it in here."

"We got the gate in here, and it weighs considerably more than a Kiowa, even fitted out to transport casualties," Hammond said. "Which I'm hoping we won't have, but let's cover all our bases."

"We don't have a Kiowa, sir," Walter said. "Would you like me to call around?"

"Try the National Guard," Hammond said. "Tell them we've got a situation involving limited space for takeoff and landing."

"It'll go through the gate, but the other side of the gate has steps down," Siler said. "We're going to need to build a platform for it to rest on when we put it through."

"How long will that take once you're on site?"

"How fast do you need it done?"

"That depends on whether we're doing it against the protests of the local authorities," Hammond said. He broke off as the sirens sounded for an unscheduled offworld activation.

"It's Saday, sir," Walter said. "We're getting a radio transmission."

As unlikely as it was, Hammond hoped for a moment to hear that SG-1 had made it back to the gate on their own. It wouldn't be the most unlikely escape they'd pulled off, not by a long shot.

"It's from Walat, sir." Hammond had left a radio set with the High King's minister of trade, not feeling inclined to drop in for another visit himself.

"Put him on," Hammond said.

"Great General Hammond of the Tau'ri, I bring you the greetings of the High King, the great Bull of the Heavens, glorious among rulers—"

"My greetings to him, too," Hammond said, without much patience. "Has he found SG-1 yet?"

"The goddess Asherah has departed on her tour of the temples of the high places, but she has not yet left our world. If the pirates are bold, we may hear from them in the next few days, but if not, I am certain that once the goddess departs—"

"If Asherah isn't anywhere near the Stargate, you won't have any objection if we look for our people ourselves," Hammond said. He mentally crossed his fingers. If the Goa'uld had left a ship sitting next to the gate, they'd have a problem. If they'd just strolled through, they might not.

"That is out of the question."

"I wasn't asking a question," Hammond said. "I was willing to be patient while there were Goa'uld in the capital, but you say they've moved on. Did they leave Jaffa to guard the Stargate?"

"It has never been necessary," Walat said unhappily. "Our own men guard the gate, but if Asherah were to return earlier than is customary—"

"Has that ever happened?"

"I will consult the records," Walat said, sounding relieved by the idea. No doubt he could make 'consulting the records' take as long as was necessary to get the Goa'uld entirely out of the way.

"I'm going to take that as 'not in as long as we can remember,'" Hammond said. "Now let me tell you how it's going to be. My team will be ready to move out in six hours." He could see Walter's eyebrows go up at that, but the man didn't protest, and Hammond had every confidence that he'd find them a spare helicopter in less time than it took most people to order a pizza. "If you can tell me by then that you've found my people, it'll spare us some considerable trouble. If not, we'll go find them ourselves."

"This may have serious consequences to future trade between our people," Walat said huffily.

"I'm sorry to hear that," Hammond said. "We'll just have to get along somehow. Hammond out." He motioned Walter to cut off the radio signal, and after a long moment, in which Walat was probably waiting for a better apology, the wormhole's blue flare sputtered and died.

"I'll start working on that platform," Siler said.

"Do that." Walter was already on the phone, and Hammond headed back to his office to call down to the infirmary.

"Dr. Fraiser, we believe we've located SG-1, and we have plans underway to extract them by helicopter. I'd like you to ride along in case they're in need of medical attention."

"Yes, sir," Janet said, sounding greatly relieved. "By helicopter?"

"We'll make it work," Hammond said.

"I'm sure we will," Janet said. "I'll be ready when you are."

Daniel Jackson returned more quickly than Teal'c had expected, but from his expression as he was manhandled down the stairs by one of Reba's men, it was not because he had been successful in his search.

"Reba got impatient," he said after the man had shoved him inside the cage and locked it behind him. "She thinks her people can find the device more quickly than I can."

"Was it not at the coordinates you determined?"

"It wasn't." It might have been taken away, or... I don't know, maybe I made a mistake in the translation. Of course, I can't check now, because Reba won't let me see the tablets again. She's not a very patient person."

"It is also possible that there is no device."

Daniel Jackson adjusted his glasses without speaking for a moment. "That's possible," he said finally. "If so, I'm not sure Reba's going to take it well."

"And if she is successful in locating the device without your assistance?"

"I've assisted," he said. "Hopefully she'll keep her part of the bargain."

That seemed unduly optimistic to Teal'c. "And if she is not inclined to do so?"

"Well, she still doesn't know how to use the device."

"Nor do you," Teal'c pointed out.

"No, but I'm going to say that I do. Look, all we have to do is keep stalling for time. If that was Sam on the radio, then they can't be far behind us. In the mean time, if Reba finds the device, or if she changes her mind and lets me go look for it again, we can see if it works, and maybe even find out where Amonet hid Sha're's son."

"You are certain that is your heart's desire?"

Daniel Jackson frowned. "What do you mean?"

"The device is said to grant one's heart's desire. I merely wonder if finding the boy is really the thing you wish for most."

"Of course it is. Besides, I already said I think the whole 'heart's desire' thing is just poetic license. There must be some way to communicate with the device, to let it know what it is you're actually looking for." He frowned again. "Why would you think I would want something different?"

Teal'c hesitated, unsure of how to answer. He knew that his friend wished to find the child because the boy was Sha're's son, and that he was determined to do so because she had asked it of him with her dying breath. He was only unsure that obligation was the same thing as desire. It had been his first duty to serve Apophis even after it had ceased to be his greatest desire.

"Look, obviously if it were possible the thing I would want most is Sha're back," Daniel Jackson said, the words coming a little too fast, as if he thought that if he spoke quickly enough he could outdistance his own feelings. "But that's not possible, so this is what I want most that I can actually possibly have."

It was difficult for Teal'c not to take the words as a reproach, whether or not they were intended as one. "As you say."

Daniel Jackson slid down to sit with his back to the bars. "At least it's warm in here."

They waited some hours, the time seeming longer because their captors had not bothered to offer them food since the night before. Eventually Reba came downstairs, shaking snow from her hair. She stood considering them both, her expression hard to read. "Bring them up," she said.

"Did you find anything?" Daniel Jackson said.

"You know the answer to that," Reba said, and her voice was sharp enough for Teal'c to suspect that her expression was barely leashed fury.

They were prodded up the stairs by men with zats, and backed against the rail. Teal'c looked around the deck, wondering if there was any chance of overpowering Reba's men. That seemed unlikely, as none of them were foolish enough to stand where he could reach them before they could fire. It might be possible to go over the rail without taking more than a glancing shot, though, and that would not knock him unconscious. He might scale the superstructure and make his way far enough down the rope by which they were anchored to jump without injury.

He was less sure that Daniel Jackson could do the same. If the man were hit by a zat going over the rail, he might well fall. Better to wait for now and count on Reba's knowledge of their value to the Goa'uld.

"You lied to me, Daniel," Reba said.

"I didn't lie. If we haven't found the Ancient device yet, that doesn't mean—"

"Do you think I'm a fool?" Reba snapped, glaring at them. "You knew it was likely that the treasure had been found already. You invented this tale of a fabulous device to delay me, to make me lose precious time in this detour."

"You believe there may not be time now to trade us to Asherah," Teal'c said.

"I meant to approach her at the temple where I served," Reba said. "I'm known there, and it's always one of her first stops. That would have been easy. Now I'll have to hunt for her party among half a dozen smaller temples, or go back to the capital where they're no doubt hunting *you*—"

"Sorry about that," he said with a half-smile that Teal'c felt was unwise.

"You should be! Because if you've lost us the time I needed to bring this Jaffa traitor to Asherah, he's of no further use to me." Reba armed her zat, pointing it squarely at the middle of Teal'c's chest.

"You could still trade us back to our own people," Daniel Jackson said quickly. "General Hammond will reward you handsomely for our return—"

"I was promised a treasure greater than anyone could desire," Reba said. "A handsome reward doesn't sound that impressive anymore."

"You still think the treasure's down there," he said, still talking fast. "You expect that this will persuade me to tell you where it is, but I don't know anything more than I've told you. If you'll just let me go look for it, if you'll just *listen*—"

"No more stalling," Reba said. Two of her men were covering Teal'c, moving in so that there was no chance of escape. "You've wasted my time, and you don't seem to believe that I mean business. Maybe losing your friend will teach you some respect." Her fingers tightened on the trigger.

"He's not my friend," Daniel Jackson said sharply. Reba hesitated, the zat still pointed at Teal'c's chest. "You think that killing him is going to be some kind of punishment for me? You'd be doing me a favor."

"You don't seriously expect me to believe that."

"Believe it," he said, his voice cold. "This is the man who killed my wife."

CHAPTER TWENTY

REBA hadn't disarmed her zat, but she was hesitating, and Daniel had to keep talking. The story had to be good, or she'd shoot. He could imagine it all too clearly, Teal'c falling as Sha're had fallen, crumpling to the deck before Daniel could make a move. He kept his eyes on Reba, unable to risk glancing at Teal'c.

"I told you she was taken by the Goa'uld. Teal'c is their enemy, and when we found her, he wasn't willing to try to capture her, to see if we could remove the symbiote. He killed her in front of me." He didn't dare stray too far from the truth, relying on the pain in his voice to give weight to the words.

"And you still work with him?" Reba sounded skeptical, but she was still listening.

"I have to. Only a few people on my world know about the Stargate. If I'm going to fight the Goa'uld, it has to be as part of SG-1. I promised..." He nearly said *Sha're*, and forced his thoughts a little farther from the truth. "I promised our commander that I wouldn't take revenge on Teal'c except in an honorable duel."

"What's stopping you?"

"We have to wait, I... I'm still in mourning for my wife. The customs of my people say that I can't fight a duel until a year after her death. But believe me, you'd be doing me a favor."

He wondered for one heart-stopping moment if he'd made a terrible misstep, if Reba might shoot Teal'c as a misguided way of earning his gratitude. Instead, she lowered the zat ever so slightly.

"Is this true?" she demanded of Teal'c.

Daniel thought he could see Teal'c's jaw tighten, but his expression didn't change. "What Daniel Jackson says is correct."

Reba glanced at Daniel, a hint of skepticism still in her tone. "You didn't seem to like the idea of me trading him to Asherah," she said.

"She'd torture him for information, or sell him to someone who would," Daniel said. "However personally satisfying that might be, I still don't want my world's secrets in the hands of the Goa'uld." He shrugged. "Besides, at the time you were talking about trading me to Asherah, too."

Reba let out a frustrated breath. "So tell me, treasure hunter, how do you suggest I motivate you to find my treasure? I could always just fetch a knife and cut off anything that you don't seem to have a use for."

"I need to go back and look," Daniel said. "You said yourself it's probably too late to sell us to Asherah. The option of ransoming us back to our own people isn't going anywhere, and for that matter neither is the option of throwing us overboard. We've still got hours before it gets dark. The device may be very near where I was looking. Just let me try to find it."

"We looked," Reba said, but she lowered the zat. Daniel relaxed a tiny bit, and risked a glance at Teal'c. His face was entirely impassive, the stern mask he'd worn in the service of Apophis.

Surely Teal'c could see the game Daniel was being forced to play, he told himself. He couldn't possibly have believed there was any truth behind Daniel's story. Daniel was almost entirely certain of that.

"So we'll look again," Daniel said. He was aware that he wasn't going to have much time, even if she let him go back down to the ruins. He was missing something, he thought, something he should have noticed. He couldn't afford to make that kind of mistake, not now.

"One more look around," Reba said. "But there's nothing there."

"Perhaps I may be of some assistance," Teal'c said.

"That's not necessary," Daniel said, hoping he sounded convincingly irritated by the idea. Reverse psychology seemed to be working so far.

"You'll both come," Reba said. "That way if you don't find anything, you'll spare me the trouble of dumping both of you over the side. I'm starting to get tired of you both."

She brought two of her own men as well, and insisted Daniel and Teal'c climb ahead of her, which gave them little opportunity to attempt to break away and make a run for it down the slope. They stopped below one of the steepest pitches, where he'd found it impossible to climb before without a rope.

"I can ascend if you will give me a rope," Teal'c said.

"Thanks, but I'd rather not trust to your rope," Daniel said. If they could get Reba ahead of them, and get her distracted—

"It's a shame when crewmen fall out," Reba said. She strode past them, but one of her men drew his zat and stepped forward to guard her as she worked her way up the rocks. There wasn't much chance to make a run for it, not unless one of them wanted to be zatted at point-blank range.

Making a run for it seemed like a bad idea anyway. There was no real path downwards, just a steep slope patched with loose rock that might be climbable or might slide away under their feet. They didn't have their radios, and he was fairly sure that without shelter, night in these mountains would be killing.

His shoulders ached more sharply by the time they'd reached the wall at the top of the ridge, and he would have suggested they stop and rest a minute if he hadn't suspected it would make Reba start threatening to shoot something again.

"Those coordinates have to be right," he said. "That section of the tablets isn't ambiguous at all. The device was five streets — well, ways, pathways, anyway — down and to the south of the north wall, on this row of buildings. It should be here." He paced around the front of the building he'd investigated before. "In which case either it was here, and it was removed, which I think is unlikely, because if someone had made that kind of find it would have been hard for them to keep quiet, or it was never here, and it was…" He turned a slow circle, noting that in several places they'd tumbled stones that had been standing when he'd first been here. "Where?"

"That's what I want you to tell me," Reba said. He heard the sound of her arming her zat again.

"Yes, and stunning me will definitely help me figure this out."

"I wasn't planning on stunning you."

He set his jaw and tried to ignore the possibility that she would simply run out of patience and kill them both. It wasn't helping him think. "Down and to the south. Why say both? Unless the word order… it could be 'to the south and down.'"

"I fail to see the difference," Teal'c said.

"Maybe it doesn't mean downhill," Daniel said. "Toss me a rope."

Reba did, although he wasn't sure how hard she'd try to hang onto him if he fell. He made his way cautiously to the very edge of the chasm that split the courtyard, edging around that side of the building, bracing himself on its stones and willing them not to choose this moment to fall.

"Here," he said.

Reba crowded behind him, and he fought to keep his balance. "Where?"

"Don't *do* that. Here. I think this used to be…" He crouched carefully and could see that he was right. "See? There were stairs carved in the rock here, stairs leading down into some kind of tunnel or underground room. And then when the courtyard split apart, part of the rock on both sides crumbled — you can see that the rock edges on either side don't fit together — and most of the stairway was destroyed. Leaving just this little edge of the stairway, which shows where it used to lead… somewhere."

Reba backed up a step, considering the gap in the rock. "You think there's still something down there?"

"I think there very well might be." The remains of the steps were no more than an inch or two wide, and while they might widen lower down, they also might have crumbled entirely. "If you want to find out, someone's going to have to climb down there."

Reba hauled Daniel back from the edge unceremoniously and turned to Teal'c. "Can you climb, Jaffa?"

"Oh, no, I was…" Daniel began, and then hesitated, unsure whether arguing that he should investigate for himself would make him sound overly concerned for Teal'c's safety or merely greedy about being the one to get his hands on the device. Neither was likely to persuade Reba.

Before he could come up with a reason that might, Teal'c was already answering. "I can descend the cliff, if the ropes are secured well."

"Good. Find out if there's a safe way down there. And don't get the idea that you can make off with the treasure yourself. We'll be waiting at the top."

"He doesn't know how to work the device," Daniel said. "I'm still the only one who knows that."

"All the more reason for you to stay right here where I can keep an eye on you."

"Let us not waste any more time," Teal'c said. He sounded out of patience himself, or perhaps just not enthusiastic about the climb. "I am prepared to descend."

Please be careful, Daniel wanted to say, but he couldn't risk saying a word.

Teal'c braced himself against the cliff face as he slowly worked his way down the remains of the broken staircase, resisting the urge to test the rope yet again to see if it would truly hold his weight. He was at least grateful that he was not attempting the climb in the armor of a Serpent Guard. He remembered one particular battle on an icy glacier that had ended in pursuing the enemy down a treacherous icefall, in which more than one of Apophis's Jaffa had lost their footing and fallen to their deaths.

This was probably not the best thing to bring to mind while descending a sheer cliff. He steadied himself, shifting his hands before reaching out carefully to find the next foothold with his foot. He kept his eyes on the rock in front of him, because looking down was unpleasant, and looking up of no value.

If O'Neill were here, he would say that Teal'c was a pilot, and so should be entirely used to heights. Teal'c had pointed out more once that there was a significant difference between flying in an aircraft and falling from one, but O'Neill seemed constitutionally incapable of understanding it.

It was easier to think of O'Neill than to think of Daniel Jackson waiting above. He had said what he had felt he must say in order to keep them both alive. Teal'c was well aware of that, and also aware that this particular story had been the first to come to mind. He would have understood it if Daniel Jackson had sworn revenge against him for Sha're's death, perhaps better than he did his forgiveness.

He had not expected to be forgiven. Or, to be more exact, he had not thought of what killing his friend's wife would mean after it was done, only of immediate necessity. He had been unwilling to allow Amonet to kill Daniel Jackson, both because he was a friend and because his skills were irreplaceable in their fight against the Goa'uld.

That was probably a good thing to bear in mind at the moment, because it was easy to feel that, as this was Daniel Jackson's plan, he should be the one currently dangling over the edge of a cliff, trusting himself to a rope held by someone who had not an hour ago threatened to kill them both. O'Neill had the knack of imposing his own will by argument alone, but Teal'c had found that nothing short of flat refusal to proceed would serve him when Daniel Jackson felt he knew the best course of action.

All of this was a distraction from taking the next step

downward. He gripped the rock with his fingers, clinging painfully hard to the spurs of rock he had found, and reached with his foot for the next step.

It wasn't where he expected it, and for a moment he could only flatten himself against the rock, trying to hold fast. He risked a glimpse downward. The stairs ended, in what might have been a switchback that had crumbled when the rock split. He would have to work his way down the bare rock from here.

Teal'c had to trust to the rope, leaning out over open space and holding onto the rope with his hands, walking his way down the wall. It was at least a faster means of descent, although ascending would take longer. More than once he was held up when whoever was above failed to play out the rope fast enough, and once the rope went abruptly slack, and he slithered down several meters, unable to arrest his fall, before it went jarringly taut.

He braced himself for a moment to catch his breath, ducking his head as loose pieces of rock continued to rattle down from above. When he looked down, he could see what looked like a ledge several meters below him, much wider than the stairs. It was hard to tell whether the rock opened above it, but he thought it was possible.

He continued his careful descent until he ran out of footholds. The rock below him did open up into a tunnel or cave that penetrated into the rock face. He tugged on the rope for more slack, and pushed himself off from the cliff face. He swung out and then back, catching himself on the tunnel's roof and scrambling down until his feet touched the tunnel's floor.

It was clearly manmade, its walls squared and dressed in finished stone, although the opening was uneven as if the tunnel's original mouth had fallen away. He took a deep breath, grateful for solid ground under his feet, and then shrugged out of his makeshift rope harness. He extracted their flashlight from his pocket — Reba had threatened dire consequences were he to break it — and shone it down the tunnel.

He could see nothing except that the tunnel continued for some distance and ended eventually in a right-angle turn. Curiosity warred with his reluctance to let go of the rope, but after a moment he let it swing free. He walked down the tunnel to the bend where it turned the corner, and followed it some distance further, far enough to see that there must be a maze of tunnels under the ruins of the city above.

The air was fresher than he would have expected so far from the entrance, although he had seen no air shafts set into the rock, which suggested that some of the turnings he passed might end in passages back up to the surface. It was tempting to see if he could find another way of ascending, but he knew Reba would be growing impatient.

It would be all too easy now for her to believe that Teal'c was looking for a means of escape and intended to leave. Not that he would do such a thing, but Daniel Jackson's story had made it seem plausible. It was what Teal'c would have done if they were truly enemies.

Instead he retraced his steps back to the entrance and refastened his rope harness, grasping the rope and beginning to haul himself up it back toward the top of the cliff. At least his find would provide Reba with a reason to be patient with their search a while longer. It would take some time for them to descend to the tunnels again, perhaps the time that O'Neill and Carter needed to find them.

What O'Neill and Carter would do if they came upon the pirates gathered at the top of a ravine with Teal'c and Daniel Jackson nowhere in sight, he was unsure, but they would, as O'Neill was fond of saying, cross that bridge when they came to it.

He looked up, mentally measuring the distance back up to the top of the ravine, and began hauling himself higher.

"I've got your helicopter, sir," Walter said. Hammond set down the sandwich that someone had brought him and went to look over Walter's shoulder. Below them, their usual ramp was being rebuilt under Siler's direction with a sturdy platform stretching level from the gate to the room's front wall.

"Good work," Hammond said. "Where are they coming from?"

"The Colorado National Guard is lending us one of the Kiowas they use for drug enforcement," Walter said. "I wasn't sure what you wanted me to tell the pilot they're sending along."

"I'll take care of briefing him when he gets here," Hammond said. "I expect this one will come as quite a surprise."

He shook his head. That was one more person who was going to have to know about the most closely guarded secret on the planet. And he was going to have to explain, one more time, why it was necessary to let down that guard enough to add one more person to the increasingly long list who knew that the SGC wasn't a facility for deep-space radar telemetry.

That was going to be half the challenge in getting Janet the new personnel she was requesting. It wasn't only their budget that kept increasing in size, but the number of people exposed to information that would be incredibly valuable to any news organization on the planet, let alone to other governments.

Still, right now they needed a helicopter and a pilot who wasn't feeling his way around an unfamiliar craft, and that was all there was to it. He had wide discretionary authority to grant security clearance to essential personnel in emergencies, and he intended to use it. It was a pity that they probably couldn't come up with a reason why adding a physical therapist to the staff constituted an emergency.

He left Walter checking on the helicopter's ETA and headed down to the gate room, standing back out of the way as another metal panel was carried in.

"How's it coming?" he asked Siler.

The man turned and shrugged. "We're working on it," he said. "They're getting the crane into position so that we can use the silo entrance up there to bring it in." He jerked his chin in the direction of the ceiling. "The tricky part will be setting it down, but it'll fit nose to tail in the space we've got."

"I'm afraid this may be a little conspicuous," Hammond said.

Siler shrugged again. "It's not like bringing in the Stargate wasn't," he said. "We'll call it some kind of readiness drill."

"And leave aside the question of what kind of military readiness drill involves needing a helicopter deep inside an underground base," Hammond said.

If Jack had been standing there, Hammond was fairly sure he would have pointed out that being a military project by definition meant it didn't necessarily have to make sense. Siler might have thought the same, but he wasn't about to say it.

"Leaving that aside, yes, sir."

"Very well," Hammond said. "Have you got the platform set up on the other side of the gate?"

"We've got it set up," Siler said, but he looked unhappier about that. "I wouldn't like to use it more than a couple of times, though. It's very hard to anchor something securely on that piece of rock that'll take the kind of weight we're talking about. It has to be level, so that we can put the thing through on a wheeled handling platform and know it's not going to roll, and if we can't drill permanent anchors and level the actual rock—"

"I'd prefer that we be able to put the site back the way we found it," Hammond said. "We are guests on this planet, and right now we're already uninvited ones."

"We'll get it done, sir," Siler said, although he looked like he'd rather argue. Hammond had noted a certain tendency in engineers to want to begin solving problems by leveling anything in their way. It was one he didn't feel like encouraging.

"I'm sure you will," he said.

Janet emerged into the gate room in field gear, shouldering an oversized pack. "I'm ready to go, sir," she said.

"I'm afraid your ride's not here yet," Hammond said. "I'm told it should be incoming soon. I'm sure SG-1 will be glad to see you."

"I'll be glad to see them," Janet said. "I hope all we need to do is give them a ride home."

"I hope so, too," Hammond said. "However, the last information we have suggests that SG-1 may be being held prisoner. Even fitted out with jump seats, the biggest helicopter we can get in here is only going to seat eight, and that's counting you and the pilot. I'll send two Marines with you for backup, but you're not going to be able to fight your way into any kind of highly guarded facility."

"Understood, sir," Janet said. "I'm hoping that we can make radio contact when we get in range and get a better idea of their situation. It may be that SG-1 can escape on their own if they've got anywhere to go once they do."

"Knowing Dr. Jackson, it's also entirely possible that they've talked their way out of the situation, and you'll find them having tea with a bunch of pirates," Hammond said. "Just watch yourself. It's an unknown situation."

"Sir, if you could just step this way," Siler said, steering them tactfully out of the way of the helicopter handling platform that was being wheeled into the room. Hammond didn't know where Walter had gotten his hands on one of those so quickly, but he wasn't about to ask.

"Come along, Dr. Fraiser," he said. "Let's let these people work."

CHAPTER TWENTY-ONE

DANIEL expected Reba to insist that he make the second trip down the cliff to fix a rope for their descent — he was getting the picture from Teal'c's expression that asking him to repeat the climb first might not be a good idea — but she shook her head and hammered in spikes at the top of the cliff herself, clipping the rope to them securely before swinging herself easily down over the edge of the ravine.

"Don't think it's out of the goodness of my heart," she said, still hanging onto the edge. "I'm not about to trust myself to your rope."

Daniel refrained from pointing out that she'd expected Teal'c to trust himself to the even more dubious security of a rope held by her men. Now that it seemed there was some chance again of actually finding the Ancient device, he didn't want to strain her temper too far.

He waited impatiently while she made the descent, which took long enough that he was considering trying to lean out far enough over the ravine to tell whether she had begun exploring the tunnel system without him when he heard her call up from far below, a wordless yell that her men seemed to take as a signal.

"You two go down first," Yassi said, brandishing a zat at them.

"I would really like it if you didn't threaten us while we're climbing," Daniel said.

"I won't need the thunderbolt while you're climbing," Yassi said, his scarred face twisting in a smile. "I can just kick rocks down on your heads if you make trouble."

"I am uncertain how much trouble you expect us to cause while descending a rope," Teal'c said, but he moved to the edge of the cliff. Reba had grudgingly leant them carabiners to clip themselves onto the rope she'd anchored at intervals down the cliff, so that if they lost their grip on the second rope they were using as a handhold, there was only so far for them to fall. Assuming that her anchors held, and that their makeshift rope harnesses did.

Unfortunately, there wasn't any way to find out other than trying it. Daniel waited for Teal'c to start his descent, and then lowered himself carefully over the edge of the rocky ledge, and began making his way down.

It was a nerve-wracking climb, made no easier by having to watch where he put his feet to avoid kicking rocks down on Teal'c's head. He was glad when he could finally unclip from the fixed rope and swing himself into the safety of the tunnel mouth, letting go of the other rope and stretching his cramped hands.

"I think this is my workout for the week," Daniel said.

Teal'c's mouth quirked, and he looked for a moment as though he were going to make some teasing reply about what Daniel considered strenuous activity, but then he remained silent, his expression sobering. Daniel wished again he'd been able to think of some better story to tell Reba. Teal'c was no doubt right that showing too much friendliness to Daniel would be bad for their cover story, but it was still disheartening.

"I thought I'd have to wait all afternoon," Reba said. "Maybe we should have just dropped you off the cliff. Tied to a rope, I mean, don't start with the complaints again."

"Nice of you to make that clear," Daniel said. He backed out of the tunnel entrance to let Yassi and the man who followed him unfasten themselves from the rope. Turning to Teal'c, he held out his hand, and Teal'c handed over Daniel's flashlight wordlessly.

"You two stay here," Reba said to her men. "Make sure no one else comes down behind us to try their luck."

"Do you not trust your crew?" Teal'c said.

"I'm not that much a fool. All right, treasure hunter," Reba said. "Lead the way."

"Okay," Daniel said. "Let's go see what we can find." He didn't feel it necessary to mention that the tablets hadn't provided any specific directions for navigating the tunnels in front of them. He'd explored much more elaborate mazes before, and he set a brisk pace, confident that he and Teal'c would both remember how to retrace their path and hoping that Reba might not.

The tunnels were squarely built, clearly not any kind of natural cave system. Not that extensive natural caves were likely in these mountains. Daniel stopped to examine one wall; its facade of dressed stone seemed thin, and he wished there was time to pry one of the panels off and see if there was any evidence of how the rock behind it had been cut.

"What's so interesting about the wall?" Reba said.

"Just wondering how the Ancients built this place."

"Wonder on your own time."

And that was a familiar enough sentiment, although Jack didn't generally threaten to shoot him. Daniel turned reluctantly back to the corridor. He stopped as they passed the next doorway, motioning the others to be still.

"What?" Reba demanded.

He could feel the whisper of moving air against his outstretched hand. "Air's coming in here from somewhere. This might be another way out of these tunnels."

"We'll check it out on our way back," Reba said.

Teal'c glanced at Daniel, and he suspected they'd both had the same thought. If there was a way out, it was also a potential way in, if Jack and Sam ever showed up. The entrance above might be fairly easy to stumble on, for all he knew, having never gotten the chance to search the city himself. On the other hand, if there had been another entrance to the tunnels, Reba and her men might have tumbled rocks over it and blocked it in their own haphazard search.

There was no point in dwelling on it either way. He led the way further down the hallway, and then stopped in the archway that ended it. Beyond it, the tunnel opened out into a wide chamber, its roof supported by pillars. He swept the light across the room, but it was hard to see much. Something flashed in the light's beam, and he shone it on what proved to be a metal panel curved around part of the pillar.

"That's interesting," he said, moving in to investigate. "Some kind of light fixture, maybe."

"It's not shedding any light," Reba pointed out.

"There may not be a working power supply down here after so long," Daniel said absently, feeling for any kind of catch or opening in the panel.

"Then how do you expect this device to work?" There was a dangerous note in her voice.

"It's supposed to have its own self-contained power source," Daniel said quickly. "According to the tablets." Actually, they said no such thing, and he frankly had no idea whether they'd be able to power the device if they found it, but saying so seemed like a bad idea.

"Hmph. What are we looking at, here? Some kind of palace?"

"More likely a temple," Daniel said. "Or some kind of place for meditation, or a center for scholarship... it's so far out of the way of the Stargate, it's not like this could have been a center for trade."

There were archways along both side walls of the chamber, but the largest opening was on the opposite wall. He made his way toward it, the pillars throwing their sharp shadows against the wall as he passed them.

Something white gleamed in the flashlight's beam, and he stopped in the large archway, playing the light across the floor of the chamber on the other side.

"Well, this is interesting," he said. There were bones lying on the stone floor of the chamber near the opposite wall, what looked like several well-preserved skeletons. Even from here, the patchy remains of wool clothing clinging to one of them removed any doubt that they were human.

Jack jerked awake, momentarily disoriented by the odd shadows around him and the lack of a hard surface under his outstretched hand. *Hammock*, he thought muzzily, and for a moment before he rolled over he expected to see the crowded hammock deck of an Amazon riverboat, and to smell strong coffee and sweat and river water.

The movement cleared his head, even if it made his knee ache threateningly. Not South America, but another planet, and a cold one this morning. Not ten years ago, and this morning he thought he could feel the difference in every sore muscle. He did smell coffee, though, and pursued the smell.

Carter was on the lower deck, nursing a cup of what still smelled like coffee. She smiled when she saw him, and then frowned. That was probably because he was limping, but there wasn't much he could do about that until he worked out the stiffness from spending a couple of hours sleeping in a hammock in the cold.

"Is that coffee?" he asked before she could say anything.

"Instant," Carter said. "I had some with me, and apparently Keret hadn't worked up the nerve to try it yet."

"The big chicken," Jack said. He found another mug, wiped it out with his sleeve, and poured from the kettle of instant coffee that Carter had left to stew on the stove. It was the most terrible coffee he'd had in recent memory, but it made the day easier to face. "I take it Keret's flying the ship?"

Carter nodded. "He traded with me right after you went to sleep. It's stopped snowing, and the wind's calmed down a lot. I think we're out of the path of the storm."

"I like hearing some good news," Jack said, taking another swallow of the steaming coffee. "You got any more of that?"

"The radio signal's definitely getting stronger. In fact, if you'd slept any longer, I was planning to go wake you up so we could talk about what we're going to do if we actually find Daniel and Teal'c."

"I take it you mean the part before 'go home and take hot showers.'"

"I mean the part where we find the other pirate ship. They have a full crew aboard, and given that Keret and the captain of the *Heart's Desire* seem to have some recent history here, she's likely to think that we're here to try to steal her treasure. Or her prisoners, which happens to be true."

"Did you figure out if we're carrying weapons?"

"We've got several harpoons they use for boarding or to damage the canopies of other airships, and the staff weapons mounted on the rail that I disabled earlier. The problem with using the staff weapons is that there's a not inconsiderable chance of causing an explosion on the other ship. Keret says they usually don't use them except as threats, because they don't want to lose the chance to capture another ship and its cargo."

"Neither do we, especially if the cargo is our people."

"That's what I figured," Sam said. "So what do we do?"

"We're pretty sure they're aboard this Reba's ship?"

"I think so, from the way the radio signal strength and direction have been changing. It looks like they've stopped for the moment, though. It's possible they were damaged by the storm, or that they're taking on supplies."

"Or else Reba found her treasure," Jack said.

Sam looked skeptical. "Keret says he doesn't believe there's any such thing."

Jack shrugged. "This place is apparently full of ruins that were here before these people's ancestors showed up. I'm inclined to believe that if one of the locals thinks there's something significant to find, then there's something, even if it's just some kind of Ancient pencil factory."

Sam smiled a little bemusedly. "Daniel's wearing off on you."

"God forbid," Jack said. "No, the thing that's important right now is that if she thinks she knows where this treasure is, she's going to stop and... what? Look around, at least. Maybe set up a dig. We know from painful experience how long that can take."

"Which will at least mean that her ship isn't as heavily guarded."

"And which gives our people a chance to escape so that we can pick them up."

"Assuming that the crew doesn't raise an alarm and keep a close eye on their prisoners the moment they see us coming."

"Assuming that." Jack frowned. "All right, if they've stopped, we should be able to triangulate their signal and get some idea of where, right?"

"We've already done that."

"Good. I'll go up and see if Keret can suggest an alternate route that would get us nearby but hopefully not put us down on top of the *Heart's Desire*." He put down his coffee mug and regarded the stairs unenthusiastically.

"Or I could go up and do that," Carter said.

He started to say that wasn't necessary, but he knew there was a time to conserve resources that weren't inexhaustible. "All right, you go up and do that."

"Yes, sir," Carter said, and trotted up the stairs.

She came back down after a while looking cold but not half-frozen. "Keret says that if we circle around and don't take the easiest set of passes between us and the *Heart's Desire*, we should be able to approach from the opposite side of a high ridge. Of course, that's assuming that Reba did take the easiest route in the first place."

"Which she might not have if she assumed she was being pursued."

"But she might have assumed we'd assume that she'd assume..." Carter trailed off, looking like she'd gotten tangled up somewhere in the middle of that sentence.

"We can make ourselves crazy that way, but it doesn't change the fact that basically we've got two ways to get to where X marks the spot: the short way and the long way. Unless you want to flip a coin…"

"We figure they went the short way, and we go the long way. Anyway, both of those are relative terms. At the speed we're traveling right now, even if we go the long way, we'll be there in a couple of hours."

"I'll go keep an eye out for the big X," Jack said.

Daniel crouched to investigate the skeletons more closely, careful not to crush any of the smaller bones underfoot. "Well, what happened here?"

Reba nudged one of the skeletons with her foot. It wasn't quite a kick, but Daniel had to bite his tongue not to snap at her to be careful of the site. Who these people were and what happened to them was probably important, but it wasn't as if he was going to be stopping to document the find properly.

It was lousy archaeology. He was resigned to doing a lot of that these days, work that he could just barely justify calling archaeology rather than treasure hunting. He took pictures of visible features and sketched sites — when no one was shooting at them — but the kind of slow excavation and preservation that so many of the things he saw deserved was usually impossible.

That was perversely easier to bear when it was because people were shooting at them. He had to admit that surviving was a bigger priority than sticking around to take pictures of an archaeological site that currently happened to be inhabited by angry people with guns. He'd had the chance to learn that lesson long before he ever saw a Stargate.

It was the times when they could have excavated properly if there were only enough time and enough money and enough interest from a military hierarchy that could be myopically focused on the question 'can you shoot people with it?' And when they did find something you could shoot people with, or that Sam said would somehow advance their knowledge of science, the orders were usually 'grab it and go.'

And that *was* treasure hunting. He was the first to admit that it had to be done; all questions of advancing human knowledge on Earth would be moot if the Goa'uld leveled the planet and enslaved the surviving population. It was just one more stone dropped into the water, one more thing to weigh heavily on his heart.

The ancient Egyptians — and the people of Abydos — believed that the heart of a dead man was weighed against a feather, to see if the dead person was too weighted down by sin to be able to enter the afterlife. There were times when he wondered if grief and tiredness and a litany of petty dissatisfactions might not be all it took to outweigh any lightness of spirit that he had ever felt —

"We're too late, aren't we?" Reba said. "They must have found something to fight over, but unless we're very lucky and they're very unlucky, the winner walked out of here with whatever it was."

"Surely the discovery of a great treasure would have become known, especially if it had been the cause of so many deaths," Teal'c said.

"Maybe," Reba said. "Men fall out over prizes all the time, and if whoever won the fight was bright enough not to tell anyone what they found…" She shook her head. "It's a rare pirate who can resist the urge to brag forever, though."

"Including you?" Daniel asked absently.

"If this thing is still here for us to find, I'll have reason to brag."

"I don't think these people died in a fight," he said. He hoped they also hadn't died of some kind of incredibly virulent space plague or toxin, because he didn't even have rubber gloves with him, let alone proper hazmat gear, but there was no point in worrying about that. "I don't see any broken bones or obvious signs of wounds, although I suppose it's possible that they were strangled or stabbed and that at this stage of decomposition we just can't see the marks anymore."

"Perhaps they were zatted," Teal'c said.

"It's possible," Daniel said. "It's a weird placement of the remains, though. They're not lined up, not like someone buried them or like they were lined up against the wall and shot. It's like they were clustering around a specific point, so maybe they were fighting over something, but…" He shook his head. "The thing is, these remains aren't anywhere the same age. There's no way this was a single fight. I'd say from the earliest to the latest deaths we're talking hundreds of years difference. Maybe more."

"Some kind of trap?" Reba said.

"Maybe. In which case we should be very careful about how we go from here."

"Should you be standing on the same part of the floor where they apparently died?"

"Probably not, but it didn't kill me when I did, so that's probably not the trigger for the trap," Daniel said. All the same, he stood up very cautiously, listening for any noise that might suggest a mechanism working in the floor or behind the walls. "Assuming it is a trap."

"It hardly seems likely that so many visitors to this spot died for coincidental reasons," Teal'c said.

"Well, no, but it's still possible that these bodies were brought here for some ritual or practical purpose. I don't think it's that's likely, because people tend to either pile bodies in a heap or lay them out neatly, and this is… not exactly either one. More like everyone who was standing in this part of the room eventually just… fell wherever they were standing."

"Perhaps we should not remain in this part of the room," Teal'c said.

"You may have a point. Let's look around, see what else we can see."

The other three walls of the chamber were the same featureless stone they'd seen so far, but when he played his light across the wall against which the skeletons were lying, he could see that it was heavily inscribed with line upon line of Ancient. Some of it he recognized from the tablet, but some of it was new to him.

"Have you seen this inscription before?" Daniel asked.

"No," Reba said, and he could hear his own excitement mirrored in her voice. "No, not all of it. The beginning, there…"

"But not starting here. This might be more directions, or…" He squinted at the inscription. "I think these might be instructions."

"For getting at the treasure without springing the trap?"

"That would be logical, wouldn't it? That way, if you can't read Ancient…"

"That's not very nice," Reba said.

"Well, I expect they thought that anyone seeing these carvings who wasn't an Ancient was one of their enemies," Daniel said.

He kept playing the flashlight's beam up and down the lines of the inscription, trying to get a sense of how hard it would be to translate. It used the same abbreviated forms of common words that he'd seen on the tablets, but he thought he was starting to understand how they were constructed. It wasn't any worse than trying to read some of the Air Force forms full of abbreviations he still had to look up.

"It's still a bit careless."

"We have no idea why they abandoned this place," Daniel said. "For all we know, they had to leave in a hurry. They might not have had a chance to come down and disable the trap. If it is a trap."

Reba looked at Daniel sideways. "How long does it generally take you to commit to a theory?"

"Theories aren't facts," Daniel said. "When we find something, we'll know for sure what it is. Until then, we need to keep an open mind. It's too easy to get hung up on a particular idea of what you're going to find..."

He trailed off as the flashlight beam reached the center of the wall.

"Does that count as something?" Reba said.

In the center of the wall, framed by the inscription on all sides, the stone had been carved into the shape of an enormous heart. It was more anatomically detailed than either a Valentine's heart or the Egyptian iconography of a heart, with the chambers and major arteries clearly drawn, although within them curled lines that might just have been artistic detailing, or might have represented blood, or smoke, or the spirit.

"That's something," Daniel said. He reached toward it from the side, trying not to step on any of the fallen bones.

"Daniel Jackson," Teal'c said, alarm clear in his voice.

"I'm not going to touch it," Daniel said. "I just want to see..." He stopped with his palm inches from the stone, sure that he felt the air near it warm against his skin. He moved his hand away, but the rest of the wall was cool. "It's warm," he said. "If this is the device, or a control panel for the device, I think it still has power."

CHAPTER TWENTY-TWO

"YOU THINK that's where Reba's gone to look for her treasure?" Keret said, looking skeptically up at the ridge. They were approaching slowly, keeping low in the valley between the mountains that towered on either side.

Sam squinted, shading her eyes to see. "I can't see anything there."

"I've never heard of anything there. Not that old ruins are rare enough for anyone to have mentioned them, particularly."

"No, wait." The ridge was cracked and split by numerous fissures in the stone, but Sam could just make out lines that seemed too regular to be the way wind and shifting earth had tumbled natural stone. "Is that a wall?"

"Might be," Keret conceded. Behind them, Jack came out on deck, coming up to the rail to see for himself.

"No sign of the *Heart's Desire*, but the radio signal is very close," Sam said. "I'd say the radios have to be on the other side of the ridge."

"They might have anchored there," Keret said.

"Assuming they didn't throw the radios overboard. Or…"

"That's a cheery thought, Carter," Jack said, giving her a sideways look.

"Sorry, sir."

Keret shrugged. "There's no way of knowing, unless you want to go over the ridge, which takes away the point of coming from this direction in the first place."

"No, let's take a walk and see what we can find. How do we anchor this thing?"

"On this hillside, with only the three of us? Can't be done," Keret said.

Sam looked at him sharply. "You never said that."

"Maybe if we took a couple of hours to drive in a mooring ring, and tied up to that, and the wind didn't shift direction and batter us against the hillside while we were wandering around looking at old rocks, maybe we could do that," Keret said. "Excuse me if I don't feel like taking the chance with my ship."

Jack looked at Sam. "Carter?"

"I don't know, sir," Sam said. "My experience with landing these things is limited to when we put down before."

"Which was on a big, flat plateau," Keret said. "Do you see one of those around here?"

Jack frowned, looking tired. Neither of them had gotten much sleep to speak of in the last few days. "What are you suggesting?"

"You two go find your people," Keret said. "I'll stay here with the ship."

"And cut and run if the *Heart's Desire* comes over the ridge," Sam said, shaking her head.

"You'd prefer us all come back and find out that Reba's men have this ship as well? If I have to leave, I'll come back for you two. You saw yourselves how hard it was to fly this ship with only two of you. How far do you imagine I'd get on my own?"

"I don't know," Sam said.

"We don't have the time to stand here and argue about it," Jack said. "We can't hold him at gunpoint and climb at the same time."

"Speaking of weapons…"

"You took my thunderbolt already," Keret said. "I admit it, I did pick up a knife from the galley, just so as not to feel quite so entirely unarmed." He slid his sleeve back to show the knife handle. "If you're really afraid I'm going to drop it on you once you're down there…"

Jack shook his head and patted Keret down for weapons despite Keret's protests. "He's clean," Jack said. "What did you do with the zats we took off his crew?"

"I found a pack to put them in, along with some of our supplies," Carter said. "We can take them with us."

"All right," Jack said. "Get it and let's go."

When she came up with the woolen pack slung over her shoulder, Keret was guiding the airship closer to the rocky slope of the ridge, adjusting its course carefully. They'd already restored the gravity drive to its usual settings, although now that she'd gotten used to its forward pull, the deck still felt like it was tilting, only in the other direction. She hoped that little side effect would wear off promptly.

"I can't get you any closer without getting overfriendly with the rocks," Keret said. "There's a ladder stowed by the harpoons if you don't feel like going down hand over hand."

"Very civilized of you," Jack said. He found the rope ladder and unrolled it, tipping the end of it over the side. The bottom end skidded slowly across the rocks.

"Can you hold the ship steady?" Sam said.

"You want me to stop the wind?"

"Never mind." Jack was already climbing over the side, lowering himself down pretty nearly hand over hand, clearly reluctant to trust his weight to his injured knee. She waited until he'd made it down to the rocks below before she started climbing down herself.

The ladder swayed treacherously under her feet, still drifting across the rock face. There was a large fissure in the rocks approaching faster than she wanted to see, and she climbed down faster, managing to scramble off the end of the ladder before it swept off the solid rock and out into empty space.

"Whoa," Jack said, catching at her pack to steady her.

"I'm good," Sam said.

Jack smiled sideways, a flicker of good humor coming through his tiredness. "At least we didn't have to parachute."

"I don't mind parachuting," Sam said. She didn't much like it, either, but admitting that was one of those things she wasn't in a position to do. It was one thing for Teal'c to imply that you would have to be a crazy person to enjoy jumping out of perfectly good airplanes, but that wasn't a good Air Force attitude for her to have. And no one was going to think that Teal'c was just being a girl.

Jack considered the slope up to the wall, which was still a disheartening distance above them. "How do you feel about climbing?"

"I packed a rope," Sam said.

"Good," Jack said. "Let's hope we don't need it."

"You know," Jack said, "when I woke up this morning, I said to myself..." He gritted his teeth, wrestling himself up a nearly vertical boulder. "Rock climbing, that's what I'd really like to do today."

"I'm sorry, sir," Carter said from below him. He found a stable place to stand and braced himself with his good leg, tossing the rope down to her, and held it as she scrambled up the same rock. "We're getting close, though."

They were at least getting close to the stone wall that seemed to mark the lower edge of the ruins, although whether that meant they were getting any closer to Daniel and Teal'c, there was no way to know. It was a painful hike the rest of the way, but it didn't involve any more serious climbing, and Carter coiled her rope and tucked it away in her pack again.

They had just reached the waist-high wall when Jack heard the sound of voices. He motioned Carter silent at once, and they both dropped behind the shelter of the wall.

The voices were faint, a conversation between several people much farther up the slope. He motioned Carter up, and she crouched to peer over the wall, and then dropped down behind it again.

She signaled three, maybe four people. Not SG-1. He pointed along the wall, to a point where it looked like they could cross while remaining in the shelter of a largely intact building, and Carter nodded.

By the time they reached it, Jack was reconsidering whether having a firefight might not have been a better decision than anything that required crouching. He straightened gratefully once on the other side of the wall, and motioned Carter toward the next building up the slope that promised to block the view from above.

He was already looking for the next piece of cover when Carter caught his arm, pointing out what looked like the top of a stairway half buried in rubble. She extracted a flashlight from her pack and shone it down there, but it revealed nothing other than that the stairs extended down and out of sight.

There was no obvious sign that anyone had been down that way, and in fact Jack thought not; it would have been hard to climb down the stairs without leaving visible footprints in the rubble. He shrugged and leaned cautiously out from behind the corner of the building.

Just past the building they were sheltered behind, the ground was split in a deep crack. It looked crossable here, if not comfortably, but further along the slope it widened to a ravine a good three meters across. No chance of crossing that with the tools they had on hand.

He froze as he saw movement on the slope above the ravine, ducking behind the corner and peering out cautiously. They were dressed much like Keret's pirates, two of them sitting on the ground near the widest point of the ravine, and another leaning on a fallen stone. It was hard to tell from this angle whether there were others sheltered behind the ruined building they were loitering around.

A metallic gleam caught his eye, and when he looked at the edge of the chasm he could see that there were metallic anchors of some kind pounded or drilled into the rock, with ropes fastened to them and hanging down into the ravine. He backed around the corner and leaned in to talk in a whisper.

"It looks like somebody climbed down there," he said, nodding toward the ravine. "I see two ways that could have gone down. One way, Reba's headed down there, and her ship's lightly guarded with Daniel and Teal'c aboard. The other way I figure it, Daniel and Teal'c either escaped or made some kind of deal, and they've gone looking for this treasure too."

"Why would they do that if they'd escaped?"

"This is Daniel we're talking about," Jack said. "If there's some kind of Ancient treasure hoard down there, you do the math. Anyway, there's no shelter out here. If they did escape, getting underground would be smart."

Sam glanced at the stairway. "You think this connects?"

Jack shrugged. "No way of knowing."

"It might," she said. "I mean, they wouldn't build a treasure chamber so that you had to climb down a cliff to get there. Would they?"

"That's a Daniel question," Jack said. "This could be somebody's basement, but let's check it out."

Piecing their way down the stairs around the rubble wasn't easy, but it was easier than the climb had been. At the bottom of the staircase, a squared-off tunnel ran past the crack in the rock and into the distance further than Sam's flashlight beam could reach.

"Well, it's not a basement," Sam said.

"Let's take a look around."

The crack was narrow enough here to be an easy jump. Or, at least, it should have been one. He stumbled on the landing, expecting for a moment to end up going sprawling, but Carter steadied him.

"I could scout ahead," she offered.

"Negative," he said, taking an experimental step and gratified when the worst his knee did was hurt rather than buckling.

"You're on your way to the infirmary when we get back, you know. Sir."

"Not the kind of vacation I had in mind."

"You could always apply for actual vacation time," Carter

said, playing her flashlight over the walls ahead of them.

"I have," Jack says. "They keep cancelling my leave on the theory that saving the world is more important."

"It might have been a better bet than trying to find us a non-stressful mission."

"Yes, but that wouldn't have gotten *you* to go on vacation."

"Well, no, but I just..." Carter trailed off. "Did you hear something?"

He thought he did, the indistinct sound of distant voices. They made their way forward in silence, and the voices grew clearer, but still not clear enough for him to make out who was speaking or what they were saying.

They rounded a corner, and he thought he saw something, too. He held out a hand to stop Carter and motioned to her to turn off her flashlight.

In the sudden darkness, he could clearly see the light coming from a doorway far down the corridor. The light shifted like someone moving around inside, and he could see from here that it wasn't the warm flicker of torches or a lantern; it was the cool glow of a flashlight.

Daniel Jackson and Reba were still examining the inscriptions when Teal'c heard a noise from outside. He turned, quietly making his way along the wall, and was taking up a defensive position near the door when he was greeted by an unexpected and welcome sight.

"O'Neill," he said gratefully. "Major Carter."

"What?" Daniel Jackson spun, turning his flashlight on O'Neill and Major Carter.

"Hi, kids," O'Neill said. He was holding a zat, covering Reba with it even as he smiled in greeting. "What did we miss?"

"Oh, we found this amazing... well, I'm not sure exactly what it is, but I think it's a device used by the Ancients to locate things, and if I can just translate these inscriptions—"

"I take it these are your friends," Reba said. She had her

zat drawn as well.

"Reba, Colonel Jack O'Neill and Major Carter. Jack, Sam, this is Reba. She's the one who kidnapped us."

Major Carter was also covering Reba now, of which Teal'c was certain she was aware. "Maybe we could renegotiate that," she said.

"You think?" O'Neill said. He armed his zat. "Daniel—"

"Whoa, wait. Actually, if you could not stun her yet, we're kind of still working on these inscriptions. She actually reads some Ancient, which is a big help in trying to figure out some of these abbreviated verb forms that..." He trailed off at O'Neill's expression. "Let me guess. 'Let's go, Daniel.'"

"Let's go, Daniel. Our new friend Keret is out there playing hide and seek with this lady's ship, and despite what he promised, I don't trust him to stick around forever."

"You brought Keret here?" Reba threw up her hands in disbelief, startling Major Carter into arming her zat. "Don't waste your shot. You don't have to blast me. You can just wait until Keret turns up to blast us all and take the treasure for himself."

"Keret doesn't even believe in your treasure," O'Neill said.

"Is that what he told you? He can't be trusted. Believe me, I know that from personal experience."

"How personal?" Major Carter asked.

Reba shrugged. "Does it matter?"

"No," Daniel Jackson said. "But deciphering these inscriptions does."

"We can handle Keret," O'Neill said. "But we need to get out of here. Daniel, come on."

"No."

O'Neill's eyebrows went up.

"I mean, please, not yet. I translated the tablets from the palace. They're copies of this inscription, which was left here by the Ancients. According to the inscription, this device can be used to locate anything that you want to find."

"It's, what, some kind of tracking device?" Major Carter said, stepping forward with interest lighting her eyes.

"More than a tracking device, a kind of… universal locator for anything that exists. Now I know that may sound impossible, but…"

"I don't know," Major Carter said. "We know that on a fundamental level, everything in the universe is connected in ways we don't even begin to understand. The part that I'm not sure is even theoretically possible is identifying things in a way that would make it possible to search for them. It's not like there's some great cosmic index of all the individual objects that exist. If you wanted to find, I don't know, all the naquadah in the universe, then maybe you could do that, but…"

"We could find all the naquadah in the universe?" O'Neill said, looking suddenly more interested.

"I'm just saying I think that's not theoretically impossible."

"That would be useful," Daniel Jackson said, his eyes on O'Neill. "Wouldn't it?"

"Obviously. How likely is that?"

"I don't know. I need more time."

"We could come back."

Daniel Jackson's eyes flickered to Reba. "I think now that people have found this place, there's a pretty good chance that if we leave and try to come back, whatever is here may be gone."

"We could deliver those with knowledge of the device to the proper authorities," Teal'c said.

"Assuming we can capture her crew, and Keret, and get them all the way back to the capital, sure," O'Neill said.

"And then the High King will come looking for the same thing, and Reba will lead him straight to it as part of a deal for her freedom," Daniel Jackson said.

Reba smiled a little. "You're beginning to get a feel for how things work around here."

"You think he'd want this thing, Daniel?"

"Who wouldn't? Everybody wants something."

O'Neill let out a breath, considering. "Okay," he said finally. "See what you can make of this stuff. You've got an hour."

"Jack—"

"The clock is ticking. You want to argue, or you want to translate?"

Daniel Jackson turned back to the inscription without further protest, although his shoulders were set in angry lines.

"Hand over your weapon, and you can help Daniel geek out over this stuff," O'Neill said to Reba. She looked like she was considering the offer for a moment, and then handed over her zat to Major Carter.

"I want this back when we're done here," she said.

O'Neill shrugged. "Play nicely, and we'll see."

Reba joined Daniel Jackson in inspecting the inscription, the two of them muttering together over certain lines.

"What's with the dead guys?" O'Neill said, shining his flashlight on the scattered bones that lay underneath the carved heart at the center of the wall. "Should we be worried about something?"

"Daniel Jackson believes there may have been a trap intended to prevent unauthorized persons from using the Ancient device," Teal'c said.

"Daniel?" Jack said.

"Yes, I do, which is why it's important that we translate this," he said without turning around. "We've been standing here for a while and nothing's happened to us, but I don't think trying to yank that thing out of the wall without reading the manual first would be a good idea."

"You think the device is behind the carving?" Major Carter said.

"Or is built into the carving somehow. The stone in the carving is warm, and the rest of the wall isn't."

"Huh," Major Carter said, making her way between the

bones in order to get a better view.

"Carter," O'Neill said sharply. "Just as a wild guess, I'm thinking it's a bad idea to touch that thing."

"Yes, sir. I got that far, sir. I wonder if this opens up somehow, if there's some kind of interface…"

"You mean like the one that grabbed my head that time?"

Major Carter nodded. "I promise, if something tries to grab my head, I'll get out of the way."

"Those head-sucker things move fast."

"I'll be alert for that, sir."

Daniel Jackson closed his eyes for a moment, his jaw set, and then opened them and focused resolutely on the inscription.

"Perhaps we could assist the translation by remaining quiet," Teal'c suggested.

O'Neill looked sideways at Teal'c. "As long as we've covered anything that we know about that could suddenly kill us or invade our brains."

"That's all I know of," Daniel Jackson said absently, his eyes on the carved lines in front of him. "If I find out about anything else, you'll be the first to know."

CHAPTER TWENTY-THREE

THE COLONEL'S hour was almost up and he was getting visibly twitchy when Sam saw Daniel tense, running his fingers back along the last few lines he'd been working on. She watched him as he backed up, looking over the whole inscription, his expression changing from tense concentration to something much bleaker.

"What?" she asked.

"Well," Daniel said, turning with a wincing smile. "The good news is, I've finished translating the inscription."

"That's good," O'Neill said, clearly waiting for the other shoe to drop.

"The bad news is, it's clear to me now that I mistranslated the inscription on the tablets. I was focusing on the system of abbreviation that they used, which, yes, was tricky, but it wasn't the only challenge in translation. Some of the language that looked very straightforward —"

"Daniel," Jack interrupted, not sharply but seriously. "What's the bad news?"

Daniel took a deep breath. "I don't think this is a device for finding things. Not in any literal sense."

"You swore there was a treasure," Reba said, reaching for the zat she wasn't holding anymore. She settled for folding her arms with a stormy expression.

"There is," Daniel said. "At least, there is depending on your definition of 'treasure.' I think this is a device for producing very realistic illusions."

"Like the Tok'ra memory recall device?" Sam said. That was the last thing she wanted to think about right now, but she couldn't help making the connection.

"Maybe," Daniel said. "More like whatever Apophis did

when he made us see altered memories."

He'd taken the form of her father. He'd played her most painful memories for her, over and over again until she'd screamed in her head, begging him not to make her relieve the moment when she learned of her mother's death one more time. And then he'd pretended to be her father. She hadn't told anyone about the dreams she'd been having since then, the ones where her father turned to her and raised the pain stick and smiled while she screamed—

"Only for much more altruistic reasons," Daniel went on, and Sam dug her fingernails into her palms. She couldn't afford not to stay focused on the here and now.

Teal'c frowned. "You believe this to have been some kind of reward?"

"You probably could use it that way, and I'm sure that's what the Goa'uld would do with it if they had it — use it to dispense fantasies to their servants like some kind of drug. I think what the Ancients used it for, though, was as a kind of aid to self-knowledge."

"Self-knowledge," Jack said skeptically.

"A way for people to find out what it is they want most."

"I know what I want most," Jack said. "Right now, it's to go home and take a hot bath. Does this thing have any actual practical purpose?"

Daniel looked like he was trying to think of one and failing. "It would be interesting to study," he said. "But I'm not sure it's worth the risk of trying to disconnect the device and move it. There are instructions here for turning it on, but not for removing it safely, and if that's what these people were trying to do when they died…"

Jack looked at Sam. "Carter?"

"I think Daniel may be right, sir," she said. "Even if we found a way to pull the device out of the wall, if it's as big as that carving, I don't know how we'd get it out of here without any equipment. And I'm afraid it would destabilize this wall, which given how much the rock these tunnels are built in has shifted... I don't think we can take this thing out safely."

"So we pack up," Jack said.

"I should have known," Reba said. "You were lying to me from the start, weren't you?" Her tone of voice made Jack raise his zat to cover her.

"I made a mistake," Daniel said.

"A very convenient one for you!"

"Well, yes, since you were planning to sell us to Asherah —"

"Hello," said Jack.

"She was planning to sell us to Asherah. Well, mainly Teal'c, but also me. Which means that even if I had known what was here — which I didn't — I wouldn't have had a lot of motivation to tell the truth, would I?"

"We had a deal," Reba said. "I swear to you, you're going to regret treating me this way. One of these days —"

"Yes, you will absolutely come through the Stargate and wreak terrible revenge," Daniel said. He sounded like he'd been fighting to keep his temper in check for a long time, and was finally losing it. "The thing is, at this point you're going to have to get in line."

"We have many more powerful enemies than yourself," Teal'c said, sounding like he was perversely proud of that.

Sam heard a faint noise. It might have been nothing, only one of the rocks they had disturbed when they came down settling, but it occurred to her that according to Teal'c, two more of Reba's people were down here in this maze of corridors, and that while they were arguing, no one was keeping watch.

She turned in time to see Keret framed in the doorway.

"So you did find your treasure," he said, his eyes on Reba.

"There's no treasure," Daniel said. "There's nothing down here worth a fight."

"I thought you said you couldn't land your ship," Sam said.

"I lied," Keret said impatiently. "Hand it over."

"He's right," Reba said. "There's nothing to hand over."

"You expect me to believe that? After the way you betrayed me? You ran off with two very valuable captives after I did all the work to set up their capture."

"I'm very sorry it worked out that way for you, I really am, but there's no treasure," Daniel said, pointing to the stone heart. "There's just this thing, which —"

"Shut up," Keret said.

Reba spread her hands in what might have been self-mockery. "What are you going to do, Keret? Fight me for a treasure that was never really there?"

"You think you've made a fool of me again," Keret said. "Not ever again, Reba." He twisted his right wrist, and Sam remembered the knife. If he threw it—

It wasn't a knife blade flashing in his hand, but a zat. She had all the weapons she'd taken from Keret's crew, but there could have been a hundred hiding places aboard the ship, and Keret had been on every deck alone at some point during the long night.

She was still arming her own zat when Keret fired.

Daniel watched Reba fall, thrown back by the zat's blast, sprawled across the floor with her long hair trailing. Like Sha're. Sha're had fallen like that, and he had crawled to her, touched her face and watched her die.

He felt strangely unreal, like he was watching the scene unfold in slow motion, from somewhere outside himself. Jack was turning to cover Keret, but there was something wrong with the motion, a stagger off balance that even Daniel could see was going to make his shot go wide. He could hear Sam's zat arming, but Keret was aiming again with a wolf's smile of satisfaction, his hand already tightening around the zat for the second shot.

He couldn't reach Reba in time, but there had to be something he could do, some way to buy a few seconds. He could feel the warmth under the stone, inches from his fingers, and he thought, all we need is a distraction.

He pressed his palm to the stone, fingers spread to touch all four chambers of the heart as the inscription directed, and felt the stone shift under his hand, bathing the room in pulsing waves of scarlet light.

Well, that ought to be a distraction, he had time to think, and then everything changed.

Daniel was rifling through stacks of papers, pulling out the articles he wanted to read over the weekend, when there was a tentative knock on the half-open door of his office. A young man with a backpack slung over his shoulder leaned in hopefully.

"Dr. Jackson? I was hoping I could talk to you about my paper."

"Absolutely, but not right now," Daniel said. "I'm on my way to lunch, and I have classes all afternoon. How about signing up for an appointment during my office hours next week?"

The kid shrugged philosophically and retreated out into the hallway to find the sign-up sheet. Daniel stacked another photocopied article on top of the teetering stack and glanced at his watch.

"Oops," he said, and grabbed for his coat. He dashed out the door, narrowly avoiding a collision with his student, who was scratching his name onto the sign-up sheet with its dangling pen.

He tried to remember what paper this was. The kid was researching Mayan pyramids — was that it? Or had he been proposing possible explanations for that strange find Daniel had read about, a perfectly preserved sarcophagus in a Mayan ruin?

The thought made Daniel uneasy for some reason as he shouldered his way out the front door of the Archaeology building and headed for the parking lot. He shook the feeling off. It was an amazing find, and one that certainly supported his own theories about connections between various cultures in pre-modern times.

He'd have to see if he could make time to see it. Between his classes and the lecture series he'd committed to, it was a busy spring, but since he wasn't going on a dig that summer, he could probably make a day trip. He'd have to find that article again, see where they had sent the sarcophagus after its excavation...

He tossed his briefcase into the car and peeled out of the lot, braking abruptly a couple of times as students wandered across the road. He'd been teaching long enough to learn that students as a species had no sense of self-preservation, and it was probably better to be late to lunch than it was to mow down undergraduates.

It was nearly 12:30 when he scrambled into the little Thai restaurant, hanging up his coat and waving at Mrs. Suprija, who was taking another customer's order and gave him a scolding look as he went by.

"I am sorry," he said, sliding into a seat at his usual table. "I was trying to find some stuff to take home this weekend, and then Peter Utkin showed up wanting to talk about the thing he's writing about the Mayans..."

Sha're shook her head at him in tolerant amusement. "Someday I will teach you to be on time, my Daniel." She had a cup of tea at her elbow, still steaming — Mrs. Suprija had probably been solicitously refilling it — and the remains of a rice-paper wrapped spring roll on a plate in front of her. "You must excuse me for starting without you," she said, smiling and cupping her hand protectively over her belly. "Your son was hungry."

"Well, let's order him some curry," Daniel said. "Although I really think milk is more traditional."

"Plenty of time for that," Sha're said. "And while we are speaking of it, my father called this morning to tell the flights he will be taking from Egypt. You can pick him up at the airport?"

"Assuming you're not in labor at the time," Daniel said. He felt that undercurrent of uneasiness again, and frowned as Mrs. Suprija put a cup of tea in front of him, although he murmured thanks to her. It was probably just nerves. Everyone said that was normal for a first-time father. "I'll have the red curry."

"He is not coming until nearly a month after the baby is due," Sha're said. "Surely even your son will not be as late as that."

"I hope not," Daniel said. "The suspense is killing me."

"All is well," Sha're said. "You are more nervous than I am, I think."

"I'm not nervous," Daniel said. "It's just the idea of actually having an actual baby..."

Sha're shook her head, smiling at him. "That is the point of the process."

"I know."

"And your parents will be here as well."

"I hope they don't drive you crazy."

"They will not," Sha're said. Her smile was teasing. "And I will know that in a few days they will go home, and then I can put my house back in order as I like it."

"I know my mom has a bad habit of rearranging cabinets," Daniel said. "It's some kind of organizational archaeologist gene."

"Perhaps it will inspire your son to keep his toys in order."

"I don't remember that it ever did that when I was a child."

"Daniel," Sha're said. "You worry too much."

"It's just that I'm happy," Daniel said. "I'm happy and I don't want anything to screw that up."

"I am happy, too," Sha're said. "Although I am ready for this baby to be born. And if it would make you more content to be less happy, wait until this summer when you are fetching things for a yelling baby, instead of in Egypt up to your elbows in sand."

"We'll go next summer," Daniel said. "My parents took me on digs when I was a year old. We'll just have to make sure that he doesn't fall in a hole or try to chew on anything pre-dynastic."

"My father is used to keeping children from harm at the dig sites," she said. "Although I think I gave him much gray hair."

She had told him the story many times, of slipping away from her father to wander among the half-excavated pyramids as she had been strictly forbidden to do, descending the stairs with a makeshift torch until she found a chamber richly inscribed with hieroglyphs that had fascinated her for years afterwards.

"If you hadn't, we would never have found the Abydos wall paintings," Daniel said. She had led him to them soon after they met, and the moment he had seen them, he'd known this was what he was looking for, a perfectly preserved account of the coming of the pyramid builders to the city of Abydos in Upper Egypt, and their eventual and hard-won defeat at the hands of the native Egyptians.

It had raised more questions than it answered, of course, as every significant discovery did. The identity of the invaders was still in question, and some of the theories were off the wall enough that even Daniel couldn't believe them. The extent of contact between societies in the ancient world had been far greater than anyone had previously believed, but to suggest as his grandfather was now doing that the pyramid builders had been aliens...

But if his greatest annoyance was the very public argument that he'd been having with Nick for years in archaeological journals, that wasn't much for him to complain about. It wouldn't stop Nick from turning up when the baby was born with a bottle of advocaat. Probably he'd start trying to persuade the baby that his own theories were correct while it was still in the cradle.

"Daniel?"

"Sorry," Daniel said. "Just thinking about how we met."

Sha're smiled. "You were so reluctant," she said. "I cannot believe how you made me chase you. It was very unseemly."

"Well, your father was throwing you at me, and I wasn't sure…"

"That I knew my own mind?" She shook her head at him as one of Mrs. Suprija's sons put plates down in front of them. "Believe me, Daniel," Sha're said. "It is not so easy for anyone to make me do anything I do not want."

"I've figured that out," Daniel said, but he felt the same unexplained shiver down his spine. He told himself firmly to cut it out. It was a beautiful day, he still had more than an hour before his next class, and although he could probably find something to worry about if he tried, he couldn't really complain about very much at all.

"Eat your food before it is cold," Sha're said. "And before you are late again and leave your students waiting in their classroom like so many lost little sheep."

"It's all right," Daniel said, sampling the curry. It was hot and delicious, as always. "Right now there's nowhere else I ought to be."

CHAPTER TWENTY-FOUR

JACK pulled into the school driveway and into what seemed like an endless line of minivans. At the school entrance, kids were climbing out, opening umbrellas against the driving rain, with occasional umbrella collisions ensuing. "You got your lunch?"

"I'm going to buy lunch," Charlie said. "It's cheeseburgers today."

"Didn't I see a lunch that your mother packed sitting on the counter?"

"I'll take it tomorrow." Charlie wrestled his backpack up from the floor of the car into his lap. Jack wasn't sure what he had in there. The kid packed for school the way Carter packed to explore other planets.

"Be sure to get ketchup," Jack said. "So you'll have a vegetable."

"Is mustard a vegetable?"

"No, it's more of a..."

"Mineral?"

"Condiment," Jack offered.

"Okay. What about mayonnaise?"

"It has eggs. So it's animal."

"Works for me," Charlie said. "Thanks for the ride." He shrugged out of his seat belt and threw open the door, rain gusting into the car. He splashed out, the hood of his sweatshirt still hanging down his back, and his umbrella God only knew where.

Jack shook his head as Charlie slammed the door, and fished his cell phone out of his pocket as he pulled out of the school's driveway.

"What did Charlie forget?" Sara asked, her voice amused.

"He left his lunch on the counter."

"I put it away before I left," Sara said. "I take it I'm competing with pizza day."

"Cheeseburger day," Jack said.

"Oh, well, then."

"I may be late tonight," Jack said.

"And that's different from every other night how?"

"It's really not, and yet I say it anyway."

"And I appreciate it anyway," Sara said. "See you when you get home."

He tucked the phone back into his pocket as he changed lanes, wipers thumping against the rain. Sometimes he felt a little guilty about talking to Sara like he was going to be spending the day behind a desk at the mountain when he was actually going out to get shot at again. This wasn't going to be one of those days, though. This mission was one he'd been looking forward to for a while.

Besides, he was pretty sure she knew he didn't have a desk job. He didn't explain it when he came home bruised or banged up, or provide much of an excuse for the times he had to spend several days off-world, and he figured she thought he was doing some kind of short-term special ops work, the kind where you moved on a moment's notice and aimed to get in and out before anyone knew you were there.

He had a real, honest-to-God vacation coming up, though, and he was determined that he was going to take it, no matter how many interesting new planets Carter found for them to explore. They'd drive up to the cabin, and he and Charlie could do some fishing while Sara sat on the dock and read a book, her feet bare to soak up the warmth of the autumn sun.

The last time they'd been up there, Charlie had caught the biggest trout Jack had ever seen, and had insisted on taking a picture of it before Jack cleaned it for dinner. He had the snapshot taped to the door of his locker at work, Charlie grinning and brandishing his fish at arm's length, his cheeks red with sunburn. Sara had snagged one of Jack asleep in a lawn chair on the dock, his baseball cap pulled down over his eyes.

"You want a picture of me asleep?" Jack said.

"I want a picture of you relaxed," Sara said, and leaned up to press her cheek to his.

He didn't have as many opportunities to relax as he might have wanted, but that pretty much came with the territory of having a kid and a house and a top-secret job exploring other planets. Every time he put it that way to himself, he had to smile. He'd thought when he joined the Air Force that it would be a good way to see the world. Seeing other worlds hadn't even been on his radar.

He slowed down for security as he entered the base, and pulled into the parking lot. The rain was letting up, and he only got a little wet as he waited for the shuttle into the mountain. Inside, he made his way down to the SGC's floors, heading straight for the locker room. His chance to eat breakfast had evaporated somewhere around the time that Charlie had talked him into dropping him at school so he wouldn't have to wait for the bus in the rain.

Kawalsky was already in there, buttoning his uniform shirt. "Thought we'd have to head out without you," he said.

"Not this time," Jack said. "Next week, when we're going back to the planet with all the mud —"

"Oh, but Major Carter says it's scientifically important mud."

"Feel free to leave without me for that one."

"We need you to carry your share of the mud," Kawalsky said while Jack was lacing his boots.

"I should ask Hammond if we can go back to the place with the purple beaches."

"There wasn't anything there."

"Nice, warm beaches. Palm trees."

"Dr. Lee says the palm tree things were poisonous."

"So don't eat them," Jack said. "Come on, let's go hit the sand."

"Not exactly beach sand," Kawalsky said, but he wasn't complaining either.

Carter and Teal'c were waiting in the gate room, and shouldered their packs as he came in.

"Ready to hit the beaches?" he said.

Carter grinned. "I can work on my tan."

"I do not believe that there are any beaches within walking distance of the Abydos Stargate," Teal'c said.

"All we're missing is the ocean part," Jack said. "I can work with that."

Hammond came down the stairs from the control room. "Give my regards to Dr. Jackson, please, and also give him these." He handed Jack a notebook full of scribbled hieroglyphic symbols. "Dr. Rothman would like Dr. Jackson's assistance with some more translations."

"Not exactly news," Jack said. "I'll trade him these for the ones he's finished."

"Please do," Hammond said. "I expect we'll have plenty more after these."

"Should keep him busy," Jack said, although he privately thought that Daniel was finding plenty to occupy himself on Abydos even without the translations Hammond kept sending through for him. He and Sha're hadn't given the impression that they were bored with each other the last time SG-1 had come to visit.

He'd asked Daniel once if he was ever tempted to join them on SG-1. They'd seen a lot of pretty cool things out there. Met a few bad guys, too, although since Ra wasn't a threat anymore, most of the people they'd met were friendly. The Jaffa were still cleaning up some of the mess Ra had left behind, but Teal'c said that was coming along pretty well.

"I think one new planet to explore is enough for me right now," Daniel had said. "Maybe in a few years we'll think about it."

"Suit yourself," Jack said. It might be for the best, anyway.

Daniel was a scientist, and while he'd get a kick out of the cool parts, Jack wasn't sure he wanted to see what the bad parts would do to Daniel's general belief that people were good and could be trusted. He and Kawalsky were old cynics, and Carter would get that way eventually; it came with the blue suit, and he wouldn't trade it for a gentler life.

He didn't really feel like trying to argue Daniel out of one, though. "All right, kids," he said. "Let's go pay the Abydonians a visit."

The wormhole's chill tugged at him, and then he stepped out into heat, and the bone-dry air of the Abydonian day. There were braziers lit in the chamber where the Stargate rested, and he could smell smoke and the scent of something cooking.

"O'Neill!" Skaara said, scrambling to his feet and smiling. He'd clearly been sitting on the steps waiting for them. "Daniel sent me to wait for you. He says that he is exploring a new chamber he has discovered, but that he will return by the noon meal."

"Which means sometime this afternoon," Kawalsky said. "Hi, Skaara."

"We could come back," Carter suggested.

"Cool your jets, Carter. We don't have anything else on the schedule for today." And if they went back, they'd more than likely get roped into exploring somewhere with a lot of mud. "There's no reason we can't hang out until Daniel gets back."

"Indeed," Teal'c said. He hadn't been very enthusiastic about the planet with the mud either.

"I see I'm outvoted," Carter said. "That's all right. I've been meaning to take some atmospheric readings."

"Read away," Jack said. "Is Mrs. Jackson also looking at interesting walls?"

"No," Skaara said with a smile. "Sha're says you must come and have tea until Daniel returns. She says she is sorry for his rudeness in not being here to greet his friends."

"We're all used to him," Jack said. "Lead the way."

Teal'c stepped out into the cool of the courtyard, letting the door close behind him and dull the sound of the crowd inside the palace. The official feast had turned into long hours of celebration, and no one was showing much readiness to go home.

"Had enough of that din?" Bra'tac asked, with a sideways smile. He was standing looking up at the stars. On the other side of the courtyard, torches lit the palace stairs, and people were still coming and going, or gathering in little knots on the stairs to talk.

"A moment of quiet would be welcome," Teal'c said. "I expect there will be little sleep tonight."

"How could there be?" Bra'tac cuffed him affectionately on the arm. "We are a free people tonight. There will be time enough to sleep when everyone has celebrated our victory."

"Indeed," Teal'c said. He had last seen Drey'auc trying to bring some order to the laying out of the food and drink so many people had brought, ordering people about as if she were a First Prime and looking entirely pleased at the opportunity to do so. "Sometime after dawn, it appears."

"Or the next day," Bra'tac said.

"And then there will be much work to do," Teal'c said. "We must have a council of some kind, to make our own laws and see to the defense of our own world."

"Yes, of course," Bra'tac said. "That will be the work of many days. We may as well take these few to celebrate."

It felt strange not to feel any sense of urgency about organizing their defenses. But Bra'tac was correct that there was hardly any pressing need. The Goa'uld were defeated forever, their power broken, and there was no one now who could send a fleet against them.

"The Jaffa of other worlds..." Teal'c began, unsure for a

moment how he meant to finish that thought. Events had moved so swiftly that he was unsure how things stood for Jaffa off Chulak. Many of them had been enemies for many years, but surely they would put that aside now that their freedom was before them.

"They will be celebrating as well," Bra'tac said. "No doubt they will send their envoys to us through the chappa'ai in good time. For now, you should take pride in what you have done. You have led us to victory."

"There can be no greater honor," Teal'c said.

"Do not let it go to your head," Bra'tac said, thumping him on the arm again, a bit harder this time.

Teal'c could not help smiling. "That is unlikely, old friend."

He had feared when he turned against Apophis that even his closest friends and family would not understand his decision. He had expected to be branded a traitor, even, and woken from dreams where even his family hissed 'shol'va' and turned their faces from him. In truth, though, he had been surprised by the loyalty of those who knew him, and then ashamed to have ever doubted it.

Drey'auc had been the greatest comfort, reassuring him that he was doing the right thing even when he had sometimes doubted himself. She had borne it patiently when she and Rya'c had lived in virtual confinement at Cheyenne Mountain, and helped Rya'c to bear it patiently as well. O'Neill had helped, persuading General Hammond to let Drey'auc and Rya'c leave the mountain from time to time to learn of Earth.

He thought Rya'c might actually have been sorry to leave Earth; he had been learning its customs with the ease of a child, and had played with O'Neill's son as he would have with a brother. O'Neill had taught Rya'c the game of baseball, and shortly before they had left Earth, Rya'c had been attempting to persuade him that he should learn to play hockey, as it was a more fitting game for warriors.

But Rya'c was nearly a man, ready to begin a warrior's training in earnest rather than continuing the studies of a scholar among the Tau'ri, and in any event Earth was not lost to them. Now that peace had come, they could trade with the Tau'ri through the chappa'ai and visit them as allies and friends.

"They will be wondering where you are," Bra'tac said. "Go, find your wife and son and enjoy the evening. There will be time enough for work."

"Are you not celebrating?" Teal'c said.

Bra'tac looked up again at the stars, his mouth twitching in a smile. "I never truly believed this day would come, my friend," he said. "The best that I ever hoped was to lessen the damage done to our people by Apophis. I dreamed of no more for you. I thought that if our freedom was even possible, it would come in the time of our descendants many generations from now. It was you who had the dream, Teal'c. You who carried it like a spark in the darkness."

"Only because you trained me well," Teal'c said. "Without your example to follow, I would never have come to believe that the Goa'uld are not gods."

"You went beyond me," Bra'tac said. "As every teacher hopes that his student will go where he cannot follow. And now, look. I look up at the stars, and see world after world of free people." He smiled again. "I am in awe, my friend. Forgive me if my heart is too full as yet for celebrating."

"Should you change your mind, I am sure there are many who would wish to honor you today as well," Teal'c said.

"Perhaps that will persuade me in time. That, or the night growing cold. Go on, now. Drey'auc will be wondering how you have lost your way in a building you served in for years."

Inside, the clamor of voices was no quieter. Warriors stood about telling stories of their recent exploits to admiring audiences, and children still ran through what had once been one of Apophis's audience chambers. It had been a solemn place, and one that many people had had reason to fear.

Now the serpent mask of Apophis lay on his throne, cracked

in two and blackened by a staff blast. A little knot of children were gathered near the steps of the throne, and as Teal'c passed, he could hear them daring one another to touch Apophis's mask.

"It is nothing but metal," Teal'c said. He rested his hand on it, and beckoned one of the boys to him. "See? It can do nothing to harm you, and neither can the dead false god who wore it."

"You should all be in bed," Drey'auc said, and the children scattered, ducking through the crowd. She shook her head. "They'll run around until dawn, and then fall asleep wherever they are."

"It will not harm them for one night," Teal'c said. "Where is our son?"

"Taking a turn to guard the palace," she said. "For the sake of ceremony, mind you. Bra'tac said there was no real danger, but that it was a task to set the boys to that might keep them out of trouble tonight."

"That is well," Teal'c said. He brushed her hand with his. "Will you be long occupied here?"

"Look around you," Drey'auc said, spreading her hands in cheerful exasperation. "I have no idea when this night will end."

"Surely it is not your responsibility alone."

She smiled, the smile that had first caught his eye long ago. "Are you trying to tempt me away, my husband?"

"Am I likely to be successful in the endeavor?"

"You are," she said, the same smile in her eyes.

Outside, there was more than one couple embracing without shame in the street, caught up in the joy of the night, but he waited until they were inside their own front door before he turned to Drey'auc, and she came to his arms, her hands tightening on his sleeves.

"They all believe in you tonight," she said. "But I always have."

"Always," Teal'c said. He felt a shiver go through him as he spoke, and reached to close the door behind them. Outside the night was growing cold, but within these walls it would be warm.

CHAPTER TWENTY-FIVE

SAM sat back to consider the device she'd painstakingly assembled on her lab bench. The only thing missing was a power supply, but with a little luck and the crystals they'd found on PX2-551, she ought to be able to put one together. She reached for one of the crystals, angling it experimentally to see if it would fit, when someone cleared their throat in the doorway.

"What is it this time, a better mousetrap?"

"Dad," Sam said, swiveling around on her stool. "I wasn't expecting you this afternoon." Someday he'd learn to call first, she thought.

Jacob Carter shrugged. "Your mom and I were in town, and I thought I'd drop in and see my baby girl."

"It's an artificial gravity drive," Sam said. "You just happened to be passing through Colorado Springs?"

"General Hammond did want to ask me about a couple of things."

Sam shook her head, smiling. "You just have to keep your hand in, don't you?"

"Well, ever since I found out about the Stargate program, it is a little hard to resist checking up to see what you've found out lately by exploring other planets."

"This is pretty interesting," Sam said. "We were visiting this planet where the locals use airships for transportation. It turned out that they were using anti-gravity technology that's very similar to what Ra used in his ships. I've been reverse engineering the drive, and I think it'll really be an improvement to our X-301s."

"They're pretty hot little ships already," Jacob said.

Sam grinned. "Teal'c and Colonel O'Neill certainly had fun testing them."

"And they're still in one piece, which is saying something."

"You mean the ships, or Teal'c and the colonel?"

"Yes," Jacob said dryly. "So show me your antigravity device."

"I'm working on the power supply right now," Sam said. "I've got to make sure that the incoming power is compatible with the crystal array we're using to adjust subjective gravity."

Jacob pulled up a chair so that he could inspect the device as she pointed out the work she'd done so far. Sam wasn't sure how much of her explanation he was following, but he still seemed genuinely interested. But, then, that was her father.

Or, at least, it was her father now. There had been a time when she'd started to feel like her father was only interested in her military career, and to despair of ever explaining to him why she found science interesting for its own sake. That had been before her mother's accident.

It had been a close call, a car crash on a stormy afternoon that could easily have killed her mother instead of merely sending her to the emergency room for stitches and a cast. It had scared Sam and her brother, but she thought it had scared their father even more. He'd been determined after that not to lose an opportunity to connect with his wife or his kids while he had the chance.

She could still remember when he'd come into her room while she was working on her science project, an elaborate display of model rocketry.

"This is nice, Sam," he'd said. "It looks really good." He'd fingered the nose cone of one of the rockets, tracing its shape with his fingers. "Is this stuff just interesting to you because you want to be an astronaut?"

Sam had hesitated, not sure what answer he was expecting. "That's not the only reason," she said. "Not even really the main reason. It's the physics of it, and the whole process of creating and testing designs based on the physical limits of the various materials that it's possible to work with and the forces that are going to be acting on them. It's…" She had trailed off, feeling suddenly self-conscious. "I think it's interesting. And it's just cool that we can go into space."

"Yes, it is," Jacob had said. "Tell me what's interesting."

She'd given him a sideways look. "Are you sure?"

He'd nodded. "I have time."

She wasn't sure now how much of his interest was professional and how much was because it was his daughter's science project, but she wasn't really going to argue either way. It helped her to talk through the process of assembling the power supply, and by the time she finished, she could see how she was going to have to fit the pieces together.

"I'm hoping we'll have a working prototype in a few weeks," Sam said.

"That's moving pretty fast," Jacob said.

"We do that around here. If you'd told me three years ago that we'd have our own fleet of starships by now, and be working on fighters with anti-gravity devices…" Sam trailed off, feeling strangely uneasy for a moment.

"Sam?"

"Nothing, I guess," Sam said. "Just thinking that things could have gone so much worse when we started the Stargate program. For all we knew, the galaxy could have been full of Goa'uld like Ra."

"As far as we know, they were dying out when we first encountered them," Jacob said. "Right?"

"That's what we think," Sam said. "We've found a lot of their technology, but very few actual Goa'uld. Colonel O'Neill keeps coming up with worst-case training scenarios involving having someone on the base actually taken as a host by a symbiote, but I think that's pretty unlikely."

"Which is good to hear, for your father," Jacob said.

"Hang around here enough, and he'll come up with a training scenario where you're the Goa'uld host."

"No, thank you," Jacob said, tapping his temple. "I think having one of me in here is quite enough."

She couldn't shake her sense of unease. "I guess it just gets to me sometimes that it could have been so different. We could have had someone taken as a host the moment we stepped through the Stargate, you know? Or contracted some kind of strange space disease, or run into some kind of device that turned out to be... I don't know, addictive or something, or had hostile aliens try to invade Earth —"

"But you didn't," Jacob pointed out.

"But we could have. We weren't very careful when we started the Stargate program, and we didn't know half of what we know now. The number of things that could have gone wrong —"

"You know, Sam, there are always a million disasters that could have happened. The important thing is, they didn't. You've got to think about everything that's gone right. You're discovering some amazing things out there."

Sam smiled. "I know. We've been... really remarkably lucky."

"That's not a bad thing."

"I know that, believe me."

"So, up for going out to lunch with me and your mom? She's hanging out back at the hotel, since she doesn't exactly have the security clearance for this stuff."

"I would love to, Dad..."

"I sense a 'but' coming."

"But, I really would like to keep working on this thing for a little while longer. Can we make it dinner?"

"Okay," Jacob said. "But if you're still in here at dinnertime, I'm dragging you out into the fresh air."

"Dinner, I promise," Sam said. She turned her attention back to the power supply, and began assembling the pieces she'd collected into a configuration that she thought ought to work. It actually seemed strangely familiar.

She supposed she'd seen pictures of something similar in video taken by one of the SG teams. They'd explored a lot of worlds and found a lot of Goa'uld technology, and the only reason that they didn't have a drive like this already was...

Well, she supposed they just hadn't stumbled on one that was this easy to reconstruct. And after all, they'd been doing fine with their space program ever since the Asgard had shared their ship and weapons technology. This would just be an added refinement to the small fighters they were testing already.

She slid the last crystal into place and crossed her fingers before she threw the power switch. Of course, it might not work the first time—

The device hummed, and Sam grabbed at the lab bench as she felt herself suddenly nearly weightless. She gave the device an experimental little push and watched it drift slowly just above the surface of the lab bench as if it weren't the size of a large television set. She quickly moved to catch it; it still retained all its mass, and if it picked up speed, it would be an alarming projectile in the lab.

When it stopped, she disconnected the power and glanced at the computer screen to check the device's energy usage while it had been turned on.

"Absolutely perfect," she said, and then told herself she shouldn't be surprised.

Daniel went home intending to work on his latest paper for an hour or two before Sha're got home, so that he could eat dinner with her without being distracted by thoughts on the dating of Egyptian artifacts. Once he sat down in his office, though, he found himself strangely unable to concentrate. He typed a few words and then found himself staring out the window, watching a bird rustling the branches of a tree outside the glass.

Building a nest, he thought. Soon it would have babies to feed and protect and teach to fly. He wondered if it was uneasy about the process, too, or if it remained oblivious to the ultimate purpose of its determined gathering of twigs.

This wasn't the first time it had occurred to him that soon they would have an actual baby, though, and he felt more off-balance than he thought that ought to account for. He scrolled back to read the last couple of pages of the paper, trying to focus his thoughts. Everything he had written made sense, but it seemed strangely flat, now, as if he couldn't remember why it had seemed so important.

It might just be that his priorities were shifting. He'd always put academia first, never had any other demands on his time, but now that he had a family, things had to be different. That was a good thing, and if he felt sometimes that he wasn't sure what was important, it was only to be expected that he would feel a little confused. As if no matter what he was doing, there was some other thing that he should be doing that would have been more important.

He heard the front door opening as Sha're came in and called "Daniel!" cheerfully.

"I'm in my office," he called back.

She stuck her head in the door, her hair damp and curling wildly from the rain. "Dinner in half an hour," she said.

"Okay." He was tempted to follow her when she went out, to put aside his unsettled mood and go make himself useful in the kitchen. Making himself useful, though, that was the thing that nagged at him.

He wasn't sure why. The research he was doing wasn't exactly searching for a cure for cancer or the solution to world hunger, but most research wasn't. It was one more piece in the puzzle of the pyramid builders, and he was proud of the slow assembling he'd done so far. "There is no rush," Nick always said. "The past is not going anywhere."

He was reluctant to dismiss the feeling entirely, though. It was possible that there was some connection he was missing in the paper that would shed light on the entire subject in a new way. It had happened that way for him before, a frustrated sense that something was wrong driving him until he found a solution.

It probably wasn't aliens. Daniel shook his head, thinking that he would never have his grandfather entirely figured out. The man could be ruthlessly practical, and then come up with a wildly fanciful theory that he insisted explained all of the mysteries about the pyramid builders. As far as Daniel was concerned, it was nothing more than an example of the over-application of Occam's Razor. The simplest solution might be the preferable one, all other things being equal, but that didn't mean that "aliens did it" was the answer to everything.

The words rang false as he thought them. This was all a smoke-screen, a wall of words that he was throwing up to keep himself from figuring out... something. Something that was both scary and important. That was frightening because it was so important. Because it would change everything.

"It can't be aliens," he said, staring at the computer screen.

"What can't be aliens?" Sha're said, reappearing in the doorway.

"I was just thinking about Nick's theory about the pyramids being modeled after the shape of alien spaceships," Daniel said.

She shook her head, looking amused. "We can rule out the aliens, surely?"

"I had. I have. I just... now I feel like that connects to something that isn't an entirely ridiculous theory, and I'm not sure what it is exactly. It's really frustrating."

She smiled sympathetically. "You will think of it soon, I am sure."

"Maybe so," Daniel said as she went out again.

He tried once again to focus on the paper. Surely he'd been interested in this yesterday. He would finish it up and send it in to the Journal of Egyptian Archaeology, and it would lead to some interesting discussions in archaeology newsgroups and be a good publication to have on his curriculum vitae.

And then he would shepherd his students through their

final exams, and the semester would be over. He would spend the summer with his wife and his newborn son, and have plenty of time to poke at Nick's wild theories if he wanted to, and all would be right with the world. There was no reason to feel like there would still be something missing, some turn that he was passing that he would regret not taking, some gate that he should be passing through—

The word sent chills down his spine, and he froze, the letters on the screen blurring together into meaningless light. A gate. There had been something about a gate, one of the inscriptions on a cartouche at Abydos that he had translated that had seemed like poetic wordplay at the time. He was abruptly certain that it was important, with a cold certainty that settled like a dead weight in the pit of his stomach.

"Sealed and buried for all time," he murmured. Hadn't that been how the inscription ran? There had been something about Ra, what he had taken for a listing of his godly attributes and possessions... *a million years into the sky*, had that been part of it? And then, *His Stargate*.

He reached for the leather-bound journal he kept in his desk drawer, the original record of the inscriptions he had found in Abydos. He kept it nearby as much for sentimental value as for reference — it also included the journal entries he had made when he first met Sha're, and when they had been falling in love — but it would have his original copy of the inscription, and the sketch he could half-see in his mind's eye, a distinctive curved shape like a ring.

He flipped the pages, frowning. The inscription wasn't there.

There was no record of a "Stargate," no inscription that referred to anything as "sealed and buried for all time." There was no sketch that even vaguely resembled the carved ring of stone he expected to find. He'd kept all his field notes in this journal through the entire Abydos dig. If that inscription had ever existed, it should have been in the journal.

He must have seen it somewhere else. Maybe it had been someone else's discovery, some journal article he'd read or some artifact he'd seen in a museum or university collection. Could it have been in Catherine's collection? She'd inherited some amazing pieces that she'd shown him the same year he went on the Abydos dig in Egypt, when she was trying to persuade him to...

To help her catalogue her collection. That was how they'd met. He remembered it perfectly well, and yet he felt like there was something he was missing there, too, some conversation they'd had soon after they met that wasn't about his plans for the Abydos dig that was important now.

He picked up the phone, hesitating for a moment, and then dialed her number.

"Daniel," she said with pleasure when she answered. "What can I do for you?"

"I wanted to ask you if you remembered anything in your father's collection that might have been called a Stargate," Daniel said.

"No, Daniel," Catherine said immediately. "There was nothing like that."

That ought to settle that, but... her answer was almost too immediate, too certain. He would have expected her to ask him what exactly he was translating as Stargate, and what kind of artifact he thought it might be, and why.

"You're sure," he said.

"Entirely certain," Catherine said. "That is not a path you want to go down."

"Have we talked about this before?" Daniel asked, frowning. "Or... did Nick ask you about this? Was this part of one of his theories?"

"You would know better than I," Catherine said. "I am sorry, Daniel, I am on my way out the door and I must not be late. You will call me again, yes? And we will talk about things more important than this Stargate. Have you chosen a name yet?"

"Not yet," Daniel said. "Sha're suggests naming him after my father, but I'm not sure I can inflict 'Melburn' on another generation, and she's equally dubious about 'Kasuf,' so we're going round. He'll probably end up named something really ordinary like 'Jack.'"

"There is nothing wrong with that," Catherine said, and he could hear the smile in her voice. "Be happy, Daniel."

She hung up before he could reply.

He flipped to a blank page in the notebook and began sketching out the lines of the stone ring he remembered. There was a clear inner and outer ring, and somehow that was important. And there were symbols, some that seemed familiar, and one that he drew larger in the center of the ring, an inverted V with a circle above it and small crossbars below the strokes.

A man? No, the triangle shape was a pyramid, and above it the setting sun. *That is not a path you want to go down.* He could still hear Catherine's voice, and some part of him knew that she was right. He was close to the answer now, a few questions away from it, and when he found it, it would change everything.

"Dinner!" Sha're called.

His chest clenched in sudden unreasoning fear. He ripped out the page from the notebook and crumpled it in his hand. It would be better to throw it away and forget all about this, he thought. It would be safer that way.

He stood there for a moment, hesitating, and then unfolded the paper. He carried it with him into the kitchen and smoothed it out on the table as Sha're put a plate in front of him.

"Does this look familiar to you, Sha're?" he said. "Because I'm really sure I've seen it somewhere before."

CHAPTER TWENTY-SIX

JACK wove his way toward Daniel's hearth through the crowd of curious people gathered around to see the Tau'ri who had come to visit. They made it to Abydos whenever they could, or whenever Rothman got particularly stuck on his translations, but they still weren't there often enough for Sha're's people to be entirely used to guests showing up through the chappa'ai.

"Sha're!" Skaara called. "I have brought O'Neill and Daniel's friends!"

Sha're ducked out from behind a hanging blanket, smiling at them. "You must forgive my Daniel," she said. "He has gone to look at more writings."

"That sounds like Daniel," Carter said. "It's good to see you, Sha're."

"You must sit and have some tea," Sha're said. "Or would you rather go out to him?"

"We'll hang out here," Jack said. Sha're raised her eyebrows at him with the very polite expression she wore when he'd said something she didn't understand. "Tea would be very nice, thank you."

She smiled at that and poured the tea. Skaara dropped down to sit next to O'Neill. "You must tell me of your great deeds," he said.

Jack made a show of looking to the rest of the team for help. "Have we done any great deeds lately? I can never remember."

"We saved those people who were stuck in a virtual reality device," Carter said.

"Okay, that was pretty cool."

"And we went back in time," Kawalsky said. "You have to admit that was cool."

Skaara frowned at him skeptically. "How is it possible to

travel in time? The past is past."

"Major Kawalsky speaks the truth," Teal'c said. "We did indeed travel into the past, and observed a time of great significance to the Tau'ri."

"What time is this?" Sha're asked.

"Well, the 1960s were... it was a time when a lot of things were changing in the United States," Carter said. "We were fighting a pretty controversial war, and there were also a lot of people who wanted... well, who wanted more freedom."

"In a lot of ways," Jack said. "Not all so great."

"What ways?" Skaara asked curiously. "Surely freedom is always good."

Jack really didn't feel like explaining 'turn on, tune in, drop out' to Skaara, and looked to Kawalsky for rescue.

"Freedom is greatly to be desired," Teal'c said. "But with freedom comes the responsibility to discipline oneself. I believe that is what O'Neill meant."

"Something like that," Jack said. "This is getting a little deep for me, though. How about the story of how we kept Teal'c from turning into a giant bug?"

"You can transform into an insect?" Skaara turned to Teal'c, looking more impressed than alarmed.

Teal'c remained stoic. "I would prefer not to."

"Nobody's turning into an insect today," Daniel said, coming up behind them. "Hi, guys."

"We brought you more stuff to translate," Kawalsky said. "Rothman says he has no idea what they mean."

"Actually, he said he'd like your advice," Carter corrected.

Kawalsky shrugged. "Same thing."

"I finished the other ones," Daniel said. "I'll get them."

"No hurry," said Jack. "If we go back too soon, we'll have time to go back to the planet with all the mud."

"That mud is full of minerals we haven't found anywhere else," Carter said.

"Even so. The mud will still be there in a couple of days."

"So will Daniel."

"Thanks so much," Daniel said.

Sam smiled at him to show she was teasing. "I don't mind hanging out here. We can tell Skaara about Teal'c and the bugs."

"I'll skip that story," Jack decided, standing up. "Want to go take a walk?"

"I, too, am very familiar with those events," Teal'c said hopefully, but Skaara tugged at his sleeve.

"You must not leave," he insisted. "You must say if they tell the story truly."

"We'll be back," Jack said, and followed Daniel toward the sloping corridor that led from this chamber out to the desert sand.

They were in the lee of the pyramid, and although there was a light wind blowing, they were sheltered from the sand that skated across the ground. The sun was low over the horizon, and the air was already cooling. When the sun set, it would be cold enough out here that he'd wish for a warm wrap like the one that Daniel wore, but for now the stone was warm when he leaned back against the entrance wall.

"So how are things, really?" Daniel said after a while.

"If you wanted to hear war stories, you should have stayed in there," Jack said. "Kawalsky can't get enough of that stuff."

"I'll hear it all after you leave," Daniel said. "Skaara loves to recount the exploits of SG-1. You'd be surprised by the number of times you've single-handedly saved the entire planet, according to him."

"Ours, or yours?"

"Usually yours. The real story of how you saved Abydos doesn't need much embellishment."

"You did have something to do with that, too," Jack said. "If you hadn't been around..." He felt strangely uneasy at the thought, like it was one he didn't want to follow up for some reason.

"You wouldn't have been able to talk to anybody, to start with," Daniel said. "Besides which, you wouldn't have figured out how to work the Stargate in the first place, so you wouldn't have gone anywhere. You'd probably still be... what were you doing before you got roped into the Stargate program, anyway?"

"Special ops," Jack said. "Doing a lot of things in a lot of places I can't tell you about."

"It's not like I'd tell anyone on Earth," Daniel said.

"It's still classified."

"Come on, it's not as if I can tell anyone on Earth without sending a message through the Stargate, which would be intercepted by some of the people with the highest security clearance on the planet."

Jack frowned. "Why do you care so much?" It reminded him uneasily of some situation that turned his stomach, someone pushing him to tell them something he knew he shouldn't reveal. He wasn't sure exactly what, and figured trying to pin down the memory was a bad idea. There were enough choices, and none of them were things he'd care to remember.

"I've just always wondered how someone like you wound up in the Stargate program."

Jack shot him a sideways glance. "Someone like me?"

Daniel made what was probably intended to be a clarifying gesture with his hands. "Someone who was satisfied with a career in the regular Air Force. I mean, Sam's interest was scientific, and Teal'c wanted to free his people, but I was never sure what made this crazy idea seem attractive to you. Here's someone saying 'let's walk through this gate to another planet, and oh, by the way, we have no idea what's on the other side of it or whether we can get back—'"

"You said you could get us back."

"Yes, but there was no way to be sure that I could."

"I didn't know that."

"So, what, you had such total trust in me from the moment that we met that you were willing to risk your life and the lives of your men on the idea that I could find and translate alien writings on the other side of the galaxy to get us home?"

"Apparently so," Jack said.

"I'm just wondering if there wasn't some other reason you wanted to go on this mission," Daniel said. "It seems strange to me that when you had a wife and a family —"

"Aha," Jack said.

Daniel looked a little annoyed. "'Aha,' what?"

"You're thinking about coming back to the Stargate program."

"I didn't say that."

"You implied it. You're thinking about coming back, but you're wondering if that would be fair to Sha're. And…?" Jack added, suddenly suspecting there was going to be someone else for Daniel to worry about leaving.

Daniel shrugged, but he smiled like he had a pleasant secret. "It would be bad luck to say anything this soon, Sha're says."

"So, if at some point in the future that we're not saying is anytime soon, you had a kid, you would wonder if it was fair to him, too."

"Would it be? You've been pretty lucky so far, but you know it's dangerous out there. If I take Sha're back to Earth with me, and then anything happened to me…"

"What does she say?"

"I think she's kind of interested in the idea of coming to Earth, actually," Daniel said. "She's always been curious. Of course she'd miss people here. I would, too. But I guess I am thinking about it."

"We could use you around," Jack said. "Rothman's a lousy translator."

"He's not really that bad," Daniel said.

"He translated the writing on this scanning device Carter found the other day as 'Beware the Giant Chicken.'"

"Well, that's... probably not right," Daniel said. "He's still working on that one, though, right?"

"So he claims," Jack said. "I'm just saying."

"I'll think about it," Daniel said. He glanced over at Jack. "So there wasn't any particular reason you decided to take the Abydos mission?"

Jack felt that gnawing sense of unease again, but pushed it aside. "No," he said. "No reason in particular."

"What is this?" Sha're asked, peering at the sketch of the stone circle that Daniel spread out on the table.

"Have you ever seen something like it?"

She glanced up at him. "Have you?"

"I think so. I thought it must have been from one of the tomb paintings we found in Abydos, the ones that showed the arrival of the pyramid builders and the rebellion against the priests of Ra, but I can't find anything like it in my notes. Do you remember, Sha're?"

"I think you must have seen this thing before we met," Sha're said. "Perhaps in a museum, or in some other place where you once worked."

"Maybe so," Daniel said. He had a sudden impression of a concrete room, somewhere cold that smelled of fresh paint and lingering dampness, and of sketching out the symbols that he could see so vividly on a chalkboard. It didn't look like a museum. A warehouse, he thought, and for a moment he thought he could remember the great circle of stone standing in a tall wooden box in a warehouse, but all of the impressions flowed away like water as soon as he tried to pin them down.

He tried to pay enough attention to dinner not to look ungrateful for it, but he couldn't have said afterwards what he'd eaten. He turned his water glass around in his hand, watching the light reflect in its shimmering depths.

"You are troubled," Sha're said, taking the glass out of his hand and putting it aside on the table.

"I am," Daniel admitted.

She drew him to his feet and toward the bedroom. "Come and tell me about it."

He went to the bedroom window and drew the curtains open, looking out at the trees bowed by the rain. The streetlights glittered gold off their leaves. And yet at the same time, all he could see when he closed his eyes was Egypt. He could almost feel the blowing sand, sand that whispered against the base of an enormous pyramid reaching up toward the bright disk of the sun.

"I think there's something I've forgotten," Daniel said slowly. "Something important, something that has to do with Abydos and a Stargate and the rebellion against Ra."

"Surely if it is so important you will remember it soon," Sha're said.

"Maybe," Daniel said. "But what if it's something I don't really want to know? What if there's something connected to this Stargate that is so monumental, so earth-shattering that... that if I knew it, it would change everything."

"Surely not everything," Sha're said, slipping in front of him so that he could put his arms around her. He rested one hand on the curve of her belly.

"Everything." He took Sha're's hand and held onto it, hard enough that he thought he must have been crushing her fingers in his, but she didn't protest. She had held his hand this way when... but, no, of course that hadn't happened yet. He'd only imagined what it would be like to hold her hand while she was in labor, racked with contractions and clinging to his hand.

It wasn't the bright labor and delivery suite with its waiting rocking chair that he could picture with the vividness of memory, but a woolen pallet in a room of stone, kneeling in front of her as she cried out, insisting that she push as she shook her head in denial, telling her that she would never lose him. It felt far too real to be a dream, even if the whole scene carried the edge of sick horror he associated with nightmares.

"I dreamed you had a baby," he said slowly.

"That is only natural when the time is so close."

"But everything was wrong. I had to leave you, and Kasuf took the baby to hide it, and then I couldn't find it. I never saw it again."

"Not all dreams are true," Sha're said, but her voice was sad.

"Was this one true?"

She turned to him, looking up at him. He thought he had never loved her more than at that moment. "You already know," she said. "You know what you must do."

"No," Daniel said. "No, I won't. Because if I remember whatever it is, I'm going to lose you, aren't I? Aren't I?" He drew her back when she would have pulled away, looking searchingly into her face. "Tell me the truth."

"You can never lose me," Sha're said. She put her fingers to his lips, tracing the line of his mouth as if committing it to memory.

"It's not worth it," Daniel said. "Whatever it is I've forgotten, I don't care. I don't care about anything but you."

"That is not true, my Daniel," Sha're said, very gently. "If it were, you would not have searched the ancient writings when we were on Abydos. Or unburied the chappa'ai and spoken of how we might travel through it if you could learn its secrets."

"It would have been better if I hadn't. Sha're..."

Sha're shook her head, and pressed her hand to his heart. "If you had not, you would not have been my Daniel. But you are, and you know that this is a dream."

"I don't want it to be," Daniel said desperately.

"Neither do I," Sha're said. She smiled shakily, and he cupped her face in his hand for a long moment, feeling her face warm against his palm. "You must wake up now," she said. "There is not much time."

"For what?"

"To save your friends," Sha're said, and then he was standing in a room bathed in crimson light, his hand pressed against the warm curve of carven stone.

"Sha're!"

She was gone. She had never been there at all. He put his hands to his face for a moment, struggling to accept that he would never really touch her again. Then memory flooded in, impossible to ignore. Reba, and Keret, and his momentary distraction.

He turned to see Reba still sprawled on the floor, her chest moving softly as she breathed; stunned, not dead. Keret was standing with his zat still in hand, his expression that of a sleep-walker. He didn't glance at Daniel, but his eyes moved as if he were dreaming, or as if he saw something that wasn't there.

Daniel looked around, and wasn't surprised to see that Jack and Sam and Teal'c were also standing stock-still where they had been when he'd activated the device. He quickly took the zat from Keret's unprotesting hand, tucking it into his own waistband, and then went to check on his teammates.

He waved his hand in front of Jack's eyes and shook him by the arm, but Jack didn't move or speak, his eyes looking past Daniel to some internal world of his own. The others were no better. He considered the idea of trying to carry one of them out of the chamber, in hopes that its effects would wear off when they were removed from its proximity, but when he tried to lift Sam, she stayed standing like a statue, making it hard for him to lift her except by putting his arms around her waist and lifting her feet off the ground.

Wrestling her out of the room that way would be hard, and wrestling Jack out would be harder. Moving Teal'c that way would be a challenge, and getting any of them back up the cliff presented an interesting problem. He supposed that if he went up, he might be able to persuade Reba's men to help hoist them up like sacks of grain, but if the effects didn't wear off with proximity, and he had to persuade them to lower them back down instead of just leaving them all as more trouble than they were worth…

"Okay, this is a problem," Daniel said, pleased that his voice was mostly steady. He was still shaking, he thought for a moment, and then realized that it was the floor that was shaking. The device was vibrating, rattling against its housing in the wall and sending dust and chips of rock showering down from the ceiling.

Maybe more of an immediate problem than he'd thought. There was no way to tell how stable this chamber was. This whole hillside was riddled with cracks and fractures in the rock that wouldn't take much added stress. Even if the roof of this room stayed up, it wouldn't help if their route back to the surface collapsed.

As if in answer to the thought, he heard an ominous rumble like thunder, although they were far too deep into the hillside for it to actually be the sound of an oncoming storm. It was the sound of rock moving, somewhere too close by for comfort. They had to get out of here.

He couldn't move all of them while they were still under the influence of the device, at least not quickly. He wasn't sure how he'd escaped from its influence himself, and couldn't afford to wait and see if they could do the same. He had to turn the thing off. The only problem was, he hadn't found instructions for that. He had hoped it would be obvious.

He probably should have thought that through a little more. He hadn't been thinking clearly, and when Reba had fallen, all he had been able to think about was Sha're. And yet when he'd gotten what he thought was his heart's desire, he'd immediately started prying up the loose corners of the fantasy world he'd constructed, unsatisfied with anything but the truth—

And if he didn't put all of that aside now and think fast, a ton of rock was about to fall on his head. Right.

He pressed his hand against the carved heart again, careful to touch every chamber with his fingers, hoping that it would be as simple as that. The red light still filled the room, and when he glanced back, none of the others showed any signs of stirring.

"Okay, not that simple," he said. There was another clatter, and loose rock and dust showered down from a corner of the room. Maybe it was a sequence, some kind of code. He could probably figure it out if the roof stayed up long enough. Another threatening rumble made him less than optimistic that it would. Of course, there might be a mechanical means of disabling the device, one that Sam could probably figure out if she weren't currently staring blankly at the wall.

"Have I mentioned that now would be a really good time to wake up?" he said, but the only sound was the distant thunder of tumbling rock.

CHAPTER TWENTY-SEVEN

SAM finished noting down the results of the last of her tests on the gravity drive, and frowned. It was performing just as expected. Almost perfectly as expected. For a first trial, that was a little strange. She would actually have felt better about seeing some strange results, a few spikes in the power consumption or some sign of incompatibility between the power source she was using and the alien power crystals.

She opened a few more files on her computer, flipping back through her last few experiments. All of them had worked just as smoothly. They'd really been remarkably successful reverse engineering all the Goa'uld technology they'd found so far. Even the hand devices, which at first she'd suspected might require some kind of protein marker specific to the Goa'uld in order to use, hadn't been that hard to modify.

For a moment, she couldn't remember exactly how. It was a funny thing to blank on; she remembered working with Janet on the problem, and their mutual excitement at the idea that they might be able to heal damage that couldn't be cured by any current human technology. She searched further back through her files, hunting for the records of those experiments.

They'd had no success in their first handful of trials, and then they'd tried injecting trace amounts of naquadah into the user's bloodstream. That had apparently created the energy signature that the hand device was looking for. It seemed a little strange when she thought about it, but it had clearly been the right idea.

What she couldn't find was any indication of how they'd originally come up with the idea. She frowned, and called up to the infirmary, asking for Dr. Fraiser.

"Hi, Sam," Janet said after a minute. "What can I do for you?"

"Do you remember when we first started working on the hand devices?"

"Of course," Janet said. "Believe me, I'm not likely to forget it. It's made such a difference in what we can do."

She was right, of course. While they were lucky not to have encountered hostile forces in their exploration of the galaxy, there were still some accidental injuries that might have been a lot more serious without the ability to heal them easily. Jack's recent knee injury, for instance, or… she had the hazy impression of a mission somewhere hot, with air that stung her throat, but she couldn't pin it down.

"I'm not sure what's the matter with me today, but remind me — what made us think that injecting a naquadah solution would make the Goa'uld hand devices start working for us?"

"We already knew that it was possible for someone with trace amounts of naquadah in their bloodstream to detect a Goa'uld symbiote," Janet said. "It seemed reasonable that it might also allow some amount of control over Goa'uld technology."

"And we knew that because…"

"Because of Cassie," Janet said, sounding surprised that she didn't remember. "The people of her planet all naturally possess trace amounts of naquadah in their bloodstreams. That's how they were able to detect the Goa'uld who were trying to infiltrate their people and infect them with what could have been a deadly plague."

"But we were able to stop it in time," Sam said. "I knew that." She and Janet had both formed a special bond with Janet's youngest patient on that mission, and they'd visited numerous times since then. It was always great to get to spend time with Cassie, and to see her growing up happily with her parents.

Sam shook her head, unable to shake the sense that something was wrong. She could clearly picture Cassie in her mind's eye the way she'd looked the last time Sam had seen her, but when she tried to remember talking to Cassie's parents on her last visit, she couldn't even clearly imagine their faces.

"We're just lucky that it didn't actually require a protein marker that could only be left by the presence of a Goa'uld symbiote," Janet said. "That would have made it pretty much useless to us, unless we felt like letting someone become a host."

"Probably a bad idea," Sam said.

"Is everything all right?" Janet asked. "You sound like you're worried about something."

"I really don't know," Sam said. "I'm having a hard time remembering things today that I feel like I should be remembering. Everything from what I said to Cassie's parents the last time we visited to how you found out about the naquadah."

"Hmm," Janet said. "You know, you've been putting in some pretty long hours lately. Maybe you should take the rest of the day off, get some rest."

"I guess," Sam said. "I really want to take another look at these numbers I just ran, though. And tomorrow we're supposed to—"

"I know," Janet said firmly. "There's always something, but you also need to take care of yourself."

"Colonel O'Neill was just saying that we needed a vacation," Sam said. "He actually suggested that we all spend the weekend up at his cabin."

"I think that's not a bad idea at all," Janet said.

Sam smiled and shook her head, even though she knew Janet couldn't see. "Don't you think it might be a little... I don't know, inappropriate?"

Janet sounded amused. "Do you want it to be?"

"I am not answering that question," Sam said. Now she was glad Janet couldn't see her face.

"I think Teal'c and Daniel count as chaperones," Janet said.

"Be that as it may," Sam said. "I'll think about taking the afternoon off, I promise. My mom and dad are in town anyway, and I was planning on taking off a little early so I can have dinner with them."

"Have fun," Janet said. "And come by and see me if you're not feeling better tomorrow."

"I will," Sam said.

She should have felt reassured. It ought to be a good thing that Janet didn't think her apparent memory lapses were a sign of anything other than overwork. Instead, she only felt more unsettled, and couldn't stop herself from questioning the conversation they'd just had.

You've been putting in some pretty long hours lately, Janet had said. But had she? Of course there had been missions, but as far as she could remember — and as far as she could tell, flipping back through mission reports — a lot of them had been routine. She'd spent a couple of days checking on the progress of the new X-301s, and she'd spent a couple of evenings in her lab, but it wasn't like she'd been pulling all-nighters lately.

And she couldn't help feeling that Janet ought to be taking any hint of a weird symptom a little more seriously. They hadn't yet encountered an alien substance that had caused a serious health problem — it wasn't as if her symptoms were likely to be a sign that she was developing amnesia or some kind of contagious disease — but that was really pure chance. They were exploring alien worlds, and the fact that so far they hadn't had to deal with any serious consequences just meant that they'd been lucky.

A lot luckier than she would have expected. Not that it was possible to calculate the mathematical probability of something going seriously wrong on an SG team mission, but the fact that they'd been exploring the galaxy for over two years and nothing had gone seriously wrong yet seemed… wrong.

Right, Sam said, shaking her head at herself. *Way to appreciate your good fortune, there.* It was an amazing opportunity to start with, getting to explore the galaxy and discover things she would never even have dreamed of before she joined the program. It would have been worth... well, a lot more than just putting in a lot of overtime... to get to see things no one else from Earth had ever seen.

And if she could see those things, and make most of the technology they found work the first time she tried it, and go home at five o'clock without leaving anyone in the infirmary for her to worry about while she was gone, why in the world was she complaining?

And why was she wondering whether she was being ungrateful when she'd started out wondering how they'd gotten the Goa'uld hand devices to work? It was too neat a distraction, the kind of unanswerable question about feelings that she had hated in school. There was at least one genuine problem here: the unexplained gaps in her memory.

She also wasn't entirely satisfied with Janet's account of how they'd gotten the hand devices to work. It sounded plausible, except that she could remember being certain that the only way to use the devices was to have the protein marker that showed that you'd once been a host. More than that, she was almost as certain that controlling them would require some element of skill. Somehow they'd managed to learn to use the hand devices without hurting anyone in the process, without ever having even talked to anyone who'd learned to use them as a host.

It was certainly lucky.

Or unbelievable.

Teal'c woke before dawn, unsure what had disturbed him. The sound of people celebrating still carried from the street outside, but there was nothing alarming in it, only the quiet sound of conversations and laughter now hushed out of some respect for the hour. The shrieks of excited children could no longer be heard; all but the oldest must be asleep by now, whether in their beds or in quiet corners of the palace.

Beside him, Drey'auc was still sleeping, although she stirred a little against him, pulling a blanket up higher against her shoulder. He slipped out of bed without waking her and dressed quietly, prompted by some inner restlessness it was hard for him to put a name to.

Perhaps it was only that on such a night, it was hard for him to sleep, even after such a long day. They had returned to Chulak in triumph in the early hours of the morning, already weary from the long night's battle. Their ships had defeated the forces still loyal to Apophis, and then they had boarded his ha'tak.

He remembered vividly making his way into the chamber where Apophis cowered on his throne. He had waited until Apophis saw him, until he was sure that the false god recognized his former First Prime, and then he had fired and watched the light go out of Apophis's eyes forever.

There was something strangely unsettling about the image, a feeling that only strengthened as he glanced back at Drey'auc, still curled sleeping under the covers, her dark hair spread across her pillow. Teal'c went out as quietly as he could, hoping that the evening air would clear his head.

He walked, head bent to avoid being drawn into conversation by anyone still celebrating. He had heard his fill of congratulations, and while he could not deny his pride in them, he doubted they were the balm he sought for his mood. He gave little thought to the direction he walked, and found himself at the gate of Bra'tac's house without being aware of having decided to go there.

He shook his head at himself. He could hardly wake Bra'tac in the cold hours of the morning to tell him of a sense of nameless unease. There was the flicker of a lit lamp on the house's veranda, though, and as he hesitated, Bra'tac called to him quietly, "I thought you might come."

Teal'c went in through the gate and ascended the steps to the veranda. "Why is that?" he asked, settling onto one of the stone benches that overlooked the side garden.

"You seemed troubled, earlier," Bra'tac said.

"I have no reason to be," Teal'c said slowly. "This is the day that we have long dreamed of. Perhaps it is only that I regret that we could not achieve our victory without the deaths of other Jaffa."

"Very few," Bra'tac said. "Almost all had already come to see the wisdom of our cause."

"So they had," Teal'c said. "In so few short years…"

"The truth is obvious once it is laid before us," Bra'tac said.

"It must be so," Teal'c said. "And yet I remember that for many years I struggled with the idea that the Goa'uld were not gods, even once I knew that you believed the same."

Bra'tac smiled sideways. "Perhaps you are more persuasive than I was. You cannot argue with the results you have achieved. You have led us all to freedom."

"And the Goa'uld to their destruction," Teal'c said.

"Surely you do not regret it."

"Never. I suppose I have been thinking of the words of Daniel Jackson."

"The Tau'ri overcomplicate things," Bra'tac said.

"Even so. He spoke once of his regret that to destroy the false gods, we must also kill the hosts that they have taken. He remembers well that his wife was nearly taken by the Jaffa who searched Abydos for potential hosts for the children of the gods."

"We must make some sacrifices," Bra'tac said. "Besides, they did not take Daniel Jackson's wife, did they?"

"They did not," Teal'c said. "But I would have, had I been the one who was sent to Abydos. She was both beautiful and brave." Apophis had praised him for bringing strong hosts, believing them the most likely to survive the implantation process, and had never known that Teal'c had hoped that the strong-willed ones would become thorns in the sides of the gods who possessed their bodies.

"Many things could have happened that did not," Bra'tac said. "You must think of our victory, and of the work still to come. It will take time for us to build a new government for our people."

"More time than it has taken to achieve this victory," Teal'c said.

Bra'tac gave him a sharp look. "What are you implying?"

It would have been easy to say that he was implying nothing. Easy, but untrue.

"Think back to where this rebellion began, in the days when I first left our people to join with the Tau'ri."

"It did not begin with you," Bra'tac said, a warning heat in his expression. "Or in your time."

"Very well. To when we first openly took up arms against the Goa'uld. It has been mere months—"

"Longer than that," Bra'tac said. "Nearly two years."

Teal'c frowned. "And yet I remember Drey'auc standing by me when few others would rally to my cause. If there were so few who believed, how were we able to face the Goa'uld without being destroyed?"

He broke off at a low rumbling in the distance, glancing up at the sky by force of habit. There were no ships there, only the flash of heat lightning across half the sky. It might not be a bad thing for it to rain, to drive the last of the celebrating people indoors to their beds.

"A few is not none," Bra'tac said when the sky quieted. "Not every attack requires an army. With stealth and good planning—"

"I think not," Teal'c said.

Bra'tac frowned. "You cannot argue with what was accomplished," he said. "Unless you imagine that this is all somehow a great trick." He shook his head, quiet anger in his voice. "You cannot imagine that I would deceive our people in such a monstrous way."

"I know you are true," Teal'c said. "But it would not be the first time that the false gods have lied."

"No reason you took the Abydos mission?" Daniel asked, still looking like he wasn't satisfied with Jack's explanation. Jack shook his head. When Daniel got his teeth into some mystery, he hung on like a terrier, worrying at it until he wrung answers out of it. It wasn't a very comfortable process if you were on the other end.

"No reason," Jack said firmly. "My number came up for the mission and I did what they told me to. Like you said, why would I volunteer for a mission like that when I had a wife and kid?"

"Why do you think they picked you?"

Jack shrugged. "My winning personality?"

"I'm just wondering," Daniel said. "If we hadn't been able to defeat Ra, was there a back-up plan?"

"Go home and bury the gate," Jack said. "Or blow it up, although Carter says now that wouldn't be as easy as we thought it was."

"I'm just wondering if it might not have seemed like a better idea to some people to blow up the gate on this end."

"So now you're an expert on military strategy? How about sticking to translation?"

"I'm getting some idea of how the military mind works," Daniel said. "And you're avoiding the question."

"It wasn't a suicide mission," Jack said. "And I wouldn't have volunteered for one."

"I thought you said you were assigned the Abydos mission. You didn't volunteer for it. Right?"

"Either way," Jack said. "You think General West would have sent a team through that gate never intending for me to bring them back? You're out of your mind."

"No," Daniel said. "I mean, why would he think you would go along with that? It's not like he thought you were suicidal. It's not like he thought you were the kind of man who wouldn't really care if he blew himself up and took anybody who was on this side of the gate with him."

Jack gave Daniel a sharp look. "What's the matter with you?" There was something in Daniel's tone that made the back of his neck prickle. *Someone walking over my grave*, he thought, and frowned.

"It's not me I'm wondering about. It's all this." Daniel waved a hand, apparently taking in the entire landscape around them. "Think about how things worked out. We defeated Ra, and everybody went home in one piece and lived happily ever after."

"That's how it works sometimes," Jack said. "Those are good days."

"Doesn't it seem maybe just a little too perfect?"

Jack shook his head. "It's not perfect. Perfect would be nobody ever getting stung by a giant bug or stuck in an ice cave for days or trapped in a virtual reality device that's sucking out our brains. Perfect would be Charlie cleaning his room without me asking him to."

"That'll never happen," Daniel said.

"Tell me about it. I don't believe in perfect. I just believe in pretty damn good, and that's what things are these days, and I'm not about to argue with that."

"And how can I argue with that?" Daniel asked quietly, as if he wasn't even really talking to Jack.

Jack frowned at Daniel, trying to figure out what had gotten him into this mood. "What's got you acting like this?"

Daniel shook his head as if to clear it. "I'm really not sure. I just have this feeling that there's something wrong with... well, with everything. Doesn't something feel wrong to you if you really think about it? Like all of this is just a little unreal?"

Jack looked out across the pyramids. The sun was setting over the desert, staining the sun red, and the evening air was growing cold. The torchlight from the nearest entrance to the pyramid shed a welcoming glow.

For a moment, it did feel unreal, like looking at a picture postcard of somewhere he'd been stationed and knowing that the real place was dirtier and colder. He had the sudden feeling that unless he turned around right now and walked back into the pyramid, when he did, Kawalsky wouldn't be sitting by the fire bragging to Skaara, and Sha're wouldn't be shaking her head and offering to go find her wayward husband for them. Because…

He wasn't going to finish that thought. Absolutely not.

"There's nothing wrong," he said. "Except maybe that you've been out in the sun too much." He clapped Daniel on the shoulder. "Come on, Sha're's probably ready to march up here and drag you in by the ear."

"She wouldn't do that," Daniel said. "Probably."

"You don't want to find out," Jack said. He headed down the stairs with Daniel behind him. Halfway down, there was a faint rumbling in the distance, the grumble of thunder like the sound of stone moving on stone.

"Storm coming?" Jack asked.

"We get them from time to time," Daniel said. "They can be pretty dramatic."

"So let's not go out in it," Jack said. "We'll stay nice and dry and have another cup of tea before we have to go home."

"You're probably right," Daniel said as they came back out into the biggest of the rooms where the Abydonians made their homes. Jack could see his team from across the room, sitting cross-legged at Daniel's hearth, Kawalsky still apparently telling some lengthy story with Skaara and a handful of other boys as his admiring audience. "We'll probably be fine in here."

CHAPTER TWENTY-EIGHT

THERE was a knock on the doorframe, and Sam spun around, startled.

"Ready to go, kiddo?" Jacob said. "Your mom's waiting out in the car."

"Almost," Sam said. "I just want to finish looking over these experiments one more time. There's something that really bothers me."

"Sam," Jacob said, shaking his head at her. "It can wait, right? Ask your friends to come along if you want."

It was tempting. There wasn't any urgency in a sense that things had been too easy for them from the beginning. Not unless it meant that everything she thought she knew about the last two years was the result of something that was currently affecting her mind.

"Actually, I don't think it can," Sam said. "I think there may be something seriously wrong, and I need to figure out what it is."

Jacob frowned, and then shrugged rueful agreement, his expression softening. "What can I say to that? Of course the job comes first."

"That's right," Sam said, with a sudden sense of relief she couldn't explain. "Not that I wouldn't like to take the evening off, but right now what I want most is to figure out this problem —"

The floor suddenly shook violently under her feet, and she reached frantically for the gravity drive. She had been sure she'd shut it off, but maybe it had malfunctioned. She hadn't really meant it that she'd be happier if something went badly wrong.

She stumbled as something hit her in the shoulder, knocking her off-balance, and then threw up her hands for protection against a shower of dust and chips of stone from above. In the distance, there was the ominous rumble of stone.

I'm in the caves under the Ancient ruins, Sam realized, *and we have a problem.*

"It is the kind of trick the gods might well play on our people," Teal'c said. "To allow us to believe that we are free of them, only to betray us into showing them open rebellion in order to crush us utterly." The thunder rumbled again, closer and more menacing.

"And then where would they be without us? We were the source of their power," Bra'tac said. "They would never destroy our whole people. And even if they tried —" He spread his hands. "Here we are, strong and whole, with ships to serve us and an army at our backs. The hand of the gods is not raised against us. They are dead, Teal'c. Nothing more than stories to tell our children's children about the days when we were not yet free."

"There is nothing I want more," Teal'c said.

"Then stop worrying."

"Tell me how we were able to achieve such a great victory in so little time," Teal'c said. "Or why it was not done generations before, if it were so easy. You said yourself that I am hardly the first to believe that the Goa'uld are not gods."

"Can you not believe that you are the first with the skill to lead others to believe it as well?"

"And what of weapons? How were we able to arm ourselves, and to take possession of so many Goa'uld ships while losing — as you said — only a few Jaffa? How is it that we can survive now without the symbiotes that have enslaved us for so long?"

"The knowledge of the Tau'ri," Bra'tac said easily.

"Perhaps," Teal'c said, but the answer did not satisfy him. He remembered well Major Carter telling him that the creations of the Tau'ri were science, not magic, and that they required time for understanding and testing before anything new could be created. There was something wrong here, some deception, and it troubled him more than anything that Bra'tac would not see it. "If so, why do I not remember it? Why is today's celebration more clear in my mind than last night's battle?"

"You are weary," Bra'tac said.

"Not so weary that it should be affecting my mind," Teal'c said firmly. "I remember boarding Apophis's ship, but not the planning of the battle. Tell me of that, if you can." He hesitated, but a cold weight in the pit of his stomach made him press on. "Or can you not?"

He expected a stern rebuke as Bra'tac stood, but instead Bra'tac came to stand before him, laying a hand on Teal'c's arm and looking down at him with solemn eyes. "Let it be, Teal'c," he said. "There is no more need for so many questions. Be content."

"If we have traded the lies of the false gods for another lie, we have won nothing."

"We have won our freedom," Bra'tac said. "That is what we have spent long years fighting for."

"There can be no freedom without the truth," Teal'c said.

He felt himself jolted, and for a moment he thought that Bra'tac had struck him. Then he realized he was standing in a stone cavern bathed in a blood-red light, and that the room was shaking as if it would collapse at any moment.

"This is a problem," Major Carter said, shielding her face from chips of stone that were now showering down on her.

"Nice of you to join us," Daniel Jackson said, the words coming out in a rush. "Help me figure out how to turn this thing off."

"It appears the device of the Ancients was indeed effective," Teal'c said. It had seemed vividly real, every detail, Drey'auc's hair warm against his face and the sounds of his people celebrating their freedom...

"How about we agree not to talk about that right now," Daniel Jackson said, his voice sounding strained.

"Agreed," Teal'c said as Major Carter moved forward to investigate the device. He glanced around the chamber. Keret was standing gazing blankly at the wall, his open hand still held in front of him as if he gripped a weapon. Reba lay sprawled on the floor, her eyes now open but as blank as Keret's.

A few steps away, O'Neill stood staring into space, his own face empty. "Colonel O'Neill," Teal'c said urgently. "You must wake up."

"I tried that," Daniel Jackson said. "It's the device. I think there must have been some kind of safety measure originally, probably some kind of priesthood or staff for this place who could turn the device off if the user... well, if the user didn't want to come back."

"Which implies there is a way to turn it off," Major Carter said.

"Yeah, but we don't know how. And I think that's the problem. After the Ancients left, people kept finding this place and turning on the device. They just didn't have anyone who knew how to turn it off, or who could even break free of the illusion long enough to try to turn it off, and so I think a lot of them just... stayed here." He nodded pointedly toward the skeletal remains on the floor.

"We could just take Colonel O'Neill and leave," Major Carter said.

Daniel Jackson looked skeptical. "What if that doesn't snap him out of it? If we leave and can't get back down here later to disable the device —"

"We snapped ourselves out of it," Major Carter said. "Presumably the colonel can too."

They looked at O'Neill, who was still staring contentedly at the wall.

"Presumably..."

"If I can't figure out how to turn this thing off, we're going to have to try it," Major Carter said. "This whole cliff could collapse over our heads pretty much any time now."

"And then we what, rappel up a cliff with three unconscious people during a landslide?" He frowned. "I mean, not that they didn't repeatedly threaten to kill us and each other, but I would feel bad about just leaving Reba and Keret here to be crushed by falling rocks or eventually starve to death."

"We came down the stairs," Major Carter said without looking up, her attention on the device.

"Okay, so maybe we can—"

"Here's the thing," Major Carter said, turning. Her voice was very deliberately calm, the tone that Teal'c had learned to associate with imminent explosions. "I have no idea how to turn this thing off without pulling it out of the wall and taking it apart, and even if I had the tools to do that, I don't think we have the time."

"What do you suggest?" Teal'c said.

"We shoot it," Major Carter said. "Daniel, I know it's an incredibly old alien artifact—"

"That's turned into a deathtrap," he said. "I think you may be right."

"What of Colonel O'Neill? If he is still under its power when it is destroyed—"

"In a couple more minutes, it's not going to matter, because the roof is going to come down and crush this thing," Major Carter said. "We can destroy it now, or we can watch it be destroyed while we get killed by falling rocks."

"Your point is well-made," Teal'c said. He armed his zat'ni'ktel, wishing for the greater firepower of his staff weapon, and aimed it at the center of the violently-shaking heart.

Jack opened his eyes to the sound of thunder. No, not thunder, but an ominous rumbling that was growing louder. It felt like it was raining, though, although when he stretched out his hands, what was showering down on them was dust.

"Sir! We have to get out of here!" Carter shouted, tugging at his arm.

He shook his head, taking in the scene in disjointed images. The heart-shaped carving on the wall was blackened and charred, as if it had been struck by lightning. Keret was dashing for the entrance, his hands protectively over his head as stone showered down, and Daniel was hauling Reba up by the arm, propelling her toward the doorway.

At the same time, he could still see in his mind's eye the flickering torchlight on Abydos. It still felt like he could steer Daniel across the room to his hearth to sit down and drink some tea, and trade war stories until it was time to walk back to the room where the gate rested that would take him swiftly back to the mountain. He'd be able to get home in time for dinner—

"Sir!"

He started moving, then, driven by the urgency in her voice, and after a few steps rational thought kicked back in. He started choosing his path more deliberately, heading for the entrance while trying to avoid the columns that were visibly toppling. "Did you shoot that thing?" he yelled, raising his voice to carry over the din of falling rock.

"Teal'c shot it!"

"Good!"

He hung back at the doorway, making sure Daniel and Carter were out before he ducked under the archway himself, willing it not to collapse on him as he did. Teal'c was in the hallway waiting for them.

"We must hurry!" Teal'c said, and headed in the direction of the stairs Jack and Sam had come down.

"This isn't the way we came in!" Daniel protested.

"It is the way Keret went," Teal'c said as he ran. "He did not seem inclined to wait for us."

"We're going the right way," Jack said. "Watch your step!" He followed Teal'c at as fast a run as he could manage. Reba seemed to have shaken off the effects of the device well enough that she could keep up with Teal'c and Daniel, but Carter dropped back, apparently intending to make sure he wasn't falling behind.

"Move!" he demanded, but he pushed himself harder, ignoring the pain that radiated from his knee with every step. His ideal world had certainly not included having a stupid injury that was slowing him down just when —

He felt the stone shift under his feet before he saw it, and reeled backwards, throwing out his arms both for balance and to stop Carter from dashing past him. In front of him, the crack they'd jumped on their way in was quickly widening into an abyss, the other side dropping as the side he was standing on rose. The ceiling was cracking as well, showering down rocks the size of boulders.

"Jump!" he yelled to Carter, and after a bare moment's hesitation she did, flinging herself into space and landing with a scramble on the other side, Teal'c's arm going around her to steady her. Jack gritted his teeth, not sure if he could make the jump, but not seeing any other choice. If he hesitated, he'd lose any chance of making it.

He flung himself toward the other side of the chasm, aware almost at once that he was going to fall short. He threw out his hands desperately, grabbing for the rock face on the other side. The rock smacked hard against his fingers, his own weight smashing him into the rock and then swinging him out away from it, and he couldn't hold on, his fingers grating across the stone.

Then Teal'c's hand locked warm around his wrist, and he was being hauled up, getting one foot under him and then the other. Carter had him by the other arm, and he let her steady him for a moment.

"Hurry!" Daniel called from further ahead. Jack could see

daylight filtering down from above, but it was at the end of a very long corridor, and parts of the roof were already collapsing, showering down stones. "I don't know how much longer—"

"We're hurrying!" Jack yelled, and took off toward the end of the corridor. A pile of rubble blocked the way, nearly waist high, and Teal'c scrambled over it and then half-dragged Jack over it behind him. Jack wasn't in a position to argue. "Get your ass out of here!"

He ducked as another stone hit him on the shoulder, wishing for once for a helmet. Or at least for his tac vest. Teal'c hauled him over another blockade of fallen rock, his own face bloodied. Carter scrambled over it on her own, and then narrowly dodged as a huge strip of the stone facade peeled away from one wall, crashing down in front of her.

The end of the corridor was in sight. He ran for it, throwing himself at the stairs, which were now not much more than a steep slope of fallen rock and masonry. He started hauling himself up them, using his hands to take the weight off his injured leg, trusting Teal'c and Carter to get themselves up.

Near the top, the rubble began to clear, and a hand abruptly gripped his wrist, hauling him up to his feet on a clear expanse of step.

"I told you to get out of here!" Jack snapped as Daniel shoved him up the remaining stairs.

"I'm sorry, I didn't hear you because the roof was collapsing!" He sounded anything but apologetic.

"I swear to God—" Jack began, and then realized that he was out in open air, the ruined buildings casting long shadows in the afternoon sun. He backed out of the way of the building's wall, which was now rocking alarmingly, and looked around. "Everybody out?"

"Everybody's out," Daniel said. He was still retreating from the shaking building, and Jack did the same, scrambling even further back as the building's roof collapsed, thundering down to block the entrance to the stairs and making the ground tremble under his feet.

He managed one more step, and then sat down hard. The ground under him was finally stilling as the last stones in the building's roof settled. Jack looked around, but he couldn't see anyone heading toward them threateningly, which was nice. They could all use a moment to breathe.

Daniel was steadying Reba, although Jack wasn't sure which of them looked more shaken. Her dark hair was gray with dust. Keret was staring down at the remains of the staircase with an expression of angry disbelief, and Teal'c and Sam were brushing dust from their clothes and assessing what looked thankfully like fairly minor cuts and bruises.

"Keep your eyes open," Jack said. "When we came down here, we had company."

"My crew were waiting for me," Reba said. "I expect they didn't stick around down here when the ground started shaking, though. They've got more sense than that."

Keret rounded on her. "This is your fault! You and the blasted Tau'ri. We'll never get back to the treasure now."

"There wasn't actually any treasure," Sam said.

Keret shook his head with an unfriendly smile. "There might as well not be now. What were you thinking, shooting off thunderbolts down there! If you'd just waited, we could have hauled the treasure out—"

"Sam's right," Daniel said. "There wasn't actually any treasure. Just the Ancient device, which turned out to be really dangerous and have nothing to do with—"

"I saw it!" Keret shouted.

Daniel glanced at Jack, who shrugged. "You explain," Jack said. "This was your bright idea."

"Yeah, I should probably say that I'm sorry if..." Daniel began.

"What about my treasure!"

"Deal with him," Jack said. He turned his face up to the

sunlight, feeling it warm on his face after the chill of the caverns below. "We'll debrief later."

"I just know that —"

"*Daniel*," Jack said. "Later."

"Right," Daniel said after a moment, and turned back to Keret. "I know you may have believed you saw a treasure. I can explain that."

"Of course you can," Keret said.

"Sir, I think it would be better if we all moved so that we weren't standing right on top of the tunnels we just partially collapsed," Carter said. "If we went a little further up the hill, I think we'd be on much more stable ground."

"You had to say up," Jack said, but he reached up a hand and let her haul him to his feet. "Let's move, people."

CHAPTER TWENTY-NINE

"LOOK," Daniel said once they'd worked their way far enough up the hill that Sam seemed satisfied they weren't all going to fall into a hole in the ground. "The treasure you may think you saw back there was only an illusion."

"I saw it with my own eyes," Keret said. "Enough precious metal that we could give up raiding forever and live like the High King. And you had to come and ruin it! Your people may be rich enough that a hoard like that is no consequence to you, but those of us who have to work for our keep —"

"Oh, give it up," Reba said, but her voice was ragged. "There or not, it's lost now."

"Lost because you couldn't keep your prisoners after you ran off with them. Where's your ransom for them now?"

Reba smiled sharply. "And where's your thunderbolt, Keret? For that matter, where's your crew?"

"We had to let them go," Jack said, leaning back against one of the tumbled slabs of masonry. "They weren't working out."

"You probably shouldn't lean on that," Daniel said. "Unless you want that wall to fall on your head."

"That would be bad," Jack said, shifting his weight, although he looked like it hurt to do it. Daniel thought about asking him if he was hurt, but decided that in Jack's present mood the best he was likely to get was *You think?*

He shrugged instead. "Not to mention that this is an important archaeological site that ought to be preserved for future exploration, but given that we've already destroyed what was probably the most interesting part of it —"

"You did not object when I proposed to fire at the Ancient device," Teal'c said.

"I know," Daniel said. "I'm not saying we shouldn't have.

I'm just saying that we did."

"Now you admit there was a treasure," Keret said.

"Well, no, that's not exactly…"

"Just shut up and keep out of trouble," Jack said. "Or do I need to zat you?" He brandished his zat in Keret's direction, looking like he would be happy for a good excuse to zat somebody.

"We probably do need him to fly the ship so we can leave," Sam said. "Speaking of which, we might want to think about doing that."

Jack gave her a look. "Then why did we climb up the hill instead of down? I'm assuming that's where we parked."

"Sorry, sir, I was just thinking that we shouldn't climb over the most unstable part of the hillside, because of the danger of falling into a sinkhole and dying." Daniel was getting the picture that everyone's tempers a little strained by this point. "I think maybe if we head that way, we can climb back down pretty safely."

"What about her?" Jack said, jerking his head at Reba.

"We should probably bring her along," Daniel said. "If we run into trouble getting out of here, I think she could be a useful bargaining chip in dealing with her crew."

"We had a deal, treasure hunter," Reba said. "You gave your word I'd get to ransom you back to your people, the ones you promised — endlessly and tiresomely — were going to pay handsomely for your return. And after all the trouble you've caused me…"

"I thought it was that if we didn't find any treasure, you were going to throw us overboard," Daniel said. "Forgive me if I'm not eager to hold up my end of that bargain."

"Not such a great deal," Jack said.

Teal'c glanced in his direction. "The terms of our arrangement seem to have been extremely flexible."

"Bring her along," Jack said. "Let's get moving before anyone else starts poking around here or more rocks become falling rocks."

Reba frowned, but moved out in front with Keret in response to Jack's emphatic gesturing with his zat. She looked like she was considering making a break for the ridge, but since it would have involved more sprinting than climbing, he wasn't surprised when she seemed to decide against it.

Of course, she was probably planning to hijack Keret's ship once they got aboard it. Daniel was pretty sure that Jack and Sam were aware of that, though, so he let them take care of covering both Reba and Keret as they hiked, hanging back with Teal'c to take up the rear.

"I'm sorry," he said in a low voice. "I screwed up, and I think we all know it."

Teal'c shook his head. "You could not have predicted that the effects of the device would render us unaware of our surroundings even when they became hazardous."

"Or that it would be so tempting to stay unaware. It felt like... getting everything I've ever wanted." Daniel shook his head. "I'm actually not sure what it says about me that I was willing to give that up for anything. I would have said I'd do pretty much anything to be with Sha're again."

"You prefer the truth, however painful, to illusion," Teal'c said. "That is hardly a thing to be ashamed of."

"I know you do, too," Daniel said. "I can only imagine how hard it must have been to give up your belief in the Goa'uld as gods, when the reality is so... well, so awful. And whatever you saw, which, I'm not asking, I'm just saying..." He glanced over at Teal'c. "I guess I just want you to know that I've always respected that about you."

Teal'c inclined his head. "As I respect you, Daniel Jackson."

"The story I told Reba..."

"Was in part true."

"Some of it," Daniel said. "I just hope you know that the part where I said that I hated you and was waiting for the opportunity to kill you wasn't one of those parts."

There was a glimmer of humor in Teal'c's expression. "You would find that difficult."

"Tell me about it."

"Had the device worked as you hoped, it would have been a useful weapon in our fight against the Goa'uld."

"That would have been nice, wouldn't it?"

"We will continue in our efforts to locate Sha're's son."

Daniel closed his eyes for a moment against the slanting afternoon sunlight. "Yeah. We will."

Whatever happened if they found him, it wasn't going to be anything like his fantasy life. The child had the genetic memory of the Goa'uld. Daniel wasn't sure what they were going to do with that, but he was pretty sure it wasn't going to involve his getting to take the boy home to Abydos, or for that matter to an ordinary apartment on Earth. It wouldn't be safe for anyone on Abydos if he did. Or for anyone on Earth.

And the child would still be Apophis's son and not his, and Sha're would still be dead, and all the paths that he'd thought had opened up for the rest of his life when he married Sha're would still be closed. All but the one that led, endlessly and demandingly, through the Stargate.

"And we will defeat the Goa'uld," Teal'c said. "In time."

Daniel glanced at him, realizing some part of what he must have seen. "We will," he said. "Just apparently not today."

Sam pieced her way downhill, trying to cover Reba and Keret without tripping over her own feet in her weariness. She stopped as they did, and glanced past them to see the deep ravine that cut across the hillside, wider than she remembered it being at this point on the slope.

"This may be a problem," she said.

Keret considered the expanse. "If we threw a rope, we might catch it on those rocks, there."

Reba gave him a scornful look. "That wouldn't take a child's weight, let alone yours. And we don't have a long enough rope."

"We may have to double back the way we came," Sam said. She glanced at Jack, trying to gauge whether he could make it back without help. He'd done a lot more climbing than she bet Janet would have recommended, and they were both dead tired. Daniel didn't look much better, although Teal'c seemed his usual steady presence.

"Let's think this through first," Jack said. "So we aren't climbing back and forth all afternoon. Teal'c, how about you go scout and find us a way down?"

Teal'c nodded. "I will do so."

"Blast the lot of you," Reba said, and sat on one of the more stable-looking rocks nearby, resting her forehead against her fists; after a moment, Daniel sat down near her, looking warily sympathetic.

"You could sit down," Sam said to Jack.

He gave her a sideways look. "And then I'd have to get up."

"Point," she said.

"I really did think the device was for locating things," Daniel said. "I'm sorry. I think maybe I wasn't exactly at my best when I was doing those translations."

Reba laughed, a bitter, humorless bark. "I should have known I couldn't be so lucky. And then when you did whatever you did back there, I thought—"

"Let me guess," Daniel said. "You'd found a fabulous treasure."

Reba looked up, her eyes stormy. "What do you know about treasures? You've never served the goddess. You don't even believe in her."

"You're not impressing me as the God-fearing sort," Jack said.

"I would have been her most loyal servant if she had only looked my way. If Saba hadn't left me behind, if they hadn't left me—"

"Who's Saba?" Sam asked.

Daniel glanced up at her. "Reba's childhood friend.

Apparently they hoped that one of them would be chosen to be her host and the other one could be her servant, but she just took Saba as a host and left."

"My supposed friend," Reba said. "I learned better."

"Your friend Saba probably had nothing to do with what happened," Daniel said. "Once she was a host, she wouldn't have had any control over what Asherah did with her body."

"I should have been her host," Reba said. "I worked and studied, and got nothing for it, and just when I had another chance, you people had to ruin it."

"Another chance," Daniel said, sounding like the words left a bad taste in his mouth.

"I thought at first that if I brought her the prisoner, she might change her mind, but then when you told me of the Ancient device, well. Everybody wants something, don't they? Even the gods."

"You were planning to sell the device to Asherah, weren't you?" Daniel said wearily.

Jack looked exasperated. "That's just what we would have needed. A Goa'uld with the ability to find anything they wanted. Like, say, us?"

"That would have been bad, yes," Daniel said. "I thought she wanted treasure."

"Keret may not be able to see any further than a full hold and a full belly, but we're not all like him," Reba said.

"At least it would have been my full hold and my full belly," Keret said.

"I saw the goddess," Reba said. She set her jaw angrily if she were trying not to show some more revealing emotion. "She said she was pleased at my gift, and she smiled at me. She said she saw now that she should leave Saba and take me as her host instead. We were going to sail her ship among the stars."

"She would have controlled your every action," Daniel said, but it seemed to fall on deaf ears.

"And I would have sent Saba back to the temple to sweep

floors for the rest of her life and look up at the stars where she would never be."

"Saba would have been dead," Sam said.

Reba glanced up. "I prefer my revenge."

"It wouldn't have mattered what you wanted," Sam said. "The Goa'uld don't let their hosts live after they have no more use for them." That was one difference between them and the Tok'ra. Even dying, Jolinar had protected Sam, who she hardly knew, who meant nothing to her but a refuge taken in desperation.

She understood now how hard that must have been for Jolinar, who never gave up, who wanted so much to live that she had taken two unwilling hosts against her own most sacred principles. It must have been so tempting for her to keep fighting for her own life until she was too weak to prevent her death from causing Sam's as well. But in the end that had been what mattered most to Jolinar, that she die as she had lived, as a Tok'ra and not as a Goa'uld, and she had comforted herself at the last with the thought that Rosha would be proud of her...

"You're lying."

"She's not," Daniel said. "Have you ever heard of anyone taken as a host returning? Even in old age? Are there even any legends about it? Because I can tell you, it doesn't happen."

"They live out their lives in service to the goddess," Reba said, but there was a note of uncertainty in her voice.

"No," Teal'c said. Sam looked up to see him standing a little above them on the slope. "If you will not believe the Tau'ri, believe me. I know the ways of the Goa'uld well. They do not release their hosts willingly except at great need, and they would never permit a former host who might reveal their secrets to live. If you had persuaded Asherah to abandon her current host, she would certainly have killed the woman at once."

"And that should matter to me?" Reba said, tossing her

head dismissively, but Sam wasn't convinced.

Neither was Daniel, apparently. "I think it does matter," he said. "Doesn't it?"

"Blast you," Reba said. "I can't even hope for it, now, can I? Not without thinking of her dead."

"It's not something you ought to be hoping for," Jack said. "Having a Goa'uld in your head, moving you around like a puppet—"

"Your god should strike you down for such talk," Reba said.

"I think he may have tried," Keret said. "You should have seen the storm we came through."

"They're not gods," Jack said, frustration clear in his voice. "They're alien snakes who like the whole god act because it gets people to bring them lots of treasure and do their laundry for them."

"You mean like the High King?" Keret said, with a sharp smile.

"There are many kinds of servitude," Teal'c said. "You cannot persuade them that they are enslaved if they wish to believe themselves free, O'Neill. They must come to discover the truth in their own time."

"I don't think we're going to be sticking around that long," Jack said.

"Even so," Teal'c said. "Perhaps the device of the Ancients may help them to find their paths."

Reba shook her head. "By showing me things I can't have?"

"By showing you what you'd give up to get what you think you want," Daniel said. "And what you wouldn't. I think that's what this thing was originally for."

Jack gave Daniel a sharp look. "You're saying this was supposed to be some kind of learning experience?"

"Probably, the way the Ancients thought about it. I think the idea was to help people figure out what they really wanted. What they really wanted most."

"Everybody knows that," Jack said.

"Not everybody," Daniel said. He looked at Sam, not quite a question, but with a definite flicker of curiosity.

"Mine wasn't really that different from real life," Sam said. "We were home, and everything had always gone really well. So well that I got suspicious about it. It didn't seem realistic for us to never have had any major problems."

"That wouldn't be realistic, no," Jack said. He looked like he was running out of both patience and energy, his jawline dark with several days' growth of beard and his eyes shadowed. She didn't ask what he'd seen, but she didn't think she had to. She didn't think any of them did. They'd all seen the picture he kept in his locker of the family he didn't have anymore.

And Sam... all right, she missed her mother, but that was an old ache, one she'd learned to live with a long time ago. That was something she'd have had to face someday anyway, something everybody did. She wished they hadn't ever made any mistakes, but that wasn't possible. They'd known when they started exploring the galaxy that it was likely to cost a lot of pain and a lot of lives, and they'd all signed on to do it anyway.

And if they'd never met the Tok'ra, if Jolinar hadn't made a desperate attempt to stay alive by taking a host who would carry her through the Stargate, her father would be dead, and they wouldn't have learned half as much as they had about Goa'uld technology. If she hadn't been Jolinar's host, personally, they all would have died on Ne'tu.

She thought Jolinar would have agreed with her completely that it was worth it to still be alive.

"I think maybe I understand what you're saying," she said to Daniel. "It's not such a bad thing to think about what's really important."

"Which right now would be getting out of here," Jack said.

"I believe I have found a path," Teal'c said. "We must go carefully. The ground near the ravine still shakes."

"You mean it's shaking *now*?" Sam said. "Oh, that's not a good sign."

Jack turned to her. "Carter?"

"We may have seriously destabilized this hillside," she said. "If enough of the underground chambers have collapsed—"

"Up," Jack said, and no one hesitated in starting to scramble up the hillside.

CHAPTER THIRTY

SAM was still hoping she was wrong when she began to feel the ground shaking underneath her, and heard a growing rumble like thunder that was all too close for comfort. She couldn't afford to stop and look back, but she risked one glance over her shoulder even as she was climbing. Down the hill buildings were collapsing, the earth beginning to buckle and slide, the chasm widening as rocks splintered.

"Major Carter!" Teal'c called, and Sam looked up just in time to dodge a tumbling block of stone that could have flattened her. Even far up the slope, stones were showering down, the ancient buildings coming down like badly-built towers of blocks.

She climbed faster, finding a path between the ruins, entirely occupied for a while with the struggle to keep her footing and avoid loose rocks that were sliding downhill. Finally she reached a level patch of ground near the top of the ridge. It wasn't what she would have called safety, but the ground wasn't sliding under her feet and there wasn't anything higher to fall on her, so she stood her ground, turning to see what was happening below her.

The rumble of thunder had turned into a roar, as earth and stone slid and cracked. As she watched, the ravine widened into a gaping chasm, and then the stone below it began to slide, toppling out into space as if an enormous hand had chiseled it away from the mountain face. She saw the airship anchored low on the hillside twist in the rush of air, its canopy bright against the sky, and then tumble as the rocks it was anchored to tipped toward the gorge below.

"My ship!" Keret shouted, and took a couple of sliding steps downhill. The ship twisted in the air, its canopy billowing, and then an enormous chunk of tumbling rock struck it, smashing through its upper deck and ripping the canopy. The fabric flapped bright for another moment, and then burst into flames, one rising swirl of fire that blazed up and then plummeted out of sight.

"My ship," Keret said again, numbly.

"I'm sorry," Sam said. She really was, too; it had been a pretty ship.

"Okay," Jack said. "I think we're going to need a different ride home."

"That would be my ride," Reba said, pointing upward. Jack followed her gaze to see another airship hovering at a cautious distance beyond the ridge, its banners flying in the wind. "Now are you willing to make a deal?"

Jack armed his zat. "How about, you get your people to pick us up, and I don't shoot you?" He knew it wasn't a good deal, and wished he had a better one to offer. Staying where they were seemed like a bad idea. It was already getting colder, and the ground under their feet was still shaking even as the new, much-abbreviated hillside below them began to settle.

"If you shoot me, they certainly won't pick you up," Reba said calmly. "I might be willing to talk about that valuable reward your people were planning to pay for you, though."

"I'm sure General Hammond would be happy to pay you for your trouble in taking us home safely," Daniel said. "Especially if we made it clear to him that we'd been your guests rather than your prisoners."

"I don't have guests," Reba said.

"Your customers, then," Daniel said. "You must have those."

"From time to time."

"See? This could all work out perfectly well for everybody," Keret said.

"Not for you," Reba said. "Have fun trying to walk home."

"You wouldn't just leave me here," Keret said.

"Well, you did try to kill her," Daniel pointed out, which

Jack didn't feel was the best thing to say at the moment to smooth things over. He was beginning to suspect that Daniel liked the woman more than he was ever likely to admit, which seemed about par for the course in terms of Daniel's taste.

"I stunned her," Keret said. "As the result of a regrettable misunderstanding."

Reba shook her head at him. "What, you tripped and your thunderbolt went off?"

"More like the regrettable misunderstanding where we had a plan to capture some valuable Tau'ri prisoners, and she ran off with two of them after I did most of the work."

"If you think you can charm your way onto my ship..."

"Then what?"

"You can keep trying," Reba said.

"Excuse me?" Jack said, waving his zat wearily to get their attention. "We'd really like to go home now."

"If I were really inclined to let bygones be bygones, I might show you the modifications to the box of winds that let us catch up to you," Keret said.

"Why would you do that?"

Daniel threw up his hands. "Maybe because he doesn't want you to leave him on a cold and very dangerous mountainside?"

"Or because I'm a fundamentally helpful person," Keret said.

"Who doesn't want to be left here to dry up and blow away," Reba said. "I don't need a device of the Ancients to tell me that."

"So let's all just click our heels together..." Jack began. He trailed off, listening. "Do you hear that?"

Daniel looked downhill in alarm. "Another landslide?"

"I don't think so," Sam said, her face lighting. "I could be wrong, but..."

"But you're not," Jack said, shading his eyes with his hand to scan the sky. "That's a helicopter."

He finally saw what he was looking for, the welcome shape of a Kiowa helicopter lowering toward the most level patch of ground its pilot could find, its rotors stirring up the dust from high above them. He extracted his sunglasses from his pocket, pleased to find them still in one piece, and slid them on.

"That would be our ride," he said with satisfaction.

He was aware now of how tired he was, now that there seemed some chance of getting to sit back and let someone else handle their travel arrangements from here on out. The Kiowa was kitted out with external seating for transport, which wouldn't make for the most comfortable ride, but he wasn't about to hold out for first class seats.

They'd go back to the SGC, and Janet would lecture him about undoing all of her good work, and Carter would fall asleep in a chair until Daniel woke her up and offered to drive her home. Teal'c would go do whatever Teal'c did when he was off duty and tired — watch TV, possibly, with an enormous tray from the mess hall at his elbow and no one asking him to shoot anyone or save the galaxy for a few hours.

And eventually he'd have to go home, and walk into his empty house where no one left their lunch on the kitchen counter. He'd gotten used to that, though. He wondered about the Ancients sometimes. How much time did you have to have on your hands to build an elaborate device to tell you what anybody with any sense already knew?

He looked over at Keret. "We will be boarding shortly. You coming?"

"On that thing?" Keret said. "I don't think so."

"Besides, we would probably have to turn you over to the authorities when we got back to the Stargate," Carter said.

"I think I'd rather be her prisoner," Keret said, glancing at Reba.

"I'll bet." Reba gave him a hard look, but it wasn't one that suggested she was actually planning to leave him behind. Not that Jack would have felt that unjust, but he wouldn't have felt very good about leaving anybody stranded alone up there. "You'd better have learned something useful from the Tau'ri."

"You'd be amazed," Keret said.

"I doubt that. I'm probably going to regret this."

"No, you won't," Keret said. He flashed them his wolf's grin. "No hard feelings?"

"Don't push your luck," Jack said.

"If you ever seek a career other than piracy, consider rebelling against your false gods," Teal'c said. "It would ultimately be more rewarding."

"All that tribute," Keret said. He looked thoughtful, although Jack was pretty sure he was imagining all that tribute going straight into his own pocket. On the other hand, nobody ever said you couldn't rebel against the Goa'uld unless your motives were pure.

"Good luck," Daniel said to Reba. "I'm sorry it didn't work out the way you hoped." Jack shot him a look. "All right, no, I'm not, particularly, but I'm sorry that you didn't get anything you wanted out of this."

She shook her head, and then smiled a little. "You could pay me that ransom you promised me."

"I'm not sure it would be very safe for you to collect it," Daniel said.

"There's always some catch," Reba said.

"Tell me about it."

The helicopter was landing, sending dust and loose stones scattering down the hillside and drowning out all conversation for a moment. Jack motioned to the pilot to cut the rotors, and collected his team with a glance.

"Come on, kids," he said. "Time to go."

He began piecing his way across the uneven ground toward the helicopter. As he did, a small figure climbed down from the passenger door, and he recognized Janet as she started toward them, medical kit in hand.

"Watch your step!" Jack called.

"It's good to see you in one piece, Colonel!"

"More or less," Daniel said.

"We need to get out of here," Carter said. "This hillside's still unstable."

"I am entirely in favor of that," Jack said. "I'm pretty sure right now what we all want most is to go home."

"No argument here," Carter said.

"Indeed," Teal'c said.

Daniel cast one reluctant glance back over what was probably a very archaeologically important crumbling hillside. Somewhere under all that fallen rock might be more records of an ancient civilization, but they weren't going to find them. And neither was anybody else. No more skeletons would be piling up down there, flies trapped in the honey of a device that made promises no one could keep.

"Daniel," Jack said.

"I know," Daniel said. "Let's go home."

"So it wasn't a complete wash," Daniel said. "At least I've got my notes on the one tablet we got our hands on, and I remember a fair amount of the inscription we found in the chamber with the device. Considering how little we know about Ancient, that probably counts as a significant discovery."

"I'm glad to hear it," Hammond said patiently. As far as he was concerned, the important thing was having SG-1 back safely. After a night's sleep and the chance to wash up, they looked slightly less like something the cat dragged in. Janet had firmly insisted that Jack use a cane for at least a few days, which Hammond noted he was using, if grudgingly. Sam and Daniel were both sporting some bruises, apparently having been nearly caught in a collapsing underground tunnel, but Hammond was well aware that it could have been worse.

"And we also destroyed the Ancient device. Which, before anyone points out that it was probably scientifically important, was also killing people," Jack said.

"I'm not going to argue with that," Hammond said. "On the diplomatic end of things, I'm afraid our trade negotiations with the High King's people have been called off for the foreseeable future."

"It's a shame we won't get to try that excellent cheese," Jack said.

Daniel frowned at him across the table. "Or get our hands on any of the other writings left by the Ancients."

"It was probably all more philosophical stuff," Jack said. "What is the sound of one hand clapping and all that."

Teal'c raised an eyebrow. "How can one clap with one hand?"

"It's a kind of a..." Jack looked across the table for rescue. "Daniel?"

"It's a question that's not supposed to have a rational answer," Daniel said. "The point is to meditate and let your intuition guide you."

"More practically speaking, I'd like to take another look at that wrecked glider they've got down at Area 51," Sam said. "Playing around with the drive on the airship has given me some ideas that might help on the X-301 project."

"I'm glad to hear that, too," Hammond said. "Since SG-1 is going to be on light duty while Colonel O'Neill recuperates, you should have plenty of time to go down and take a look."

"Just find us a mission that doesn't require mountain climbing, and I'll be fine, sir," Jack said.

"I think we'll wait until SG-1 is ready to handle whatever they might run into out there," Hammond said.

"I'm sure that'll be soon, sir," Sam said.

"I might take some vacation time," Daniel said. Sam and Jack both looked at him as if that were a surprising thing for someone to do. Hammond personally felt it was about time. "Take a few days off. If this isn't a bad time."

"I see no problem with that," Hammond said. "Barring emergencies."

"Yes, always barring those."

"And do what?" Sam asked.

Daniel shrugged. "Whatever people on vacation do. It's been a while. I could work on that 'ready for whatever we might run into' thing."

"Then you won't be needing me, either," Jack said to Hammond hopefully.

"Go on vacation, Jack," Hammond said. "Again barring major threats to the safety of our planet." It was probably better for the sake of everyone's peace and quiet to have Jack O'Neill on vacation rather than Jack O'Neill limping around the base finding things to complain about. Sam and Daniel were both better at occupying themselves productively yet quietly. "Major Carter, Teal'c, if you'd like to take some personal time as well…"

"I would appreciate the opportunity to visit my family," Teal'c said.

"You should probably take it," Hammond said. "It's not as if we get a lot of down time around here."

"So I have seen," Teal'c said.

"And you, Major?" Jack said.

"I'd actually prefer to go look at that glider," Sam said. "Really. I swear." That last seemed to be in response to Jack's look of definite skepticism.

"Whatever you want," Hammond said.

"I'd like for there to be no major threats to the safety of our planet," Jack said. "Can I put in for that?"

"I'm afraid I can't guarantee that one," Hammond said. "Dismissed, people. Colonel, if I could have a moment of your time."

Jack hung back as the others left. "Sir?"

"I'm sorry you didn't get your easy mission," Hammond said. "If any of our teams deserve one right now, it's SG-1."

"Maybe next time," Jack said. "How about a planet full of nice tropical beaches?"

"Strategically important tropical beaches?"

"Well, that's the catch." Jack smiled wryly, and then sobered.

"Sir, my team can handle whatever they need to. Every one of them. They just need a break once in a while to get back to the top of their game."

"So do we all," Hammond said. "Let's see if we can give them one."

Whatever Jack meant to reply was interrupted by the sound of the alarm klaxon sounding. "Unscheduled offworld activation! General Hammond to the control room!"

"Maybe starting tomorrow," Jack said.

"That might be best," Hammond said. "Let's go see what today has in store."

STARGATE SG·1.   STARGATE ATLANTIS

Original novels based on the hit TV shows STARGATE SG-1 and STARGATE ATLANTIS

Available as e-books from leading online retailers — and in paperback from our website
www.stargatenovels.com

*Some backlist titles still available from bookstores.

STARGATE SG-1 is a trademark of Metro-Goldwyn-Mayer Studios Inc. ©1997-2012 MGM Television Entertainment Inc. and MGM Global Holdings Inc. All Rights Reserved.
STARGATE ATLANTIS is a trademark of Metro-Goldwyn-Mayer Studios Inc. ©2004-2012 MGM Global Holdings Inc. All Rights Reserved.
METRO-GOLDWYN-MAYER is a trademark of Metro-Goldwyn-Mayer Lion Corp. © 2012 Metro-Goldwyn-Mayer Studios Inc. All Rights Reserved.